The Place Between the Pillars

by Brandon Glossop

 FriesenPress

Suite 300 - 990 Fort St
Victoria, BC, V8V 3K2
Canada

www.friesenpress.com

Copyright © 2017 by Brandon Glossop
First Edition — 2017

Early editing by Kaley Walls

Cover photograph by Frances Litman

All rights reserved. No part of this publication may be reproduced in any form, or by any means, electronic or mechanical, including photocopying, recording, or any information browsing, storage, or retrieval system, without permission in writing from FriesenPress.

ISBN
978-1-5255-0038-1 (Hardcover)
978-1-5255-0039-8 (Paperback)
978-1-5255-0040-4 (eBook)

1. FICTION, WAR & MILITARY

Distributed to the trade by The Ingram Book Company

This book is for Jade.

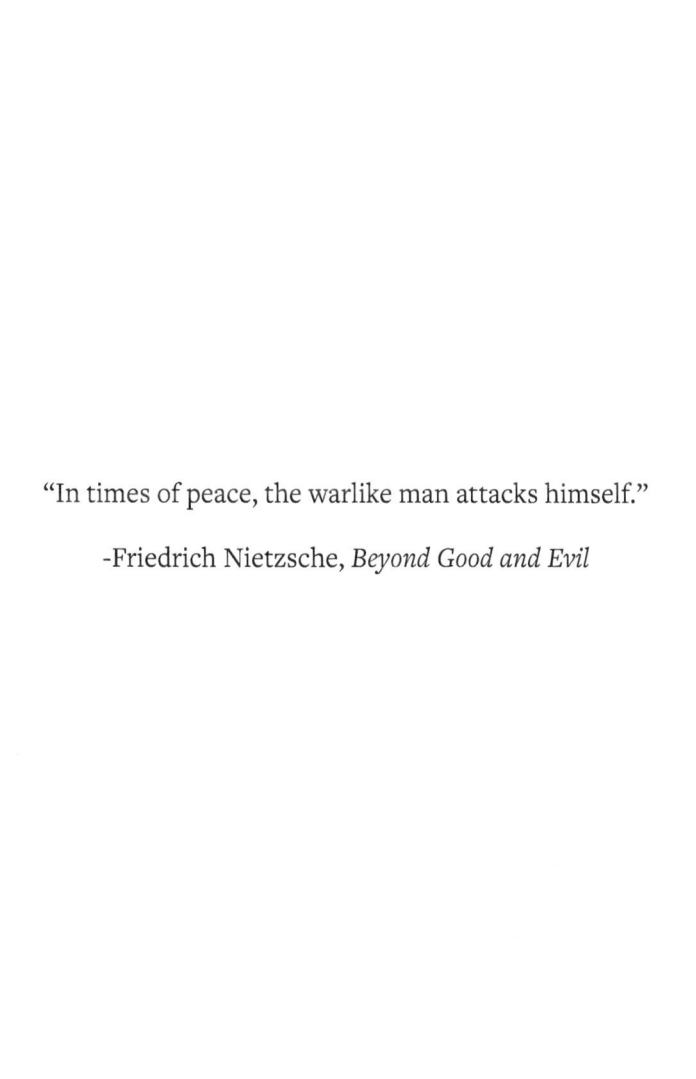

"In times of peace, the warlike man attacks himself."

-Friedrich Nietzsche, *Beyond Good and Evil*

PART I

Chapter 1

They were in the back of a LAV with the heat on, drinking vodka out of their canteen cups, and the new guy was trying to dig an ingrown hair out of Hartford's neck with a Gerber.

"If you fuck this up, I'll cut your goddamn head off," Hartford told him.

The LAV was an eight-wheeled infantry fighting vehicle and seated seven in the back between two inward-facing benches, on which they were sitting. They were nearing the end of a winter training exercise, and small packs, duffel bags, sleeping mats, weapons, cases of ammo, boxes of rations, and jerry cans of water were packed into the spaces behind the benches. Everything, including them, was layered with dirt, oil, and grime.

John Hall was in the corner near the turret. Hartford and the new guy, whose name was Franklin, were on the opposite bench near the ramp, under the best utility light.

Hartford was a big man, massive in his layers of winter kit. His hair was high and tight, and the right side of his face was cratered with shrapnel scars. He held up his head, and Franklin put pressure on the large lump near his Adam's apple with a finger, pushing the tip of the knife into the other side at the base of the lump. Franklin's hands were steady, and he was being very careful. He pulled the knife out, and a bit of blood followed. He wiped it away with a wet wipe and stuck the knife into a new place and raked it up, trying to catch the hair.

"Just fucking squeeze it," Hartford said.

"I will when it's open." Franklin stuck the knife in again and raked it out, and a thick drop of blood appeared. "I think I got it." He wiped the blood away and squeezed the lump. A lighter shade of blood came out, followed by hardened chunks of yellow pus and then more blood. He kept wiping and squeezing. Soon the thin cloth was soaked with red and yellow fluids. "You have any more wet wipes in here, Hall?"

"Hold on," Hall said. He put his canteen cup down, put his cigarette in his mouth, and found a pack under the bench on his side. He gave it to Franklin.

"Thanks."

"You're welcome. You're pretty good at that, Franklin."

Hartford snorted. "It's not fucking brain surgery. Did you get the hair?"

"No," Franklin said as he continued squeezing and wiping. "I got a lot of fluid out though. The hair might've dissolved, or it could have just been a big pimple."

"A pimple? Are you serious? It was huge."

Franklin shrugged. "They can get bigger than that."

"Get off me," Hartford growled, pushing Franklin away. He grabbed the pack of wet wipes, took out a fresh one, dabbed his neck, and looked at the yellow and red spots it collected. "Hall, make me a drink."

"Sure." Hall turned on the bench and dug the two-quart canteen out of his small pack. "You want another one, Franklin?"

"Yeah, please."

The canteen was half full. Instead of making individual drinks, Hall filled the canteen from a jerry can they had melting next to the heater. He had a few juice crystal packets saved from his rations, and he poured two of them into the canteen, screwed the cap on, shook it, and poured everyone a good drink. They all took sips and lit cigarettes. All of the hatches were closed, and the air was thick. Hall took off his toque and ran a hand through his greasy hair. He felt it stay in place where his hand left it. The skin on his hands was dried and cracked, and all of the cracks and lines were filled with dirt and grease. He tried to rub some off and then picked at a hard callous on his palm.

Franklin peeled off his winter jacket.

"Feel better now?" Hartford asked.

"Yeah, that heater works good."

"Yeah, we're lucky," Hall said.

"Is this your first winter ex?" Hartford asked Franklin.

"I did battle school in the winter."

"Good for you," Hartford said. "Did you get a medal for that?"

"Why are you such a prick, Hartford?" Hall asked.

"I'm not a prick."

"You are now. He used to be a sweetheart," Hall told Franklin, "but then he got blown up. Now he's a prick."

Hartford touched the scars on his face. The blast had caught him on his right side. There had been no major tendon or muscle damage, except for one place on his cheek, where he had a large, L-shaped scar. His mouth sagged slightly on that side, especially when he was tired or cold. It was the best wound in the battalion, and they were all jealous of the scars on Hartford's face.

Hartford started telling Franklin war stories. All of Hartford's war stories were good because you could look at the scars on his face while he told them.

Hall was pouring everyone another round when the troop door swung open and locked in place, rocking the LAV slightly.

The open door sucked away the hot air, and someone leaned in. He wore a black balaclava, and only his squinting, watery eyes were exposed. Icicles had formed on his eyebrows and lashes.

"Who the fuck are you?" Hartford said.

"Your section commander, fuck head." He pulled his balaclava up and wiped a stream of snot away from his nose.

"What's up, Sarge?" Hartford asked.

"Bad news. We got roving patrols and turret watch tonight."

"What? Are you joking?"

"Would I fucking joke about that, Hartford?"

"This is a gun camp," Hall said. "Since when are gun camps tactical?"

"We're not tactical, but we have some white space to fill, so the major wants background activity. Professional development."

"Tell that retard to suck my fucking dick," Hartford said. "Professional development? Fuck off."

"Why don't you go and tell the OC that yourself, Hartford?"

"Maybe I will, Sarge."

"You want to come in and warm up, Sarge?" Hall asked.

"No thanks, Hall. I still got shit to do. How you holding up, Fish?"

Hartford laughed.

"Good, Sergeant," Franklin said.

"That's good. Don't let Hartford rub off on you too much. He's fucking junk."

"You want to fight me, Sarge?"

"Shut up, Hartford." The sergeant's eyes narrowed suddenly on Hall and then on the canteen cups. "Are you guys drinking? I smell booze."

"No way, Sarge," Hall said. "We don't drink."

"You don't drink? Give me that." He took Franklin's cup and smelled it. "This is what I mean, Franklin. You can't let these guys rub off on you. Are you authorized to drink this,

Franklin? Is this a wet exercise? I don't remember telling you to burn my fucking diesel and suck off my heater while you get fucking wasted in the back of my fucking LAV."

Franklin stared at him, unsure of how to respond. The sergeant put it on well.

Hartford squared off with him, too. "Answer your fucking section commander, Franklin."

"That stupid fucking look on your face isn't an answer, Franklin," the sergeant said. "Who said you could drink alcohol on this exercise?"

Franklin looked to Hall for a way out, but Hall shook his head. "Don't you blade me, Franklin."

The sergeant gave Franklin the four-finger point. "Were you about to blade Hall? What the fuck did Hall ever do to you? If there's one thing I won't tolerate in my section, it's a fucking rat."

Hartford leaned in close to Franklin and blew a stream of smoke in his face. "Well, what do you have to say for yourself, rat?"

Franklin raised his eyebrows, smirked cautiously, and looked back and forth between Hartford and the sergeant. Neither of them broke. He glanced back at Hall again, starting to look nervous, and Hall let a smile slip. After Franklin saw it, he took the chance and forced a laugh.

"Fuck off," he said, and they all broke and laughed.

Hall offered up the two-quart, "You want a quick one, Sarge?"

"I'll have Franklin's." He drank the cup in two swallows and handed it back to him, blowing out a vodka breath. "Give me a cigarette, Hartford."

"Who the fuck do you think I am?" Hartford said, but he lit a cigarette and gave it to him anyway.

"Now seriously," the sergeant said, "don't get fucked up. We're rolling at 0700, so I want you guys cut off by 2300, got it?"

"Roger."

"Got it."

"Yes, Sergeant."

"Good. Especially you, Hall. You're driving this boat tomorrow. Okay boys, I'm gonna get the details about the patrols and shit, and I'll be back to let you know." He wiped away more snot that had leaked from his nose, pulled his balaclava over his face so he again was only a pair of watery eyes, and swung the door shut.

Franklin looked at his empty cup. "What an asshole."

"He's not an asshole," Hartford said. "You're just a pussy."

They drank another round and smoked more cigarettes, and Hartford got louder and meaner to Franklin. Hall called him on it—not to defend Franklin but to confront Hartford. Hall was getting drunk and he was feeling good and aggressive. He slid down the bench so that he was sitting across from Hartford.

"He's not that tough, you know," Hall told Franklin, nodding at Hartford. "He actually can't fight worth shit. He's a bitch. He's just big and loud and mean, but he's not that tough."

Hartford's eyes grew wide. It was a look that terrified most people who did not know him, with his bright green eyes, the scars on his face, his high and tight haircut, and most of all the size of him.

"Hold my cup, Fish," Hartford said, handing Franklin his canteen cup.

"You better take mine, too," Hall said.

They put their cigarettes in their mouths and leaned toward each other slightly, their hands ready. The smoke from Hall's cigarette crawled up his face, and he squinted his eyes as they began to sting. Hartford sucked on his cigarette and blew the smoke in Hall's face. Otherwise they remained frozen, poised, daring each other with their stares through the smoke.

Hartford went for it. He got one collar, Hall caught his other arm by the sleeve, and they started grappling across the benches, grabbing at loose clothing, twisting arms and fingers when they could. Hartford was stronger, but Hall had more reach. He got a hold of Hartford's collar with both hands, cinched the material, and started to strangle him. Hartford's face turned red, his green eyes furious, and he snorted, rocked backward, and came forward with all his strength and weight, and the back of Hall's head hit something sharp.

* * *

When Hall came to, Hartford and Franklin were holding him upright on the bench.

"You okay?" Hartford asked.

"You son of a bitch," Hall said. He put his hand to the back of his head, and it came back covered with blood. "You opened me up. Look at this."

"Jesus," Hartford said, laughing. "Let's take a look at it."

Hall leaned forward on the bench, and he felt them move his hair around and poke at his scalp. It did not hurt much, but he felt blood leaking down the side of his head. It was warm, and it traveled past his ear, down to his chin, and collected there and started dripping.

"It's not that bad," Franklin said. "It's just bleeding a lot. Cuts on the head always bleed pretty good, and the booze doesn't help."

"Thank you, Dr. Fish," Hartford said. He turned back to Hall. "You'll be fine, bro. Just put some pressure on it. Fuck,

I'm sorry, man. I didn't mean to do that. I just meant to loosen your grip. You almost had me."

"You tried to kill me, you son of a bitch," Hall said, and he sat up and held the back of his head.

"Don't say that," Hartford said. "I'd never hurt you. I love you. Say you love me, too."

"Shut up, Hartford."

"Say you love me!" Hartford growled.

"I love you."

"Good," Hartford said happily and then he scowled at Franklin. "Don't you fucking look at me like that, Fish, or I'll open you up too."

Chapter 2

Wright was tall and lean. His jaw and nose were sharply angled, and his eyes were sunken in slightly so that they always held shadows. His face made Hall think of a bird of prey. Tattoos crawled up his neck, and on the right side was a tattoo of some biblical demon with one hand cupped over its mouth, whispering into Wright's ear. Wright looked at each of them, jumped into the back of the LAV, and shut the combat door behind him. Hall felt the cold radiating off of him.

"How is everyone?" Wright asked.

"Good, man."

"Fucking great."

"What happened to your head, Hall?"

"Hartford happened to my head."

"Ah," Wright said. "The sergeant told me you guys were having a few back here."

"Yeah, you want one?"

"Sure."

"Pour him a drink, Hartford."

"You pour him a drink."

"I'm busy holding this goddamn head wound closed, you fuck."

"Oh, poor little princess. Franklin, pour the master corporal a drink."

"Sure."

Franklin found an empty juice bag somewhere, gave it to Wright, and filled it for him. Hall could tell that Wright made Franklin nervous. Wright used to make Hall nervous, and sometimes he still did, especially after hearing the stories about him.

"Thanks," Wright said. He took a sip of his drink. "This is good. This yours, Hall?"

"Yeah. I've got a bit more for the smoker."

"I don't think you'll need it. They have rum this time."

"It's a rum ration?" Hartford asked.

"And beer. Lots of beer," Wright said, "just like last time."

"This should be fuckin' good. You ever been to a smoker, Fish?"

"No."

"Three guys were hospitalized last time," Hartford said. "Nine needed stitches."

"I heard they get pretty crazy," Franklin said.

"Just you fuckin' wait."

"Have you heard anything else about these roving patrols and turret watches?" Hall asked Wright.

"They got shit canned."

"Thank fuck."

"Yeah, so go to ground when you guys are ready," Wright said. "Stove watch starts at 2300. Who wants first shift?"

"I can do it," Franklin said.

"Oh, you can do it, can you?" Hartford laughed. "You're brave enough to take the first shift and get six hours of uninterrupted sleep, are you? Fuck you. You're on at 0300."

"You want it?" Wright asked Hartford.

"You take it."

"No," Wright said. "Hall?"

"No thanks, man."

"It's you or Williams then," Wright told Hartford.
"Fuck Williams," Hartford said. "I'll take it."
"Okay then," Wright said. "Hartford, you're 2300, Hall, you're midnight, and Franklin, you're 0300. I'll put the list in the tent. Thanks for the drink." He let himself out the combat door.

They drank what was left in their canteen cups and smoked a few more cigarettes. Hall's head stopped bleeding and was starting to scab over, so he put his toque back on. Hartford told Franklin the story about Wright. Wright had been deployed on four combat tours, and on one tour, he had supposedly carried a wooden axe handle with him while out on patrol. What he did with the handle varied with each telling, but the version Hartford told Franklin was the most widely agreed upon and the one Hall personally liked to believe.

After Hartford had finished the story, they sat there for a while and did not talk. The engine rumbled at high idle, and the air was thick with smoke and they were heavy from the story. It was almost 2300. Hartford left for his shift, and Franklin went on his phone. Hall picked up the two-quart and swirled it around. There was a little left at the bottom. He drank it straight from the canteen. He tried to read on his e-reader for a while, but he was too drunk, and it was too hot in the back with all of his kit on. The words blurred together, and he kept losing focus.

Franklin left while Hall was trying to read. Eventually he gave up and put his e-reader away and got out of the LAV. The cold air made him cough when he breathed it in, and he felt his nose hairs freeze. The snow around the LAV was trampled and dirty. Small, leafless shrubs poked through the snow in some places. They were all broken and bent. Hall shut off the LAV and locked the hatches. In the process, he got some grease on his hands, so he picked up some snow and rubbed it into his skin. The snow melted and cleaned the grease off. He stuck his hands into his ice pants and put them near his groin for a moment to warm them.

Hall walked back to the tent line, where a few guys he knew were smoking cigarettes. He talked with them while he smoked and then went to his tent. He unzipped the inner and outer flaps of the tent and crawled halfway through.

Hartford was sitting in front of the stove with his shirt off and was shaving in front of a small hand mirror. His scars stopped at his chest and halfway down his right trap muscle and then continued down his right arm. He looked at Hall with wide, angry eyes. "Are you coming in or not?"

"What time is it?" Hall asked.

"You're on in ten."

"I'll be back in fifteen."

"You'll be back in five," Hartford growled.

"Keep your voice down," Hall said, nodding at the bodies in sleeping bags.

"Get the fuck out," Hartford said.

Hall crawled out, closed the tent behind him, lit a cigarette, put his hands in his pockets, and smoked with every breath. A platoon of LAVs drove by on the camp route, their engines whining on the hill in front of the tent line. The crew commanders and gunners stood in the turret hatches, lost in winter kit—helmets, headsets, goggles, and, under everything, balaclavas so that no skin showed. They were as dark as the dark-green LAVs, extensions of their weapon systems, only roughly humanoid in shape.

Once all the vehicles were over the hill, Hall walked down the tent line to the kit tent and dug through the bags until he found his spare. He unzipped it and took out a two-quart canteen of vodka. He took a shot, put it away, and started back toward his tent.

Halfway there he turned around, went back for the two-quart, took another shot, and took it with him.

Outside the tent he smoked another cigarette, stripped off his jacket, covered his rucksack with it, and went inside with the two-quart. Hartford laughed when he saw it. They said goodnight, and Hartford got into his sleeping bag.

Hall sat over the stove. He found a ration with orange-flavoured juice crystals and made a screwdriver in the juice bag. He took his toque off, ran a hand through his hair, and drank and stared at the ring of blue flame in the stove. Something warm started dripping down his head. He realized he had been picking at the scab, and it had started bleeding again. He looked at the blood on his hand and put his toque back on.

Once the screwdriver was finished, Hall poured more vodka into the bag and watered it down, but it still went down hard, so he scraped up some snow from behind the stove, where it was somewhat clean, put it in the bag, and the vodka went down a little easier. He turned his phone on. It was getting late, and most of the camp had gone to ground, so the service was good. He logged onto Facebook and went through the profiles of women he had slept with. One had recently broken up with her boyfriend, and there were many pictures of her at bars and restaurants and live music venues. In most of the pictures, she was leaning close to, or had an arm around various men, and in all of them she was smiling brightly or laughing. Hall sent her a message. Another one had gotten breast implants and had put up pictures of a bikini photo shoot. Hall sent her a message too, and then carried on, but the rest of them had boyfriends, or had moved away, or were ugly.

He finished his vodka and poured another one. Once that was finished, he turned the stove off, took the tank outside, and filled it. Back inside the tent he restarted the stove, and when the flame was burning good and blue again, he made another drink and found Danielle on Facebook. She had unfriended him—or he had unfriended her, he could not remember—but her settings allowed him to go through her pictures, so he went through them. Her profile picture was "The Scream" by Edvard Munch. Her next picture was of her dancing. Her hair was long and dark, and it waved across her face. She was looking down, or her eyes were closed, and she was smiling. The next picture was of her and her boyfriend, who was tall and thin and had long hair. Hall went through more of her pictures and came to one of her sitting on someone's couch and looking to the side at someone. There was love in her eyes.

He looked at that picture for a long time and thought very deeply. He decided to send her a message:

I'm in a tent on a training exercise, drunk, and it's probably bad to message you while I'm drunk, and I'll probably say the wrong things, but if I wasn't drunk, I wouldn't have the courage to get in touch with you, so even though I'm doing it the wrong way, it's good to-

He read over what he had written and deleted it. He started again:

I have no hope of us ever getting back together, but you're the only woman I've ever loved, and when—

And again:

You fucking bitch, why can't I stop loving you?

He deleted that, too. He sipped at the vodka and stared at the blue ring. After he had thought for a long time, he started once more:

The last time we spoke was very bad, but the time before that, when we met for drinks on a whim and ended up sleeping together, was so good that it overpowers all the other times, all the bad times, and it demands attention so that I can't just leave it alone. I can't just drop something that good. That was the last time I made love, and I don't mean the sex, because that was only pleasure, only fucking, and the love was made after, in the bathroom in front of the mirror with me standing behind you and us looking at each other, one of your arms up and around my neck and my arms around your waist, your head to one side, and mine against your neck. It was good when we looked at each other, but when it really happened, when the love was really made for me, was when you looked into your own eyes and I saw that you were happy with how we were. I felt love for you then, and I've never felt it since, and there may not have been any love in your happiness, but that doesn't matter now. I don't know what will happen with us, and I don't know what I'm really trying to do here. I don't know much of anything.

He sent the message and made another drink.

* * *

Chapter 3

"Wake up, you drunk fuck."

Hall was soaking wet. He was in both sleeping bags, and he was still wearing thermals, ice gear, and winter socks. The only thing he had managed to take off were his boots, and he had sweat steadily for the few hours he had been asleep. His head pounded from the inside with every sound and movement around him. He muttered something, and Hartford punched him in the shoulder.

"Come on, dude," Hartford said. "We're rolling in twenty, and you already missed breakfast."

"Fuck." Hall sat up and started peeling away the sleeping bags. His wet thermals clung to his skin.

"Jesus, you slept in that?"

"Yeah," Hall said. He started packing away his sleeping kit. "Did I do anything last night?"

"You passed out on your shift."

"I did? Fuck."

"Yeah, you're all good though. Wright woke up and covered for you. He said the stove was still going at four, so you must have passed out just before he got up. Wright told the Sarge and the guys that you took their shifts because you couldn't sleep."

Hall finished packing his gear and looked at Hartford, who smiled at him. "You fucking shit show," Hartford said.

Hall felt his chin. It was rough. "How do I look?"

"You can barely see it. You're fine."

"Good enough."

Outside the tent, the cold found his wet clothes. Steam came up from his collar, and his skin tightened. He dug through his rucksack, pulled out dry thermals, and his fingers went stiff in the process. He could not do up the buckles, so he left his rucksack undone and went to the LAV with his gear. The LAV was already running, and he threw his things in the driver's hatch and checked all the fluids while the cold dug deeper and a shiver started in his core. The sleeves and collar of his thermals froze, and the ice in his collar cracked as he moved.

"Hey, Hall."

He looked up and saw Wright in the crew commander's hatch with no face gear on. The cold had deepened the ridges and lines in his face. "Get in your hatch, dude. Warm up."

Hall nodded, shut the engine hatch, kicked the latch shut, stepped down into the driver's seat, and closed the lid. He looked through the three periscopes. They were clean but scratched where someone had tried to scrape off the frost with some kind of tool. He sat back and cupped his hands over his mouth and breathed into them. The driver's hatch was a hole with a lid in the front of the LAV, next to the 350 diesel engine. It was dark, tight, and loud, and everything vibrated.

Hall put on his headset. The plastic pads around the earpieces were cold and hard but began to thaw against his skin. He looked over the levels and adjusted the seat. Cold air blew against the back of his neck, so he reset the heater, but the air stayed cold. He shut it off.

"Heat working in the back?" he said through the headset.

"We're all good," the sergeant said. Hall tried the driver's heat again, but the air stayed cold, so he left it off. He started dry heaving, and a bit of bile came up. He spat it down the side of his seat, into the hull.

"Good to go," Wright said over the headset.

Hall put the LAV into gear, pulled the parking brake, and followed the LAV ahead of them.

The shaking settled down briefly at first, but when it started up again, it was more violent and came in quick spasms. He dry heaved again, but nothing came up. The spasms settled back down to a continuous shaking. He pulled a cigarette out of his pack with his teeth, but he could not light it. His fingers were too stiff, and the lighter was too cold, so he shoved the lighter through his fly and warmed his fingers and the lighter against his groin and drove with one hand. His fingers started to tingle and burn, so he took his hand out and lit the cigarette. The first drag was thick and stale and made him gag. He started dry heaving again and vomited down the side of the seat. The LAV went off the road a little.

"You all good?" Wright asked.

Hall flicked the switch on his headset. "Yeah, just adjusting the wheel."

"What was that sound?"

"Just coughing."

"All right, man."

Hall drove on, shivering and smoking. When the cigarette was finished, he put it out in the vomit splattered on the engine panels and threw the butt down the side of the seat.

Wright came over the headset and said his platoon net had stopped working. Hall was the only one in the LAV with a communications course, so he talked Wright through a few steps but nothing worked. He told him he would fix it at their next halt.

When they stopped, Hall got out of the hatch, and the gunner got out of the turret so he could get in next to Wright and start working on the radios.

Wright watched Hall and saw that he was shaking. "Stop," he said.

Hall turned in the gunner's seat and looked at Wright, who took off a glove, reached through Hall's coat, and felt his thermals. "You're soaked."

"I'm fine," Hall said.

"Do you have a dry set?"

"Yeah."

"In your hatch?"

"Yeah."

"Change," Wright said.

"I'm good, man," Hall said, "I can do it at the range. I won't be—"

"No," Wright said, "I'm not fucking asking you. As soon as you're done here, change in your hatch."

"All right." Hall turned back to the radios, got the platoon net working, climbed out of the turret, and went back into the driver's hatch. He changed into a dry thermal top and fleece, put his headset back on, and started working on his pants.

"Why aren't we moving?" the sergeant asked over the headset.

Hall looked through the periscopes and saw the rest of the platoon pulling away.

"Hall is sorting out the comms," Wright said.

"Can you hear me, Hall?" the sergeant asked.

"Yeah, I got you, Sarge."

"Let's fucking go then."

"Are you finished?" Wright asked.

"Almost," Hall said.

"Don't worry about the radios now," the sergeant said. "If you two can hear each other, then we're fucking good to go, so let's fucking go, Hall."

"That's my call, Sergeant," Wright said.

"The fuck did you just say, Wright?"

"I said that's my call. I'm crew commanding this fucking LAV, and she moves on my fucking orders . . . Sergeant."

"I'll be talking to you later, Wright."

"Looking forward to it."

The headset went dead. After Hall had his thermals, ice pants, and boots back on, he said he was good to go and started after the other LAVs. Wright went over the platoon net and was told to meet the other LAVs at the range. Wright took them off route, down a black track, and onto a different service road, and they were the first LAV to arrive.

There had been a miscommunication somewhere in the chain of command, and by the time the platoon had fully arrived, they were two hours late. The sergeants and warrants ran up and down the line of LAVs, yelling at the troops who jammed cold rounds into magazines with stiff fingers, stripped off extra kit, and filled their canteens from any jerry cans that were not frozen. Once they were ready, they ran to the starting point, which was two kilometers from the assembly area. When they arrived, they were all panting and sweating, and then they stood around waiting for the range safety brief for over an hour. Their sweat froze, and a deep chill settled into all of them. Hall felt much better now that the rest of his platoon was suffering like he had been all morning.

A C9 gunner was away getting treated for frostbite, so Hall was given his machine gun and was put in the firebase at the top of a small hill. On H-hour, they began firing into a line of Figure 11 targets. The C9 jammed halfway through the first box. Hall went through his drills and got it going again, but then after a few more bursts, it jammed again. He smashed at it with his hands, but the jammed round would not come loose. He took off his gloves and tried to pull it out, but his fingers were frozen and useless.

"Get that fucking C9 going!" someone yelled.

Hall used his knife to dig into the guts of the gun and stab at the round. It came loose, he swiped it away, finished the drill, and put his eye back in the sight.

"Stop! Stop! Stop!" someone screamed.

Hall stood up and warmed his hands in his groin. It sounded like the warrant was screaming at someone nearby. After a few minutes, he heard that Franklin had apparently gone outside of his arcs and nearly shot his fire team partner. The platoon warrant brought them all together in a group, yelled at them for a while, and made them run the range again from the start.

That was the last range of the exercise, and when it was over, "End Ex" was called. The platoon was cold, tired, and hungry, but now they were also happy.

Chapter 4

Hall, Hartford, Wright, Franklin, and a few other guys from another section were sitting at a table in the mess tent drinking beer and eating cold pieces of roast beef.

"This would have been good if it was fucking hot," Hartford said.

"Put some horseradish on it," Franklin said.

"Shut the fuck up, Fish."

"No, try it," Wright said. "It makes it okay."

"Really?" Hartford asked.

"Yeah."

"Okay, pass it here."

Franklin passed him the horseradish. Hartford smeared a large forkful over a slab of cold beef, rolled it up, and took a bite.

"Ugh." Hartford spit it back onto his plate. "Fuck that, and fuck this smoker. And fuck you, Franklin."

Hall was on his fourth or fifth beer. They had a two-four between them. He cracked a new one and looked at his hands. His fingers had blistered from the cold, but the colour had not changed, so he was not worried. He picked at the blisters and sipped his beer as he listened to Hartford abuse Franklin. The table was good, and they were all laughing.

"How much longer you got?" Wright asked Hall.

"Less than three weeks now."

"Are you still going to travel?"

"Yeah, that's the plan. I just have to ride out the time until I get my severance pay, and then it's a one-way ticket to Thailand."

"Jesus," Hartford said. "You're going to fucking die there."

"Maybe," Hall said.

"Not maybe. You barely survived three weeks there on leave. You were safer in Afghanistan."

"You're probably right, but fuck it."

"I like where your head's at," Wright said. "You know where you're going to go or you just going to rough it?"

"I'm going to start in Bangkok and rough it from there."

"That city is fucking filthy," Hartford said.

"Yeah, but it's wild. Cities are like people. They can't be wild and clean at the same time, and I like wild cities."

"You like the lady boys."

"There are no lady boys. Well, no more than anywhere else, anyway. I never saw any when I was there."

"Yeah, that's exactly why you're going back," Hartford said.

Hall threw an empty beer can at him. It bounced off Hartford's forehead, and he gave Hall his wide-eyed look. "Don't make me open you up again."

They all laughed.

"You're out soon, too," Hall said. "What are you going to do?"

"I'm going to get a fucking job like a grown up."

"Yeah? Buy a house, marry your girlfriend, have kids?"

"That's what grown men do, Hall."

"Fuck that."

"You don't want to get married and have kids?" Franklin asked.

"Well, I want a woman and I'm sure one day I'll want kids," Hall said, "but it's everything that goes with it that turns me off, even repulses me. Marriage, a mortgage, car payments, anniversaries, parent-teacher meetings, jury duty, soccer games, fundraisers, all that shit, fuck it. It sounds fucking awful, man."

"You fucking anarchist," Hartford said.

"No, anarchy is an opinion, what I'm talking about is . . . fuck, I don't know."

"I don't get it," Franklin said.

"Okay," Hall said, "look, how many of you guys dropped out of high school?"

"Yeah."

"I did."

"Grade ten."

"Yep."

"I went to university," Franklin said.

"What the fuck?"

"Are you serious?"

"Is that where you learned to suck cock?"

"You wanted to become an officer, didn't you Franklin?"

"I hope you get fucking cancer, Franklin."

"I went to university," Wright said, and everyone went quiet. They waited for him to elaborate, but he sat silently, looking back and forth between everyone at the table. He finished his beer, pulled a new one from the case, and cracked it. Franklin was smiling.

"Wipe that grin off your face, Fish." Hartford said. "You're still a fag."

"What did you study?" Hall asked Wright.

"It doesn't matter now. So, what were you were saying?"

"Well," Hall continued, "I dropped out of high school because I hated the path it was taking me down. It just seemed so worn out to me. So I dropped out, and I found a job and a girlfriend, and we got a car and a place together and all that shit, and then I was on a different path, but it was heading in the exact same direction, and it was just as worn out."

"So young John Hall up and joined the army," Wright said.

"Pretty much. And now the path is much more rugged, but it's just as worn out here, too. If I stick around, what do I do? Become a Jack, then a Sergeant, then a Warrant, blow through a couple of marriages, fuck my back up, and OT to the Navy? Fuck that."

"How are you going to get anywhere if you keep changing paths?" Franklin asked.

"Why should it matter?"

"I guess it doesn't," Franklin said. "Well, as long as you're happy. That's all that matters."

"Being happy? That's all that matters?"

"Yeah, being happy."

"Are you happy, Franklin?"

"Sure."

"Really?"

"Yeah, really."

"Well, good for you."

"Ah, fuck," Hartford said. "You just need a good woman to calm you the fuck down."

Hall shrugged and finished his beer.

"So three weeks, eh?" Wright asked.

Hall nodded. "Yeah, man, three more weeks. I start clearing out as soon as we get back."

"I couldn't imagine."

"Yeah," Hall said.

"You nervous?"

"Yeah."

They continued drinking beer and picking at cold pieces of beef. The mess tent grew louder as the battalion got drunk. When the case was done, they went outside, found some rum, and Hartford and Hall went over to the fire.

The fire was at its climax: a massive heap of wood sprouting flames twice the height of a man. The heat kept the soldiers back a few meters, but the drunker ones were already having contests of who could get closest for the longest, and Hall could smell their burnt hair.

Shouting broke out near them, and bodies pushed and slammed into Hall and Hartford, causing Hall to spill his rum on himself. They moved with the crowd that was forming a ring around two fighting men. They were roughly the same size and were grappling in the mud and slush, where the fire had melted the snow. It looked like a hockey fight, if hockey players had been allowed to fight on the ground. One got both hands on the other's head, lifted him up, and slammed his skull into the mud and slush. The man on the bottom went limp, and the man on top straightened his back and started connecting wide strikes that made thumps of wet knuckles against skull and splashes of slush and mud.

"Rip his fucking head off!" Hartford screamed, and then the fight was broken up. There was much yelling and cursing and a few brief follow-up fights, but then the mob settled down. Hartford and Hall went to find more rum. They found a bottle and drank near the fire with two men they had been overseas with.

Hall's phone vibrated, and he found a Facebook message from Danielle. He took a cup of rum into one of the portable plastic toilet stalls, sat on the seat, smoked a cigarette, and sipped the rum. Once the cigarette was finished, he opened the message:

You can't keep doing this to me, John. You think because you never hurt me physically you never abused me, but sometimes I wish you had. Sometimes I wish you had just broken my fucking nose, because then I could have said to myself, 'Look, look what he did to you. He's bad for you and dangerous, and you need him out of your life.' But you didn't, and what you did do, what you're still doing now, in its own way, is much worse. Do you even remember the message you sent me before this one? Probably not, since you only message me when you're drunk, so go ahead and scroll up and refresh yourself if you need to, see how many times you called me a bitch and a whore and a slut. See how done with me you are. See how horrible a person I am, how I've wronged you so terribly. And now you send me a fucking love letter? Are you serious? This is a perfect example of why we broke up, the Facebook equivalent of our relationship. One night you're drunk and kicking our furniture around the apartment and yelling at me, and the next morning you bring me flowers and take me to breakfast, and then you get drunk and do it all over again. I know I've hurt you, John, but I don't deserve to be treated like this. It's enough to drive a person mad. You're a good person when you're sober, but that other part of you is too much now, it's too strong and I can't stand it. I'm trying to make a life with someone else now, so please, John, just move on. Never contact me again.

He put his phone away, lit another cigarette, and drank the rest of the rum. He took his phone out again and read the last few messages he had sent her. He barely remembered any of them, and one, the longest and cruelest one, he did not remember at all. He put his phone back again and smoked another cigarette. There was a loud knock on the plastic door.

"Quit jerking off in there!" someone yelled.

"Fuck off."

"Is that you, Hall?"

"Fuck off."

He recognized the voice but could not place it. It was drunk and annoying, and it went on for a while. He ignored it, finished his cigarette, and then went out. The voice belonged to Franklin.

"You're an annoying little fuck, you know that?" Hall said.

"What's the matter with you? Do you realize how annoying you're being right now?"

"Oh relax, man, c'mon I'm just—"

"You're just what?" Hall said. "Happy? Is that what you are? What the fuck do you have to be happy about? You're ugly as fuck, you're a shit soldier, no one likes you, and you can't hold your liquor."

Franklin laughed drunkenly, his eyes and mouth glistening. "C'mon, Hall, what the fuck you goin' on about? Get out of here, man."

"No," Hall said, "I'm not going anywhere. Look at me. I said look at me, you little bitch. Look at me, and listen to what I'm saying to you. You're pathetic, and you look too much like a faggot to be in the army, and no one likes you. Do you understand that?"

Franklin looked away from him and shifted his weight back and forth. "What's your problem, man?"

"I should break your ugly faggot nose."

"What, Hall, what the fuck—"

Hall started laughing. He laughed for a long time and put his arm around Franklin and patted him on the chest. "I'm just fucking with you, man. Lighten up. You're all right, Franklin. I'll see you later."

Hall left him at the toilets, found some more rum, and drank it from the bottle by the fire.

* * *

Chapter 5

"Wake the fuck up, Hall, you fucking retard. Wake up."

Hall was sprawled across a bench in the back of the LAV with one arm caught behind the backrest. His vision was blurry, and his right eye throbbed. He sat up and touched it. It was swollen and sore. "What the fuck?"

"You fucking shit show," Hartford said. He was standing outside, leaning in through the troop door.

Hall rubbed his face and looked at Hartford. Hartford looked hungover, but he was still Hartford—still human. Hall felt like something less. "Give it to me," he said. "All of it."

"Well, first you sucker punched some Recce dude."

"Is that where I got this?" Hall pointed at his swollen eye.

"Oh yeah, he kicked the living shit out of you. It was great."

"Okay. Then what?"

"We came back here and hung out in the back of the LAV for the rest of the night. You cried."

"I cried?"

"Like a bitch."

"Where?"

"Right where you're sitting."

"Who saw it?"

"Me and Franklin."

"Fuck."

"Whatever, man. Who gives a fuck? You were drunk. Remember me last Remembrance Day?"

"Yeah," Hall said, and he looked away from Hartford, "but that's different."

"It's all good, man. If Franklin makes something out of it, we'll just kill him."

"You're a good friend, Hartford."

"I know. And that's why I gotta say this: You gotta watch it, man. Every time you drink is like this. I'm getting worried about you, bro."

"Fuck off."

"I fucking mean it, you son of a bitch. Don't tell me to fuck off."

"I know. Thanks."

"That being said, here, you'll need this."

He tossed Hall a Gatorade bottle. Hall opened it, and he could smell the rum.

"Oh god, I love you," Hall said.

"Love you, too, brother. Now sort your shit out, we're going to be busy today."

"Okay. I'll be out in a bit."

"All right, man." Hartford shut the door, and the back of the LAV went dark.

Hall sat still and felt his right eye throb. He tried a small sip of the rum, and it made him gag. A bit of bile came up, and he spat it on the floor. He tried again with the same result, so he turned on a utility light, ripped open a ration, took out the dessert, and poured some of the sugary juice into his mouth. He drank a shot of rum and swallowed it with the juice, and this way he was able to keep it down. After the first one, the rest went easier, and soon he finished half the bottle and started to feel better.

He thought about Danielle and about drinking. He took another drink and thought about what Hartford had said.

You don't need it, he thought. *Make this your last one. Remember how you feel right now, and that will make it easier to stay away from it. Just remember this feeling.*

He took another drink. There was one more good one left in the bottle.

This is it, he thought. *This is your last drink. Now finish it, and get on with your life.*

He finished the bottle and gagged, but he felt good and full of resolve.

Chapter 6

Three days later, Hall was drinking beer and whiskey with Wright and Hartford in a bar on Whyte Ave. It was a payday Friday, and they had been cut loose after PT and had been drinking for most of the day.

Hartford was yelling and cursing about different things, and Wright kept looking around the bar, which was just filling up. Hall laughed at Hartford and tried to follow Wright's stares as more and more women and girls came into the bar. Hall watched the shadows play on their calves and thighs, wrap around their waists, and hang in their hair.

"I want to fuck them all," Hall said.

"Get to work then," Wright said.

"Are you coming with me?"

"No."

"Why not?"

"Women don't like being approached by me. It's better if I'm introduced by someone like you."

"Someone like me?"

"Someone softer," Wright said.

"Fuck you. What about you, Hartford?"

"I have a girlfriend."

"All right, whatever," Hall said, "you'd be useless anyway."

"Women fucking love me."

"Yeah, yeah. Let's finish these."

They tapped the shot glasses together, tapped them on the table, and put them back. The whiskey hit Hall hard. He felt it coming back up and ran for the bathroom, which was close to where they were sitting, and threw up in a stall. The man dispensing soap and handing out paper towels yelled at Hall as he vomited. Hall came out, smiled at the man, gave him a twenty, and the man laughed. He gave Hall some breath mints and sprayed cologne over him. Hall washed his face with cold water and went back to their table, where another round of whiskey was waiting for him.

"Drink up, you fucking pussy," Hartford said, "and don't waste it this time."

"I was long overdue," Hall said. He took the shot and washed it down with beer. "That's better. Goddamn it. Fuck."

"What?"

"Nothing . . . Fuck."

"You've made it this far."

"Somehow."

"Get to work."

Two blondes stood by the bar in tube dresses. They were not beautiful, but their make-up worked well for them. He told them he did not have any pickup lines and that he just liked the look of them and wanted to talk. He guessed which one had a boyfriend. He was wrong, but why he had picked the one he did got them going a bit. He kept a smile on his face, and they asked about his black eye. He told them a lie that made them laugh. One of them started flashing her eyes at him. He told them he was buying a round of shots, and they said no, but he bought a round anyway, and they drank the shots.

"Let's dance," one said.

"I don't dance," Hall said.

"You don't dance or you can't dance?"

"Both."

"Come dance with us; we'll teach you."

"I don't think so."

"Fine. Maybe we'll find another boy to dance with."

"Sure. And when you're done, I'll steal you back from him."

"Oh, you think so, do you?"

"If he's the kind of a man who picks women up with dance moves, then yes, I think so. I know so."

"You're scared of dancing," the one who had been flashing her eyes at him said. She was still doing it, and she was smiling. "It scares you, because it exposes you, and you're too ignorant to see the beauty in exposing yourself."

Hall smiled back at her and looked into her wide, challenging eyes. "You . . . You go dance, and when you're done, once you've been good and exposed, I'm going to find you and—"

"And what?"

"You'll see when I find you."

They left for the dance floor, and Hall went back to the table.

"Well," Hartford asked, "how'd you do?"

"Good."

"Then where are they?"

"Dancing."

"Fuck dancing."

"Yeah," Hall said. "Let's go for a cigarette."

They left their jackets inside. The cold was sharp and felt good on Hall's skin. They smoked a meter away from the bar entrance, which was right on Whyte Ave. The sidewalks were busy. Wright had his back to the bar, and Hartford and Hall stood on the sidewalk facing him.

Wright's head followed someone walking on the sidewalk. "Don't you dare eyeball me, you fucking sand niggers."

Hall and Hartford turned around and saw four Middle-Eastern men stop on the sidewalk in front of the bar. They had close-cut hair, neatly trimmed beards, and they were all drunk, loud, and aggressive. The biggest one approached Wright with his hands held out to the sides in an aggressive way but not in a fighting stance, and he started yelling at Wright. Wright stepped out toward him, but the big man seemed to have no intention of fighting, only of bumping chests and staring Wright down. As soon as he was close enough, Wright hit him and connected well. It sounded like two wet bricks being smacked together. The big man went down.

The other three attacked Wright all at once, none of them hesitating, and Wright was beaten back quickly, but he kept his arms up and his head down, and he stayed on his feet. Hall and Hartford grabbed one each. The one Hall grabbed was his size and easy to handle, because he was wearing a coat, and Hall was only wearing a T-shirt. Hall yanked him to where it was easiest to hit him, but the first few strikes were no good, glancing off the side of the man's head or hitting the thickness of his coat, but then Hall connected a wide hook, and his adrenaline flared from the cracking sound it made, and he skipped ahead a bit in time.

* * *

Hall had the same man against a wall, and the man was crumpled up, holding the sides of his head. Hall swung hooks into the sides and back of the man's neck and uppercuts into any bit of the man's face his knuckles could find. Blood started coming out of the man, and somewhere a woman was screaming. Hall swung harder, and the man's arms fell away from his face. He slid down the wall to one side. Hall started connecting more cleanly to the nose and jaw. The woman went on screaming, and then someone came up behind Hall and hit him in the back of the head.

* * *

Hall was being picked up off the pavement. He felt no pain, but everything was soft and dull. His legs came back, and he felt himself walking. His arms came back, and he felt his right one around Hartford's neck and his left one around Wright's. They were holding his wrists and back. The back of Hall's head was swollen, and he could feel his pulse in it.

"Fuck . . . ."

"Come on, bro, we need to get the fuck out of here," Hartford said.

"Wait," Wright said. He stopped and turned them around.

A large crowd was on the sidewalk and the street watching them. The big Middle-Eastern man lay still in the same place Wright had put him, and another lay near him, also still. Blood was on and around him, and a woman was crouched over him, whimpering. The third man was crumpled against a wall and was moving slowly and moaning, but no woman was whimpering over him. The fourth man was gone.

"You see that jundie against the wall?" Wright said. "That was you. You did that."

"Let's fucking go," Hartford said.

They turned around and walked down an alley. Hall looked at the men on either side of him. Hartford's mouth was bleeding, his eye was starting to swell, and his shirt was ripped. Wright was covered in blood. Some of it had leaked from his nose and been smeared around, but most of it had been splattered and smeared from somewhere else.

"Fuck," Hall said again. "I'm good, I'm good." He took his arms back from around their necks, and they broke into a run.

Wright drove them back to his place, and they went into the kitchen and passed around bottles of beer. They drank quickly and took turns at the sink washing the blood off their hands and faces. They were loud and drunk on the alcohol and the violence. Hartford excitedly filled Hall in on everything that had happened after he had been knocked out. Even Wright was excited. He talked fast and loud and grinned with genuine happiness. They went over the details of the fight again and again—the well-connected strikes, the flat, wet thumping sounds, and the blood.

"Let's order some call girls," Wright said.

"You want to get hookers?"

"Yeah. I want to fuck a whore after that. It seems like the right thing to do."

"It does seem appropriate," Hall said. He looked at the clock on the microwave and saw that it was almost two in the morning. "I might be able to get a couple girls over here. Crystal was on Whyte Ave tonight, and I was supposed to meet up with her. Her friends are all eighteen, and they're pretty good."

"No, I don't want a girl," Wright said. "I want a whore. Hartford?"

"If you two are going to fuck whores and teenagers, then I'm going the fuck home. My girlfriend's waiting for me."

"I'll get you a clean shirt before you go," Wright said.

"No," Hartford said, "I want her to see the blood."

"That's jundie blood," Wright said.

"Yeah, that's exactly why I want her to see it."

"You don't know what you're saying," Wright said. "Get that shirt off. It's disgusting. Hall, give me yours, too."

They took off their shirts and gave them to Wright, who took off his own shirt, which had the most bloodstains, and walked out of the kitchen.

"That was fucking good, man," Hartford said.

"Yeah," Hall said, "that was something."

"Man, don't go to Thailand."

"I might go somewhere else."

"Don't go anywhere. Stay here, man. Stay where your friends are."

"I'll come back," Hall said.

"You'll fucking die."

"Pass me a beer."

Chapter 7

"Oh my god, what happened to your eye? Did you get in a fight tonight? Look at your hands. Oh my god, John, you did get in a fight, and the back of your head, oh my god, look how swollen it is, John! Oh my god, it looks like it hurts. Does it hurt?"

Crystal stood up on her toes and pressed her chest against him and touched his face. Her breasts were small and firm, and her hands were cold. He kissed her.

"No, stop it, let me look at it." She laughed, and he kissed her again. "No, let me look at it, John. Does it hurt when I touch it?"

"Don't worry about it. The black eye is from a few days ago."

"So you didn't get in a fight tonight?"

"No, I got in a fight tonight, too."

She gave him her best look of disappointment and tried to pull away, but he grabbed her waist and kept her pressed against him. "You look fucking good," he said.

"Hmm . . . ." she whined. "So who did you fight?"

"A couple of jundies."

"What's a jundie?"

"A rag head."

"John! Don't say that!"

"We kicked the shit out of them."

"You're terrible."

"You're beautiful."

"Oh, you think so?"

He kissed her, and this time she responded. They mostly used their tongues, and it was not good kissing, but it was fun and closer to fucking than good kissing. He grabbed her ass with both hands and kissed her harder, and then she moved away.

"Oh my god, I was so drunk tonight, I'm still so drunk, but I'm starting to sober up. Does your friend have anything to drink?"

Hall opened Wright's fridge and pulled out two beers.

She eyed them skeptically. "Beer?"

"Well, what do you want?"

"Does he have any vodka?"

Hall opened the freezer and found a bottle of Grey Goose and poured two glasses on ice with a small press. As he poured, his ears started ringing.

"Water? Does he have any cranberry juice?"

"No. It's Grey Goose; it's fine with water."

He gave her a glass, and she took a small sip. The ringing in his ears went away.

"Oh, you're right, that's not bad. Oh my god, that bump on your head looks so painful. Does it hurt?"

He drank half his glass and pulled her close with one arm. She was tiny—no waist, only a small curve to her hips—but she was firm. He put his drink down and swept her dirty-blonde hair away from her neck so he could kiss her there. She whined and purred, and he came away and looked her in the eyes, moved in close again, their noses touching. Her eyes were large, and he liked the way she used them—flashing them open with surprise and challenge, then squinting lazily with pleasure, then darting playfully from side to side. She was very confident for her age. Hall reached up her shirt and wrapped his other hand around her throat and kissed her hard again.

The doorbell rang. She pulled away from him and looked at the front door and then back at Hall. "Who's that?"

"Someone for Wright."

"Who's Wright?"

"This is Wright's house."

"Oh."

Wright came down the stairs and looked into the kitchen. He still had not put a shirt on. Strands overlapped strands of stabilizer muscles, and veins and tattoos crawled over everything. Hall watched Crystal's eyes go over his abdomen. She straightened her back and pushed her chest out. Hall laughed.

The demon whispering into Wright's ear had been done in a darker shade than the rest of his tattoos. He stared at Crystal.

"Hello," he said.

"Hi, I'm Crystal. Are you Wright?"

"Yes."

The doorbell rang again, and he went to the front door and opened it. The escort waiting there was skinny, the frame of fashion or sickness. She came in with a careful sway and a practiced confidence that made her skinniness lithe.

Wright talked to her quietly in the front room. She leaned into him and touched his stomach, his arms, and his shoulders. When she walked past him to the stairs, she stopped for a moment at the kitchen and looked at Crystal and Hall.

"Hello," she said softly. She had a smoker's voice, and her face was worn. She had been beautiful once. Unfairly beautiful. Doomed.

"Hi," Crystal said.

The escort smiled at her and walked up the stairs.

Wright came back into the kitchen. "Have a nice night," he said and he followed the escort up the stairs.

When he was gone, Crystal turned to Hall with wide eyes. "Who was that? She kind of scares me."
"That was his wife."
"No, it wasn't!"
"It was."
"You're lying!"
"Maybe." Hall smiled at her.
"You'd never lie to me."
"Maybe."
"Stop being so terrible." She leaned up on her toes again, pressed her chest against him, and started rubbing him. "You haven't drank too much like last time, have you?"
"I'll be fine." He gently pushed her down onto her knees and undid his belt. He leaned down and kissed her, and then she started. He stood up straight and drained the rest of his vodka and watched her.

After a while she stopped and looked up at him. "Not again, John. Come on. Please, John, come on."

Chapter 8

The ringing came back in Hall's ears. He was soaked in sweat, and his mouth felt like it had been swabbed with cotton. Crystal was sleeping beside him in her underwear. He ran a clammy, shaking hand along her side and left a streak of sweat on her dry, smooth skin. He got out of bed, leaving a large oval sweat stain on the sheets, went to the hallway bathroom, splashed cold water on his face, and drank some.

He had to keep drinking—he could not imagine doing anything else. He went downstairs and found the bottle of vodka and mixed it with some Gatorade powder he found in the pantry. After he finished the drink, he started to feel better. He kept drinking. He looked at his darkened reflection in the window above the sink and touched his black eye. He ran a hand through his hair, and it stood up from the sweat. He flexed his chest and arms in profile, took a long drink, and threw up in the sink.

Wright came down the stairs with a half-empty bottle of Jack Daniels. He put it on the countertop between them. Dark red scratches covered his abdomen, the deeper ones rimmed with white where the skin was scratched off and hung loose and dead in small flakes. "How was she?" he asked.

"I got whiskey dick," Hall said.

"You what?"

"I couldn't get it up. I was too drunk."

Wright stared at him. "That's unacceptable."

"I'll fuck her in the morning," Hall said.

Wright shook his head. "No." He turned away and walked out of the kitchen and up the stairs.

Hall drank more vodka and Gatorade and cleaned the sink. Wright came back into the kitchen and put two red-and-grey capsules on the countertop.

"Take these," he said.

"What are they?"

"Cock pills."

"No, man, I said I'll fuck her in the morning. I have a goddamn concussion or something. My head is killing me, I keep throwing up, I'm sweating and shaking; I'm all fucked up, man. I don't want to fuck her right now."

"Take the pills and fuck her, Hall."

"Fuck off, man."

Wright inhaled sharply through his nose, and Hall saw that he was angry. Wright turned and walked away and then came back and put his hands on the island and leaned forward, his muscles bunching up and flaring. "Did you kill anyone overseas?"

"What?" Hall said, "You know I didn't, what the fuck—"

"You feel bad about that? Does it emasculate you that you were sent to war and you couldn't take a life?"

"I never had the chance."

"There were plenty of chances."

"Not any good ones."

"There were plenty of good ones."

"I mean right ones."

"Right?" Wright pushed away from the counter and stood in the middle of the kitchen, squaring off with Hall. "What the fuck is right? What the fuck did you do over there that you can call good or right or anything? There was no right or wrong; there was only doing your job or not doing your job, and you could have taken any number of lives as part of doing your job, so why didn't you? You weren't defending your country; you weren't drafted into the army. You joined the army because you wanted to fucking kill people, and you had the opportunity to do it, and now you're telling me you didn't because it wasn't right? Fuck right. Men kill when they have to, but there's no telling what compels a man enough that he *has* to do something. There's no way of measuring that, so we don't really kill when we have to; we kill when we can. You could have, but you didn't."

"I get it," Hall said. "You've killed people. Good for you. Why are you being such a fucking prick?"

"Just answer my question," Wright said. He came back over to the island and leaned into the countertop again. "Does it make you less of a man because you didn't kill anyone?"

"Fuck you, man."

"Answer the question, Hall."

"No, it doesn't."

"Yes." Wright took a drink of whiskey from the bottle, swallowed it, pursed his lips, and pointed at Hall. "You're right. It doesn't make you any less of a man, because a man's primary purpose is not to kill." He shifted his weight back and forth between his feet. He was in a fighting stance. "Now, what is the primary purpose of a man?"

"I don't know, Wright. Why don't you tell me?"

"Use your fucking head, Hall. This is important. And don't give me anymore fucking lip, or I swear to fuck I'll put you out." His face was red, his jaw clenched. He took another drink, coughed, and wiped his mouth with the back of his hand.

Hall looked at the capsules on the countertop. "To procreate," he said.

"Yes," Wright said, and his shoulders relaxed, as if Hall's answer had been a great relief to him. "As a male human being, your primary purpose on Earth is to spread your seed. As a man, your purpose is to fuck. Your job in Afghanistan wasn't to kill people; your job was to show up and follow orders. You showed up, and you followed orders. As a soldier, you did your job. But as a man, here and now, you have not. You have failed. I won't stand for that, Hall, not in my house, and not as your friend. Now take these pills, drink some whiskey, go upstairs, and fuck that little bitch."

Chapter 9

Crystal went home Saturday morning, and Wright and Hall drank all day and night. On Sunday Hall went home, picking up a two-six of vodka and a couple cartons of orange juice on the way to his apartment. He got drunk, pissed himself in his sleep, and when he woke up, his alarm had been ringing for twenty minutes. His bed was wet and cold, and he was badly hung over. He made a screwdriver with the last of the vodka and drank half of it. He showered and shaved and drank the rest of the screwdriver and a tall glass of water.

It was nice out that morning, barely below freezing, and the battalion went for a ten-kilometer run.

"Jesus Christ, Hall," the guy behind him said. "You smell like a fuckin' brewery."

"Is Hall drunk again?"

"Hall, you need some black coffee in a church basement."

A few guys laughed.

"Shut the fuck up in the ranks!" a warrant screamed.

They stopped to do push-ups, and halfway through his set, Hall started throwing up. He got some cheers of approval while he finished the set and formed back up in the ranks to continue running.

After PT, they started post-ex drills, first working on the LAVs. Equipment was checked and manifested, oils were changed, tires replaced, troop compartments cleaned and organized, hauls pressure washed, weapons cleaned and oiled, and all serial numbers confirmed.

After they finished with the LAVs, they started on the toboggan groups. They ripped them apart, hung the tents up to dry, cleaned and organized the tools and kit, and repacked everything back into the toboggans. Once they were finished, one of the section 2ICs, Master Corporal Rich, said that everything needed to be laid out on the shelves in the platoon cage, so they unpacked the toboggans and organized everything to one platoon standard. As soon as they finished, the platoon warrant came out of the office. He was a lean, wiry man with crooked teeth.

"What the fuck are you guys doing?" the warrant shouted. "Who the fuck's the dumb cunt who said to lay this shit out? Where the fuck are my 2IC's?"

Wright and the other master corporals circled around the warrant. "Now whose bright fucking idea was this?"

"It was mine, Warrant," Master Corporal Rich said.

"Rich, you stunned cunt, do you not remember me saying we're preparing for IRF?" He was nearly screaming. Men from other platoons made themselves scarce, disappearing upstairs, behind lockers, and down hallways.

"Yes, Warrant."

"Then why the fuck would you spread my fucking toboggans out across my fucking cage? Is that the SOP for IRF? What the fuck does IRF mean to you, Rich?"

"It means instant reac—"

"I didn't ask what the fucking acronym stands for, you stupid fuck!" He was screaming now. "Get the fuck into the office! The rest of you, get the fuck out of my cage!"

The warrant followed Rich into the office, slammed the door behind him, and started screaming again.

"Hang out in the back," Wright told the platoon. He turned to Hall. "You got a cigarette?"

"Yeah."

They went outside to the smoke shack.

"Fuck, he's on the warpath today," Hall said.

"He's getting divorced again."

"Again? How many is that?"

"I don't know. I think he remarried one of them. If that's the case, then two. If not, three. Either way, it's three divorces. He's going to want to talk to you at some point today."

"About what?"

"The fight."

"You told him about the fight?"

Wright gave him a look. "What do you think?"

"Hartford."

"Yeah, Hartford. Half the battalion knew before PT was finished."

"Fuck. I can't handle the warrant right now," Hall said. "My nerves are shot, and my head is still fucked up."

"Don't worry about it. I doubt he'll jack you up. I think he just spent it all on Rich."

From inside the lines, the warrant screamed for the 2ICs. Wright laughed, put his cigarette out and walked back inside.

Hall was talking with a few guys in his platoon when Wright came back and told him to go see the warrant.

There were five desks in the platoon office. The warrant's desk was at the back facing in, and the others faced the warrant. Some of the section commanders and 2ICs were working at computers on the desks, and Master Corporal Rich was in a corner running a massive pile of paper through an old shredder.

Hall knocked on the door, and the warrant looked up at him. "Hall," he said, "get in here."

Hall was still hung over and concussed, and his knees were shaking. He walked over to the warrant's desk and stood in front of it. The warrant leaned back in his chair and put his hands on the armrests with his elbows raised like he was about to leap out of his seat. Hall's knees shook harder and he leaned back slightly against the desk behind him. It helped.

"Well, tell me a story, Hall."

"A story, Warrant?"

"Yes, Hall, a story. I hear you got a few of them."

"A few, Warrant." His voice shook.

"Let's start with something recent. How about something from the weekend."

"Well, I got in a scrap with a few of the boys, Warrant."

"Tell me about it."

"It was on Whyte Ave. and we got into it with a couple of jundies. There were no cops."

"Is that right, Master Corporal Wright?"

"Yes, Warrant."

Hall turned and saw that Wright was standing behind him.

"All right, Hall, do you know why I'm not pissed?" the warrant asked.

"No paperwork, Warrant?"

"That's one reason. Why else?"

Hall thought for a moment. "I notified my chain of command immediately, Warrant."

"Exactly. I'm going to give you the benefit of the doubt and assume you would have thought of that if your 2IC hadn't been right there throwing punches beside you." The warrant cracked a little and grinned. "Well, you get any good shots in?"

"He beat the living fuck out of one of 'em," Wright said. "Left him in a pool of blood."

"Good," the warrant said. "That's what I like to hear. Pass it around to the rest of the troops that if it doesn't land on my desk and you notify your chain of command immediately, you'll never get any flak from me. Now go—wait, aren't you clearing out, Hall?"

"Yes, Warrant."

"I'll tell you what, you take the rest of the day to yourself, get your admin done. Just swing by around 1530 for the O group."

"Roger that. Thanks, Warrant."

Hall left the office and walked around the lines for half an hour. He got two signatures on his clear-out papers and then went out to the parking lot and got in his car and drove to a bar. He sat in a corner booth and drank pints of beer and texted Crystal and another girl he found in his contact list but could not remember meeting. He got the girl's last name and added her to Facebook and went through her photos. After he had gone through all the best ones, he unfriended her and stopped texting her.

He texted Wright and Hartford and told them to come to the bar for lunch. Hartford said he would, but Wright did not reply. Hall was looking at flights to Spain when they arrived together. They ordered two pitchers of beer and their meals. Wright and Hartford had a 1300 timing, so they drank fast, and Hall naturally fell in step with them. As they started on the second pitcher, Hall asked Wright about the pills he had given him.

"It's a Cialis knock-off," Wright said.

"You use them often?"

"All the time. I pretty much have to now."

"Really?"

"Yeah. I haven't gotten a good, natural hard-on in years."

"Jesus, man," Hall said, "why don't you go get that sorted out?"

"Sorted out? What, go talk to some shrink about my cock? I don't think so. Those pills work fine for me. I get good hard-ons with those pills. You want a bottle?"

"Yeah. Fuck yeah."

"What about you?"

"No," Hartford said, "I don't need pills to get a hard-on."

"You do to get real hard," Wright said. He held his fist up and squeezed it, and the muscles in his forearm bunched together tightly. "Hard like you got when you were fourteen. Rudely hard. You'll tear your woman in half."

"I don't fucking need that shit."

"Well, get me some anyway," Hall said. "Can you give me a couple until you get me a bottle?"

"Sure," Wright said, "but Hartford's the one who really needs them. He's the one with a girlfriend."

"I don't fucking need them."

"Not to function, but they'll improve you."

"I don't need improvement. I fuck just fine."

"So you fuck just fine? Why not fuck greatly? It's all you have for her, so you might as well give it to her as best you can."

"The fuck is that supposed to mean?" Hartford said.

"You're a soldier. You don't have shit for your woman except your cock. You're loud and rude, you drink too much, you get paid fuck all, you're always away from home, and when you are home, you're always tired and pissed off. The only thing that makes you any good to a modern woman is your cock, so you might as well keep it nice and hard."

"You're very Freudian," Hall said to Wright.

"He's full of shit," Hartford said.

"Let's get another pitcher," Wright said.

"Okay."

Their meals came, and they ordered another pitcher. They drank quickly, and as soon as the third pitcher was finished,

Wright and Hartford paid their bills and left. Hall ordered a double rye and ginger and called Crystal. She agreed to come over later that night. After they hung up, he ordered another double and looked around the bar. The ringing started in his ears, and it was loud, but it did not last long.

Hall noticed an old man in a booth on the opposite side of the bar staring at him. He wore denim and plaid, and Hall could see he was dirty. The bar was not large, and they were not far from each other. The man had a month-long beard, and the skin on his face was blotchy and red. They stared at each other for a while, and then the man stood up and came over to Hall's booth and put one hand on the backrest opposite him.

When he spoke, there was a rasp in his voice from a lifetime of smoking and an uneasy tremble from something personal. "Thank you, son. That's all I wanted to come over and say. Thank you very much. Did you go over there?"

"Yes, sir," Hall said, "I did."

The old man held out his hand, and Hall stood up and took it. The old man had a good grip.

"Well, thank you, son. Thank you for everything."

"It was nothing," Hall said.

"Nothing?"

"It's just a job."

They were still shaking hands.

"And over there? What was that?"

"Part of the job."

"Part of the job?"

"Some loud noises and a bit of blood. That's all."

"Ah. Well, thank you for that then."

"You're welcome."

"Take care," the old man said, releasing Hall's hand.

"You, too. Or do you want to have a drink with me?"

"No, thank you," he said, "I like to drink alone."

"Me too."

"I'm sorry to hear that."

"Yeah, me too."

"Goodbye."

"Goodbye."

Hall drank another double, paid his bill, and left.

He was drunk when he got to the lines and he smoked a few cigarettes to hide the smell before the O group. After the warrant had passed on the points and let them off for the day, Hall followed Wright to his house, and Wright gave him a dozen pills in a plastic bag. They drank a few beers, and then Hall drove to a liquor store and bought three bottles of wine. He cracked a bottle of something white in the car and poured some into a travel mug. It was cold and went down nicely. He could taste a bit of the coffee that had been in the mug before. It started to snow lightly, and he turned the radio and the heat up and rolled his window all the way down. He was feeling good with how drunk he was, how early it was, that he had the pills, that Crystal was coming over, and that he would be out of the army soon.

He stopped at the grocery store. In the parking lot, two old women were trying to push a cart full of groceries through the snow and slush, and they were moving slowly and clumsily. Hall took the cart from them, pushed it to their vehicle, emptied the groceries into the trunk of their car, took the empty cart, and pushed it into a stack near the entrance. He went inside and bought a rotisserie chicken and some fresh white buns.

When he got home, he ripped apart the chicken and ate all the best parts, using the buns to mop up the grease. He drank water with the meal, and when he was finished, he washed his hands and face and drank another full glass of water so that he felt bloated. When he poured himself a glass of wine, he could only drink it slowly. He sat on the couch and watched TV, drank wine, and smoked cigarettes until Crystal phoned and said she would be over in an hour. He did 150 push-ups in sets of 25. Between sets, he tidied the apartment so that when he was finished the place looked presentable, and his chest and arms were full of blood and good and firm. He flexed in the bathroom mirror. Satisfied, he took two of the pills and had a shower.

    Crystal was late, so Hall went back to the couch, drinking, smoking, and going through Facebook on his laptop while he waited. One of Crystal's friends had tagged some pictures of her from the weekend. There were five pictures, four of her with other women posing for the camera and one of her and a man—a boy, really. They were sitting on a couch together. Crystal had her back to the boy's side, her feet up on the couch, his arm around her, her head turned toward him, her saying something, their faces close. Hall put the laptop away and poured himself another glass of wine and smoked another cigarette. The windows were all closed, and he could see the smoke in its layers—smooth waves rising and falling. He waved a pillow, and the waves disintegrated into a bland, grey haze.

    When Crystal arrived, she came in energetically, carrying her purse and two shopping bags and wearing a tight, low-cut white shirt under a loose, dark blouse and black leggings. Hall helped her take off her jacket and took her bags from her and put them in the kitchen. He turned to her. She was talking quickly about something, but he cut her off by kissing her. He pushed her against the wall, pulled her blouse off, and she laughed and started to talk, but he kissed her again, running his hands over her roughly. The pills worked well, and she succumbed to it. He turned her around, pushed her against the wall, pulled her leggings down, and took her.

It did not last long, but it was good and strong, and they were happy after it was over and slightly embarrassed. They put their clothes back on, and Hall poured two glasses of wine. They sat on the couch, and he put his arm around her, but it made him think of her and that boy, so he took it back, lit a cigarette, and did not return it. She did not seem to notice, or it did not bother her if she did. She brought up her legs, crossed them underneath herself, and started to talk. Hall nodded, laughing and talking when it was appropriate and sometimes when it was not. It was more of a monologue than a conversation, and his contributions did not do much to change the path she was on, only confirmed that he was actively listening. She was performing a function as regular and essential to her as eating or sleeping, and he was the platform on which she satisfied that basic need, more than a simple enabler, less than a source of inspiration for the process, as she had been for him when he had taken her against the wall.

Suddenly, she jumped up, skipped over to her bags, and started pulling things out. She turned her back to him and peeled off her leggings.

"You have such a wonderful ass," he said.

She slapped it for him.

"Good girl," he said, and they both laughed.

She tried on two pairs of pants and three shirts, and he told her which ones he liked best, and then she put on sweatpants and one of his old desert T-shirts and came back to the couch with him.

"So, what do you want to do?" she asked. "You've already fucked me, so now what?"

"Let's watch a movie," he said.

"What movie?"

"*Gladiator*."

"No way."

"What?"

"We are not watching that again," she said. "I hate that movie. You just get really drunk and yell all the lines at me. It's no fun."

"Good art isn't supposed to be fun."

"It's not art; it's a movie."

"That is very wrong and a terrible thing to say. Just for that we're watching the extended version and all the deleted scenes."

"No," she whined, "no, no, no!"

"Yes," Hall said, "and do you know why?"

"Why?"

"Because I'm stronger than you."

She sighed dramatically and slapped him lightly across the face. He grabbed her and wrapped his arms around her and tried to bite her ear. She hated her ears being touched, and she squealed and screamed and laughed.

"John, stop! I said stop! John!"

He let her go, and she turned on him angrily and raised her eyebrows.

"What?" he said. She slapped him again, and they laughed and settled down.

"Why don't you get us some more wine?" Hall said.

"Excuse me? What do you think I am?"

"Energetic."

She put on a cute, whiney voice. "And I'm supposed to use all my energy being your little slave?"

"Yes."

She slapped him again.

"Stop slapping me."

"Or what?" she said.

"Or I'll fucking sort you out."

"Stop being so tough. You're not so tough. I know what you are. You're just a pink, little, mushy marshmallow. You're a pink marshmallow that's been overcooked so that you're all crusty and burnt on the outside, but on the inside, you're all pink and mushy and nice."

"That was a brilliant psychoanalysis," Hall said. "You might just be right."

"I'm always right."

"How about that wine?"

"Ugh. Only if you say please."

"Please."

"Please what?"

"Please, beautiful."

"Fine."

She took their empty glasses and came close to his face. He went to kiss her, but she pulled back and smiled, came close again, pulled back once more, and went into the kitchen. She came back with their glasses full, gave him his, and sat on the couch with her back to his side. It was only natural for him to put his arm around her. So it had only been natural for that boy.

"Are you still going on your trip?" she asked.

"That's the plan."

"To Thailand?"

"I'm thinking Spain."

"Spain?"

"Spain."

"I'd love to go to Spain," she said.

He took a long sip of wine and put his cheek against the top of her head. "Well, come with me, then."

"Yeah, right."

"Why not?"

"I couldn't afford it."

"I'll help you pay for it, once I get paid out by the army."

"Why would you do that?"

"Why not?"

"You're not being serious, are you?"

"Sure I am."

She turned and looked at him, at different parts of his face, then turned back. "I don't know. Spain would be pretty cool though. Do you think I'd like it?"

"You'd love it. I'd make sure you did."

She took his hand in hers and started picking at the scabs where his fingers had blistered. "I don't know. That's a pretty big thing, you know. We're not even dating."

"Let's stop talking about it. Even if it does happen, it won't happen for a few months."

"Okay. So, what do you want to do?"

Hall put his glass of wine down on the coffee table next to hers. He grabbed her legs and pulled her around so she was facing him with her legs across his, and he kissed her.

They put a movie on, something besides *Gladiator*. She talked over it, and he opened the third bottle of wine. He was getting very drunk. She started talking about the weekend, about a house party with some old high-school friends she had went to, where he assumed that boy had been.

"Did you fuck him?" he asked.

"Excuse me?" She pushed herself away from him to the opposite end of the couch. "Are you serious, John?"

"Sure I am. Did you?"

"No, John, I did not fuck him, and even if I did, it wouldn't be any of your business. We're not dating, in case you've forgotten."

"It wouldn't be any of my business?" Hall said. "So if you had fucked him, you'd tell me you hadn't, is that what you're saying?"

"No, I did not fuck him, John. Oh my god, where is this coming from? Is it because of that picture on Facebook? You automatically assume because I was sitting beside a guy on a couch that I had sex with him?"

"Well, you two looked pretty goddamn friendly."

"We were catching up. I hadn't seen him in like a year, John."

"That's a pretty slutty-looking way to play catch-up."

"Oh my god, did you just call me a slut? You just called me a slut."

"No, I didn't call you a slut. I said you were being slutty. That doesn't mean I'm calling you a slut. I like to drink, but that doesn't make me a drunk."

"Oh yeah, John," she said, "are you sure you're not a drunk?"

"Are you sure you're not a slut?"

"Oh my god, I don't need to take this. Fuck you, John, you fucking asshole. You're a real piece of shit, you know that? My friends told me to stay away from army guys, and obviously I should have listened."

"Probably should have," Hall said.

She collected her bags and put on her jacket. When she left, she was still wearing his old desert T-shirt.

For good measure, he threw a wine bottle at the wall.

* * *

Chapter 10

Hall woke up to a loud banging on his front door. Nothing really registered until he opened it and saw Hartford and Wright standing there in their uniforms, both smiling.

"Oh, fuck," Hall said. "Fuck, no, fuck. I did. Fuck. What time is it?"

"Nine thirty."

"Fuck."

"Relax," Wright said, and they came into his apartment. "You're already AWOL, and there's nothing you can do about it, so there's no sense getting all worked up."

Hartford pointed at the wine stains on the wall and laughed. The bottle had left a dent in the drywall.

"Looks like you had fun at least," Hartford said.

"Two weeks," Hall said as he collected the pieces of his uniform. "Two weeks until I'm out, and I sleep in. Fuck, man, fuck."

"You'll be shot for sure," Hartford said. "They've already selected a firing squad. I volunteered so I can shoot you in the dick."

Hall put on a green T-shirt and combat pants. While he was looking for a tunic and his beret, he found a half-empty bottle of wine and took a drink from it.

"Now you're thinking," Wright said. He took the bottle from him, took a drink, and handed it back. "Relax for a minute," he said.

Wright sat down on the couch. Hall sat beside him and took another drink.

"So, what's it look like?" Hall asked.

"Not too bad. We kept it under the rug. None of the officers know. The sergeant major knows though, so you'll have to see him."

"Fuck."

"Whatever, man. Even if they charge you, you only have two more weeks. They might be two really shitty weeks, but you've been through worse."

Hartford came over, grabbed the bottle, and took a drink. "Ugh. How can you drink this shit?" he said and he handed the bottle back to Hall.

Hall took another two good drinks, and the bottle was empty.

Wright and Hartford talked and laughed most of the way back to the lines. Hall stared out the window. Hartford tried to bring him into the conversation a few times, but Hall could not handle it.

At the battalion lines, Wright took Hall into the office. The warrant looked up at him from his desk.

"Hall."

"Warrant."

The warrant's lips rolled from top to bottom like he was trying to find the source of a bad taste in his mouth. Hall looked him in the eyes, still a little drunk, waiting for it, ready for it, but it never came.

"Stay in the back," the warrant said finally. "Wait until the sergeant major is ready for you. Roger?"

"Roger that, Warrant."

Hall walked to the back of the lines. Most of the company was back there playing cards, reading magazines, or bullshitting. Someone started a slow clap, and when they had all seen him, it spread quickly into applause. He went for a cigarette, and Hartford followed him outside.

"So, what's the deal?" Hartford asked.

"I'm waiting to see the sergeant major."

"Shitty. He's gonna execute you."

"He's not that bad."

"No, I know he's not. He's cool. I was just bugging you. It'll be fine. Going upstairs sucks though. I hate it."

"Everyone does."

"It'll be fine though."

"Yeah."

"Two more weeks."

"Two more weeks."

Hall stayed in the back, waiting to be called upstairs, talking to some friends and telling them the story. It was fun for a while. He felt energized by it, by all the attention and the impending climb up the two flights of stairs to the offices above.

The lunch break came and went, and the wine wore off completely. Hall's heartbeat picked up an irregular, anxious rhythm. He kept feeling his pulse, trying to make sense of it. His hands went cold and clammy, and the shaking settled in. He kept thinking he heard his name being called, but whenever he asked someone about it, they said they had not heard anything or that the call was not for him.

Finally, Wright came back to him. "All right, dude."

They went upstairs. The sergeant major's office was the first on the right. His door was open. Wright stood to the side, and Hall walked through the door and tried to slam his boot down as he came to attention, but he fucked up the step into it and made a pathetic smacking sound instead.

"Sir."

The sergeant major had a square jaw, a high and tight haircut, and well weathered skin. He looked like the warrant but ten years older and with better teeth.

"Corporal Hall," he said. "Shut the door."

Hall closed the door and went back to attention.

The sergeant major leaned back in his chair and stared at him. "Look at yourself."

Hall looked down, looking for something wrong with his uniform, and then back up at the sergeant major.

"You're fucking vibrating," the sergeant major said. "Sit down before you fall down."

"Sir," Hall said, and he sat down in the single chair across from him.

"It takes a lot of alcohol to make a man shake like that the next day. Do you know why I waited until now to speak with you?"

"So I'd be sober, sir."

"That's right. It's not so fun up here when you're sober, is it?"

"No, sir."

The sergeant major looked away for a moment and rubbed his chin. When he looked at Hall again, he leaned forward in his chair. "Hall, I've been tracking you since you came to this company, and I've heard mostly good things about you on every exercise. I also know your chain of command from your tour, and they all speak pretty highly of you. But this is not the first time you've stepped on your dick here on base, and correct me if I'm wrong, but every incident you've had has been alcohol related. Is that right?"

"Yes, sir."

"Is your drinking a problem for you, Corporal Hall?"

"No, sir."

"Are you sure? We're not talking on an administrative level here. This is a personal question out of concern for one of my troops. I've been around awhile, Hall, and trust me, it's better if you're honest. So, once again, do you think your drinking is or might be a problem for you?"

"No, sir."

The sergeant major leaned back in his chair again. "All right, Corporal Hall, that's good to hear. I'm not going to charge you, but your warrant will have some extras for you. Your next two weeks are going to be very busy. Carry on."

Hall stood up and came to attention. "Sir," he said and then walked out.

On the drive home, Hall turned into a shopping center for some food but parked in front of the Liquor Depot instead.

He walked through the automatic doors. It was warm inside. A middle-aged woman was offering samples of wine. He took a sample and walked down the aisle to the far corner and looked through the bottles. A fan blew warm air through the aisle, and the draft went down the back of his neck. He picked a forty-pounder of vodka. He waited in line and moved the bottle back and forth between his hands. It was heavy. When it was his turn to pay, he was shaking so badly that he had to use two hands to get his debit card into the machine—one hand to hold it, the other hand to guide it. The clerk was a beautiful woman his age. She wore a plaid shirt that she had tied around the middle so that a bit of her stomach was exposed. He was too nervous to look her in the eye, and when she greeted him and asked him how his day was going, he could not bring himself to say anything. He just paid and left.

Chapter 11

Hall did not remember going to sleep or waking up; he simply came to with his ears ringing, lying next to a red-headed girl in a strange bed. He was in a room like his own. The paint and the blinds were exactly the same. He was somewhere in his apartment building. The redhead beside him was breaking out on her forehead, and her lips were dry and cracking.

"Good morning," Hall said.

She smiled, and he saw that she had braces. He smiled back at her.

"How did you sleep?" he asked. He tried to remember her name, but he could not. He had drank hard and fast, and the blackout was complete and left him with nothing. The ringing in his ears quieted down. He was still very drunk and he felt good. He wondered who the girl was and what he had done with her the night before. He assumed he had met her in a bar. It must have been a sure thing after they had found out they lived in the same apartment building.

"I slept so bad," she said. "You kept me up all night with your snoring. It was so loud, it was, like, terrible. You snore worse than my mother."

Hall leaned up on an elbow and moved the covers around. He was naked. Realizing this, he pulled the covers away from her and saw that she was also naked. Her skin was a perfect white, spotted with freckles, her breasts were firm and round, and she had wonderful curves and hips and wrists and everything. Hall pulled the covers completely off and stared at her body, running his hand over it. She smiled at him and hummed as he went over her. He was hard to the point it hurt. He wondered if he was still operating on the pills he had taken for Crystal or if he had taken more the night before. She grabbed him and started pulling on him, and he kissed her. He moved to her neck and started kissing her there.

"You're such a dirty old man," she said.

"I am not."

"Yes, you are!"

She really pulled on him. He got rough with his hands.

"I'm not old."

"You're, like, so old."

"How old are you?" he asked.

"You know how old I am."

"Tell me again."

"What?"

"Tell me again how old you are."

"I'm fifteen."

Hall stopped. "What?"

"Fifteeeeen," she whined.

"You're fifteen? What do you mean you're fifteen?"

"I mean I'm fifteen. I'm almost sixteen though." She kept pulling on him, but he grabbed her hand and stopped her.

"Fifteen," Hall said. He sat up in the bed and leaned his back against the wall. There was no headboard, and there was a space between the wall and the bed. He let one of his arms hang down there. He put his other arm across his lap and tried to keep himself down. He looked away from her and thought for a moment and looked around the room. It was a mess. Clothes and makeup and other things covered the floor, and magazine cut-outs of men and women, mostly actors, were taped to the walls. He looked at her again, and she was smiling with her lips open. He looked at her braces, and he did not feel good anymore.

"You don't remember anything from last night, do you?"

"It's a little hazy," Hall admitted.

"You don't remember fucking me?"

"We shouldn't have done that."

"Why not?"

"Because you're fifteen."

"But that's, like, why you wanted to fuck me in the first place," she said.

"What?"

"That's why you wanted to fuck me in the first place," she repeated, drawing out every word.

He turned over so that he was facing her better and pulled the blanket up over them. He smiled at her. "I need you to do something for me, okay?"

"Okay," she said. Her eyes went over his face, and she smiled again. He looked at her braces again.

"I want you to tell me everything about last night. Right up to this second, and don't leave anything out. I want every detail."

"Wow, you like really blacked out, didn't you? That's so weird, you didn't seem that drunk to me. You were like talking fine, and you weren't stumbling or anything. My mother is like that. She doesn't seem too drunk, but the next day she like doesn't remember anything. You two were talking about blacking out last night, but you probably don't remember. Actually, it's kind of funny that you don't." She started laughing and moving her legs around, kicking at the blankets. "You blacked out your blackout talk. I bet you don't even know my name."

"I don't."

"That's like so funny."
"What's your name?"
"Zoe."
"I'm John."
"I know."
"So can you do that for me, please, Zoe? Can you tell me everything about last night?"
"I guess so."
"Okay, go ahead."
"Okay." She turned so she was lying on her back and looking at the ceiling. "Well, you came in with my mom last night. You were wearing your army stuff—well, just your pants and your boots and a T-shirt, you know, like all that green stuff. Your like uniform or whatever. You had met my mom in the hallway at a vending machine or something, and you had this like huge bottle of vodka with you, and you and my mom drank it pretty fast. I was in my room talking to my boyfriend on the phone, or not really my boyfriend, but that, like, guy from school I was telling you about, but you probably don't remember that either. Do you remember me telling you about him? His name is Erik. But it doesn't matter. Never mind. Anyway, so I hung up and came out, and you were sitting on the couch with my mom drinking vodka, and when I came out you said I was the most goddamn beautiful redheaded thing you've ever seen, and that's exactly how you said it, you were like, 'You're the most goddamn beautiful redheaded thing I've ever seen,' and it was so funny. You were being pretty funny.

"Anyway, you asked if I wanted a drink, and my mom was like, 'No, she's only fifteen,' but then my mom was like, 'Well, whatever, she drinks with her friends anyway,' and my mom poured me some of your vodka, and I drank with you guys. I don't really remember what we talked about. You and my mom were pretty loud, and I guess she was talking about her job, and you were talking about the army. And then we finished your vodka and started drinking my mom's gin, and I got pretty drunk, like I was actually having lots of fun. You kept asking me about school and stuff and about what I do with my friends and about, like, boys in school and stuff. My mom was like really drunk at that point, and she kept, like, passing out on the couch with a cigarette in her hand, and we would take it from her and smoke it. That happened like a thousand times. It was pretty funny. I got pretty drunk off that gin. Then you asked me if I'd ever been kissed by a man, and I said I guess not, and then you just stood up and walked over to me and kissed me. It was pretty hard not to let it happen, like you came over to me and put your hand on my cheek and looked me right in the eyes, and it wasn't like you forced me to kiss you or anything, but you made it like there wasn't really any other choice. Do you know what I mean? I'm not mad about it. I liked it, but it was just how you did it, you know? I don't know. It was pretty funny. Never mind.

"Anyway, then we just sat in the chair in the living room, or you sat in the chair and I like sat in your lap or whatever, and we talked really quietly so we wouldn't wake my mom up. We made out a few times. I was pretty drunk from the gin, and I was being silly, and you must have been really drunk, too, because that bottle of vodka was already half empty when you came in, but it didn't seem like you were that drunk. And yeah, we made out. Do you remember that? No, you don't remember anything, do you? That's so weird. But whatever, anyway, you told me that I was in my, like, sexual prime and that all the boys at school didn't have anything for me. You said that boys don't turn into men until they're well over twenty, but girls become women when they're my age. You were like, 'just look at you,' and you said I had the best body you've ever seen, but you always said 'goddamn.' You were like, 'You have the best goddamn body I've ever seen.' It was so funny. You were being pretty funny. You said the Romans had it right and that too many generations of insecure fathers or, like, overprotective fathers or something like that have fucked everything up so that a woman's, like, prime or whatever is wasted on boys. Oh yeah, and you said it's not weird if you're not old enough to be my dad, and it's kind of true, I mean you're not really that old, like I told you about my friend who fucked that guy who's like thirty-five, right? That's pretty weird, if you ask me. You don't remember me telling you about that? You said it was pretty weird, too. Anyway, yeah, you said a bunch of other stuff, and then you fucked me. You were really hard. Yeah I guess that's, like, pretty much it. I can't believe you don't remember any of it."

She turned and looked at him for a moment. She licked her lips and left her tongue pressed against her bottom lip. Hall looked at her braces and smiled. She looked back at the ceiling and continued.

"And yeah, then you passed out. Like you were out, like right out. You started snoring and, ugh, you were so loud, it was terrible. I kept punching you in the shoulder, and sometimes you would quiet down a bit. Anyway, I passed out, but then your phone woke me up. I don't know what time it was, sometime in the morning, it was starting to get light out. Then, like, five minutes later, it rang again, and it kept ringing, like, ten more times, so I turned your volume off."

Hall laughed. "That was nice of you. Most people would have just woke me up."

"I know, right? So, yeah, then we woke up, and now I want you to fuck me again, but now you're being all stupid about me being fifteen."

"Yeah, I am being pretty stupid," Hall said.

She grabbed him and started pulling on him again, but he took her hand away.

"Ugh," she said. "Come on. Stop being stupid."

"I can't."

"Why not?"

"You're too young."

"You're scared of the 'R-word,' aren't you?"

"The R-word?"

"You know . . . rape."

"Rape?"

"Yeah, rape. Statutory rape. I know what statutory rape is."

"Don't start talking about that," Hall said. "I don't want to hear that again. That would not work out well for anyone."

"Yeah, I guess you're right," she said.

Hall carefully released the breath he was holding.

"So, that's it then? You don't want to fuck me, because it's illegal?"

"No, it's not just that," Hall said. "I just don't feel right about it."

"Why? Are you worried about what other people might think?"

"I guess so."

"Last night you said, like, fuck what other people think. I liked you better last night."

Hall sat up and looked around for his clothes. He found his combat pants and his green T-shirt but no socks or underwear. He put on what he found and sat back on the bed. He found his phone on her dresser and saw he had thirty-four missed calls. The time read 10:49. He told Zoe that she had to come with him so he could buy her a Plan B. She said she had never taken it before, and she seemed excited about it.

Once she was dressed, they went out into the living room. The place was in relatively good order. It was not dirty, but it was crowded. Porcelain cats, mix-and-match pieces of china, and little fake flowers covered massive pieces of antique-looking furniture. There was very little room to move around.

Zoe's mother was asleep on the couch. She was in her early forties, her face was lined with wrinkles, and her nose was a blotchy red. She was snoring. Zoe went into the kitchen and came back with two Twisted Teas and gave one to Hall.

They walked upstairs to his apartment, which was still in the shape he had left it after the night with Crystal. He shaved and put on the rest of his uniform. Zoe asked about the wine stain where he had thrown the bottle against the wall, and he told her he had thrown it to kill a spider. She laughed. His phone kept ringing, and he kept it on silent and did not answer it.

They got into his car and drove to a shopping complex with a McDonald's, a Liquor Depot, and a Rexall Drugs. He went into the Liquor Depot first and bought a mickey of vodka for himself and a twelve-pack of Twisted Teas for Zoe. They went into the Rexall together, and he bought the Plan B. It was expensive, and he had to use his debit card. He wondered if he had enough money. It seemed to take forever to process, but it went through.

Back in the car, he gave her the two pills and watched her take them. He made her show him the inside of her mouth and told her to lift her tongue and say, "Ahh." She did, and they both laughed.

They drove through the McDonald's drive-through and bought some food and a large orange juice for the vodka. They ate in the parking lot and drank the Twisted Teas and listened to the radio. Hall drank two while they ate, and after they finished, he opened a third. He was starting to feel better.

"Hey," Zoe said, "those were supposed to be for me, you know."

"Bootlegger's fee," Hall said.

"No fair. So, now what? Are you going back to the army?"

"Yeah," Hall said, "I guess I'm going back to the army. When do you get your braces taken off?"

"This year," she said. "Actually, in a couple of months."

"You're going to have really nice teeth when they're off."

"You think so?"

"Yeah. You're going to look even prettier, and you're very pretty right now."

"Thank you." She smiled brightly and finished her drink.

Hall drove her back to their apartment building. They did not exchange numbers and agreed they would see each other in the hallway someday.

"Well, it was very nice to meet you, Johnny," she said.

"Johnny?"

"Yeah, I've decided I'm going to call you Johnny. Is that okay?"

"Sure, I love it."

"Really?"

"Really."

"Awesome! Well, I'm eighteen in, like, two and one quarter years, so maybe then, you know, you won't have any reason to be so stupid anymore."

Hall laughed. "I'd be stupid not to chase after an eighteen-year-old woman like you."

"Promise you will?"

"I promise."

"Okay! Well, have fun in the army." She went to kiss him, but he turned his head and hugged her and kissed her on the cheek. "Ugh, Johnny," she said, "you're so stupid it makes me mad."

"I know, but I have to go now."

"Okay, well, see you later, but give me just one more hug, please."

He hugged her again.

"Bye Johnny!" she said and she took her box of Twisted Teas back to the apartment.

Hall drove to the lines and poured half the mickey of vodka into the orange juice and drank it before he went inside. He walked straight into the office and the warrant stood him at attention. He screamed and pointed his finger in Hall's face and Hall felt flecks of saliva landing on his forehead and cheeks. He was drunk enough not to mind any of it, saying "Yes, Warrant" or "No, Warrant" when it seemed appropriate. He watched a strand of spit attached to the warrant's lips expand and contract as his mouth opened and closed. When the warrant started losing his voice he wiped his mouth with the back of his hand and told Hall to wait in the back.

Hall walked to where most of the company was sitting around. No one applauded this time, but a few guys shouted and laughed. Hall ignored them and went out for a cigarette. Hartford was smoking with Franklin and two other new guys in their platoon.

"Look who decided to show up," Franklin said, smiling and laughing with the other new guys.

"Shut the fuck up, you stupid cunt," Hartford growled. Franklin and the other two turned away and talked in their own group. Hartford slapped Hall on the back. Hall lit a cigarette and did not say anything.

They smoked in silence for a while, and then Hartford started laughing. "Give me a hug."

Hall did, and he started laughing, too.

"Jesus, you reek like vodka," Hartford said, pulling back.

"I know. I'm wasted."

"Of course you are."

Wright came out and took Hall up to the sergeant major's office. When Hall came to attention at his door, he slammed his foot down, and his boot connected perfectly and shook the floor.

"Sir," he said.

The sergeant major looked up at him. He brought him in and told him to shut the door. Hall did and went back to attention.

The sergeant major looked him up and down. "You're not shaking today, Corporal Hall."

"No, sir."

The sergeant major did not say anything else about it. He talked about discipline and told Hall that he was going to be charged. He explained how it would work with him releasing so soon, that he would be very busy the next thirteen days, and that he was walking on very thin ice, and was very close to being dishonourably discharged.

Then, when he seemed to be wrapping things up, the sergeant major said, "Corporal Hall, you're out of the army in thirteen days. Yesterday, you told me you don't consider your drinking a problem, but I think your actions in the past twenty-four hours suggest the opposite. When it comes to shit like this, Hall, I can't do anything for you unless you want to do something for yourself. It has to be you. You have to want to better yourself, but before you can better yourself, you need to recognize where there's a problem. The army has procedures in place to help you deal with the problem you may or may not have, but it won't do you any good once you're out, so I have a proposition for you. Sign another contract. I'll see that the paperwork goes through immediately. And then go to Mental Health and get yourself into a spin-dry program. They'll send you to a center for a month or two and get you sober, and then you can come back to the lines and put in your voluntary release. I'll make sure it goes through without any problems. This is serious shit, Hall, you need to understand that. I've seen too many good men torn apart by the bottle, and it's my job to do everything in my power to ensure it doesn't happen to one of my own troops, whether you're getting out of the army or not. But I can't do anything for you once you're a civilian. You follow me?"

"Yes, sir."

"Good. Don't answer me today. I imagine you'll get at least four or five days' defaulters for this, which will give you some time to sober up and think it over. I want your answer before your last day of defaulters is up. Roger?"

"Roger that, sir."

"Carry on, Corporal Hall."

"Sir."

Hall spent the rest of the day preparing for defaulters, sorting out his kit, borrowing gear where he needed it, and working out the details with the warrant and the CQ. He bought a Gatorade from the canteen, dumped half of it out, poured the rest of the vodka into the bottle, and kept it in his locker. He came back to it throughout the day, and it kept him together. At the end of the day, the warrant told him the sergeant major had fast-tracked his charge, and he was to go in front of the OC the next day.

Hall picked up a two-six of vodka after work and went to the Rexall drugstore and bought a bottle of Nyquil, some sleeping pills, and some nighttime cold tabs. When he got back to his apartment, he bought some orange juice and 7-Up from a vending machine in the hallway and made a strong screw-up and drank it as he got the last of his kit together. When he finished, he had a shower and got into bed with the vodka on the nightstand. He propped himself up against the headboard and drank and smoked cigarettes while he watched a movie on his laptop. Once he had drunk half the bottle, he drank half the Nyquil and swallowed five sleeping pills and five nighttime cold tabs to be sure he passed out before he blacked out. It did not work right away, and he stayed awake for another hour, but it made him groggy and slightly ill so that he drank the vodka more slowly. When he finally did fall asleep, he had only drunk another quarter of the bottle.

The next morning, he poured the rest of the vodka into a 7-Up bottle and took it to work. He was to be charged at 1030 and was told to stay in combats and wait in the back while the rest of the company did PT. He sat on one of the old, tattered couches, sipped the vodka seven, and read a *Men's Health* magazine. There was a good article about retaining muscle mass in a cutting cycle and another about high-intensity training. He read them both and went out for a cigarette. After morning parade, the warrant called him into the office. He stood Hall at attention while he went over his uniform.

"Re-blouse your boots," the warrant said. "Thread here. And here. Holy fuck, Hall, were you drinking last night?"

"Yes, Warrant."

"I can smell it. You think it was a smart idea to get drunk the night before you get charged for being drunk and AWOL?"

"Probably not the smartest idea, Warrant."

"Probably fucking not. Get upstairs."

"Warrant."

Upstairs he stood outside the conference room. When they were ready for him, the sergeant major stood him to attention and marched him into the room in front of the OC, who was sitting at a desk with regimental and company flags crossed behind him. Standing on either side of him were supporting officers. About twenty soldiers were in attendance, mostly new guys on either side of the room facing the OC's desk.

Hall was drunk enough that he could stand straight without shaking, and when he said "Yes, sir" or "No, sir," his voice was steady. The OC gave a long speech about the importance of discipline. It seemed directed more to the new guys in attendance than it was to Hall.

"Five days of defaulters," the OC said finally, "and eight hundred dollars to be deducted from your pay."

Chapter 12

Hall was on defaulters with one other soldier named Laqua, who had been charged for a negligent discharge on the winter exercise. They were in front of the main building shoveling snow and chipping ice off the sidewalks and parking lot. They had been working for several hours and had a good pace going that kept up a light sweat so that they wore only their combats, wind jackets, toques, and gloves. Both men had good-sized blisters forming on their hands from smashing at the ice with five-foot prybars. They were comparing blisters when the base orderly sergeant came out and told them to get inside and start preparing their kit for inspection.

In the defaulter's room, they laid their ground sheets out in front of their beds and started setting out their kit in identical displays with everything folded carefully, all straps rolled and taped, and everything square and symmetrical. Once they were finished, they started putting on their gear, but the duty sergeant came in early.

"Room!" Laqua called.

Hall came to attention, his vest unzipped, his helmet in hand.

"Relax," the sergeant said. He was tall and bald and had a thick, black moustache. It was their first night on defaulters, and the sergeant had been screaming at them for most of the day, but when he came into the defaulter's room, he seemed deflated and tired. "You boys are done for the night," he said. "Take that shit off."

They removed their fighting order, and the sergeant just stood there, watching them quietly. Once they were dressed down to their uniforms, they turned to the sergeant for further direction. He was staring at the ground with his arms crossed. He looked up at them.

"A member of the battalion was found dead in his apartment a few hours ago."

"Fuck," Laqua said.

"Who is it?" Hall asked.

"They haven't given me a name yet; it's a standard blackout. As soon as the family knows, I'll know, and then you'll know. Myself and the duty officer are going to be busy, so you two are off the hook. We're not playing this fucking game anymore tonight."

"Roger that, Sarge."

"Roger, Sergeant."

"Okay then. You'll be hearing from me."

As soon as he left, Hall and Laqua got their phones out and started texting and calling their friends. Hall knew it would not be Hartford or Wright, but he called them anyway to fill them in.

"I hope it was Franklin," Hartford said.

After Hall finished talking to Hartford, he called Wright. "Call me back if it's someone I know," Wright said. "Otherwise I'll see you tomorrow."

"Any word?" Hall asked Laqua once they were both off their phones.

"No," he said, "no one knows anything."

"How many is that from our tour?"

"Five, I think," he said. "No, six. There was that reservist who hung himself in BC. Or maybe he was one of the five. I don't know."

They started packing up their kit. "How would you do it?" Hall asked.

"How would I do what?"

"Kill yourself."

Laqua stopped packing and looked at Hall. "Man, did you really just ask me that?"

"Yeah. If you were going to do it, how would you do it?"

"Fuck, man, I dunno. How would you do it?"

"I'd shoot myself in the heart."

"In the heart? Why not the head?"

"Too quick. When I die, I want to know what it feels like. I want to experience it. It only happens once, and who knows, it might feel good. If not, then fuck it, it wouldn't last long."

Laqua shook his head. "That's pretty fucked up, man."

"So, how would you do it?"

"How would I kill myself?"

"Yeah."

"Well," Laqua looked away and thought for a moment, "I'd say . . . probably heroin."

"Heroin?"

"Yeah, man. Like, you want to feel what it's like to die, and that's cool, maybe you're right, maybe it feels good. But I want to be fuckin' sure of it, you know? Like, if I had to kill myself, I'd want to die because I felt so fuckin' good my body just couldn't take it anymore. That's how I'd want to go."

"I never thought of that," Hall said. "Have you ever tried it?"

"Once." Laqua was smiling, but he did not look happy. He looked disquieted and unsure of himself.

"What was it like?" Hall asked. He put down what he was holding and sat on his bunk and looked up at Laqua.

"Man," Laqua said, "it was scary."

"Scary?"

"Yeah, man. Terrifying. It was like so good, man, it was so good I can't even begin to describe it to you, I just can't put it into words. I thought, like, fuck, if something can be this good, then how bad can shit get? I didn't know it was possible to feel that good, and I was, like, fuck, man, if it's possible to feel this good, it must be possible to feel just as bad, you know what I mean? It just expanded my spectrum of feelings way past my comfort zone. It just opened me up to something . . . I don't know, something that . . . Fuck, I don't know, man. It's better to leave that stone unturned. I wouldn't try it."

Hall forced a laugh. "I don't plan to."

They went back to packing away their kit. When they finished, they agreed it felt wrong to do nothing, so they drew their weapons from the orderly desk and sat on the floor of the defaulters' room and started cleaning them. Laqua pulled a bore snake through his barrel, and Hall disassembled his bolt and worked on the face with swabs and Q-tips. Hall had cleaned it several times since he had last fired it, but the white of the swabs and the Q-tips still found carbon. There was always more carbon.

"You're going through withdrawals," Laqua said.

"What?"

He pointed at Hall's hands. Hall was using his Gerber to get a swab between the ridges of the bolt face, and his hands were shaking badly.

"You ever tried to quit?" Laqua asked.

"Drinking?"

"Yeah."

"Not really. Have you?"

"Have and did," Laqua said. "I don't drink."

"What?"

"I don't drink."

"Not at all?"

"Nope."

"Why not?"

"It doesn't do anything for me anymore. It just takes away from me, you know? It always ends badly when I drink too much, and every time I drink, I drink too much, so it's nothing but bad anymore. I don't know, man, it's just like every time I drank, I'd just wake up the next morning and be like, 'Fuck, why the fuck did I do all that stupid shit? I'm such an idiot.' I'd feel so shitty, and, oh man, the hangovers got so bad they were, like, impossible to deal with. Most of the time I'd have to keep drinking just to get through the mornings, you know what I mean?"

"Yeah," Hall said. "I know what you mean. Fuck, I know exactly what you mean."

"So, yeah, man, I just stopped. I got a year and a half off the sauce now. Best thing I've ever done."

"Huh," Hall said. "So, if you don't drink, what do you do?"

Laqua smiled the way he had when he was talking about heroin, more of a smirk than a smile, but now he seemed surer of himself, and the smile was genuinely happy. "MDMA."

"MDMA? What's that?"

"You ever tried ecstasy?"

Hall shrugged. "Once or twice. When I was a kid."

"Well, MDMA is like pure ecstasy. It's the love ingredient. Man, I don't tell too many people about this shit, because you know how it is around here, but we're both getting out soon, and I think you should hear this. My drinking got really bad after tour, and then I quit, and everything was all good, but I was bored as fuck, you know? Like, drinking was all I ever did for fun, so I didn't know what to do with myself on weekends anymore. Anyway, this chick I was seeing at the time used to go to these music shows, so I went with her and did some MDMA, and man, it was awesome. It was the best time I've ever had in my life. It makes you feel so fucking good, man, but not doped up like heroin does, just like super happy and social kind of thing. I was so sick of the army party scene, you know, getting wasted with a bunch of army dudes and hitting the bars to pick fights with college kids, like fuck that, man. No one really wants that, not deep down. What people really want is real connections with other people, you know? MDMA opens the channel for those connections to be made, you know? It's wild, man, like I was making friends with everybody. I don't even party with army guys anymore. I'm done with the bar scene. I'm all about the EDM scene now."

"EDM?"

"Electronic dance music."

"Like techno and shit? So you're talking about raves?"

"Yeah, man, raves. But it's more than that, man. It's like a culture."

Hall laughed. "You fucking hippy."

Laqua smiled and shook his head. "All right, man, you can be like that, but I've heard all the stories about you, and you're just like me, man, and I guarantee you that just like me, you're not going to be able to take the bottle for much longer. Look at your hands shake, man. That's some pretty serious shit. And what are you going to do when you're out of the army? There's no defaulters out there, man. You keep showing up late to a regular job, and they'll straight up fire your ass. But going to shows and doing M, man, it's like an event. It's like . . . it's just really something, man, I'm telling you. It will open your eyes."

The orderly sergeant came in and told them the name of the man who had killed himself. Hall did not know him very well. He had done his LAV driver course with him and had gotten drunk with him once at the junior ranks in Wainwright with a few other guys on the course. He was average height and build, and he had big ears and a thick neck. They had done PT with the course, and Hall remembered the man being so hungover one morning that he threw up all over himself on a run but had caught back up and finished the run with the course. He also remembered his voice being slightly too high. He had shot himself under the chin with his roommate's hunting rifle. He had been drinking for three days before he did it, and his angle had not been good, so there would be no open casket.

Chapter 13

Hall was badly hungover on his release day. He drank a mickey of vodka before the parade so his legs would not shake when he went up in front of the battalion. It was an important parade, and the brigade commander made an appearance to personally award Hartford and Wright and a few others with medals. Hartford was given his Sacrifice Medal, and Wright received the Medal of Bravery for a time his platoon had been ambushed on his second tour.

A few more men were called up, and then the brigade commander handed the parade back over to the CO. Hall was called up with four other men. They were all dressed in their parade uniforms. The CO said something, the RSM said something, Hall held up a certificate, and they took his picture as he shook hands with the CO. Once the other four had done the same thing, they did their drill, and Hall formed back up with his platoon as the battalion clapped for them. Someone behind him grabbed his ass. Someone else whispered, "You dirty fuckin' civi," and someone else, "See you in six months." It was a Friday, and they were cut loose at 1130 because the funeral parade was being held on Sunday.

After they were dismissed, Hall drove to the headquarters building and handed in the last of his paperwork and officially became a civilian. Still in his dress uniform, he drove to the

Liquor Depot and picked a forty of vodka off the wall. The same girl was working the counter, and she was wearing a different plaid shirt that she had again tied in a knot to expose a bit of her stomach. Hall was still running well off the mickey. He looked at her stomach and then her eyes and smiled. She did not smile or say anything, except, "Thirty-seven fifty." He used his debit card, his hands steady this time, but it was declined. He tried it again, and it was declined again.

"Here, son, let me get that." Hall turned and saw a middle-aged man wearing a denim jacket and a ratty baseball cap standing behind him offering his card.

"No," Hall said. "Thank you, but there's no way. I just need to swing by the bank."

Hall went across the street to the Cash Money office. The cashiers were behind glass, and a cardboard stand-up of a kangaroo wearing an orange-and-yellow Cash Money outfit was facing the door. It was a childish thing and stood out in stark contrast to the customers, who looked worn out and beaten down. The cashier asked for his ID and if he was still employed by the DND. He said he was and showed them his online bank statement on one of their computers to prove his most recent payroll deposits. Unsure of what it was for or how he was going to pay it back, he borrowed $1,100.

Back in the Liquor Depot, he handed the girl two twenties, but she refused to take them. "That guy paid for it. He said he won't be coming back, so if you don't take it, no one will. He also said, 'Thank you.'"

"Oh," Hall said. He bought a couple cartons of orange juice and left.

In his car, he made a good half-and-half screwdriver in the travel mug and sat in the parking lot and drank for a while with the car idling and the radio on low. He called Crystal.

"What do you want, John?"

"Hey," he said, "guess what?"

"What?"

"I'm a civilian now. It feels pretty good. What are you doing?"

"I just got off work."

"Well, now what are you doing?"

"I'm going home."

"Okay. Well, look, Crystal, about that night at my place, when I threw the bottle of wine . . . I . . . shit, I feel like such an asshole for that. I don't know why I do things like that, why I act like such a goddamn child, but I want you to know that I do feel bad about it, that I don't like it when I do things like that, that I'm actually . . . I'm actually, well, really ashamed of it. When I act like that, when I get drunk and treat you like shit, I don't know why I do it. It's not because I get a kick out of it or anything or . . . or I don't know, because it makes me feel . . . I don't know, big or tough or whatever. It actually just makes me feel small and pathetic. I mean you're such a goddamn sweetheart, and I love hanging out with you. It's just that . . . Fuck, I don't know, Crystal, I don't know what I'm trying to say here. But I'd like to see you . . . Are you still there?"

"Yeah, John, I'm still here."

"Okay . . . So, I'd really like to see you."

"You don't remember calling me last night, do you?"

"No."

"You called me a cunt."

Hall flinched. "What?"

"You called me a cunt, John. And you called me a slut. Again."

"Well . . . fuck."

"Yeah, John, well, fuck."

"Look, Crystal—"

She hung up.

He put the phone down in the passenger seat and leaned back and lit a cigarette. He tried to think of something to do with the money, but spending it did not seem appealing anymore. He decided to go for a drive.

He got on the Anthony Henday and followed it around the city, and by the time he came to the airport, he had finished the drink, so he poured another half and half and kept driving south. He followed the signs to Calgary.

The sun was setting. It was cold, and the highway looked bluish and had a shine to it. Hall kept it ten over the limit on cruise control and took his parade boots off with one hand while he drove. He turned the heat to the floor and put it on max. He chain-smoked cigarettes, keeping the passenger window down a bit to let the smoke out. His wallet was thick and uncomfortable in his back pocket. He drank and drove for an hour and put a third of the forty away. Then he started vomiting. He got some of it out the window and about as much down the front and side of his uniform. He did not stop driving. He wiped it away as best as he could and made another, stronger drink.

* * *

"I'll fucking kill you!"

Hall had pulled over on a range road behind a small red truck. He was out of his car in the snow in his socks and smashing his elbow against the window of the truck. Inside the truck was a Middle-Eastern man wearing circular glasses. He was holding a cellphone to his ear and yelling.

Hall continued to scream at him. "You motherfucker! Get the fuck out of the truck! I'll fucking kill you! Get the fuck out of the truck!"

He struck the glass again, and his elbow went through it. It was safety glass and it crumbled. He pulled his elbow out, and he could hear the man clearly now. Hall reached into the truck for him, but the man put the vehicle in gear and drove away. Hall went back to his car and made another drink.

* * *

Hall pushed it to 180. His car would not go any faster. He was back on the highway, and he had both hands firmly on the steering wheel. It was snowing, and the flakes came straight toward him as he weaved in and out of traffic. The other vehicles drove well below the speed limit and left large gaps in the road. He had the passenger window all the way down, and the cold air screamed and turned the right side of his face numb. He felt the grooves of the gas pedal and the clutch through his wet socks and bits of gravel stuck between the grooves.

Something hard formed in the back of his throat—the symptom of a feeling he could not feel, because there was nothing but the hardness of the thing itself, the coldness of the air, his wet, cold socks, the gravel in the grooves of the pedals, and the screaming wind.

* * *

Hall woke up with his head against the window. The glass was cold, and he had a headache. It was dark inside the car. All the windows were covered with snow. The parking brake was on, and the car was idling. There was something crusty on his right hand. He looked at it in the dim blue light of the gauges and the radio clock and saw that it was dried blood and vomit. Vomit covered his legs and the steering wheel and was splattered over the console. He sat up and stretched and stared at the whiteness of his windshield. He remembered the man in the red truck and driving down the highway, weaving through cars, but nothing else.

The forty of vodka was on the passenger floor. About two inches was left in it. The travel mug was still in the cup holder. He picked it up. It was half empty. He sniffed it, and it smelled very strong, so he put it back in the cup holder. He stared at the whiteness of the windshield and tried hard not to think. The anxiety was digging in deep. It tunneled into every part of him, physically and mentally. He scraped his nails across his face, and a congested feeling grew behind his eyes and nose. He breathed out deeply, clenched a fist, bit his lip, and went to punch the driver's side window but stopped himself. He breathed in and out and in once more and out again. He picked up the travel mug and drank as much of it as he could, but it came right back up on his lap. He found one of the cartons of orange juice and poured it into the travel mug, and when he tried to drink it, it stayed down. When he finished with the travel mug, he turned on the windshield wipers, and they pushed the snow off the glass, except where some of it had melted and froze again, but they cleared enough away so he could see that he was on another range road, parked beside a cattle fence.

He drove home carefully, sipping the remains of the vodka. It took him two hours. When he got back to his apartment, he found some sleeping pills and some nighttime cold tabs, took a few of each, and went to bed with a movie playing on his laptop. It did not matter what movie it was. He only needed the voices and the light of the screen.

The next morning, he paced around his apartment. He sat on the couch, went back to bed, back to the couch again, and then he drove to the liquor store and bought a forty of vodka. Back at home, he mixed a strong screwdriver and sat on the couch and watched TV. After three or four drinks, he started feeling good, and after six or seven, he blacked out.

* * *

Hall was in a bar. It was dark inside, and there was screaming. Someone was hitting him in the face, and he tried to hit back, but he was being held. He was kicking and thrashing and snarling. Snot was coming out of his nose, and his face was swollen.

* * *

Hall was walking somewhere in a T-shirt. It was cold, and he was shivering.

* * *

Hall was in his bed, and his sheets were red and attached to him. His skin crumpled and cracked as he came to and moved in the bed. The sheets moved with him, pulled by his arms and legs, and when he sat up, the sheets came up with him. His entire front was caked with dried blood. He sat there looking at it all, at the red sheets dried to his skin. He moved his arms back and forth in front of him, and flakes of blood came away from the sheets as they broke away.

He peeled the material off his skin, and it came away easily from his arms and stomach, but the dried blood was thicker near his chest, especially on the left side. The sheets stretched his skin and ripped his hair out. When he tried to pull the material off his shoulder, a deep pain erupted there. He winced and felt sick from it.

He took a few slow breaths and tried again, but it was too painful, so he bunched up the sheets, held them to his chest, and went into the bathroom. He filled a glass with warm water and poured it over his chest and shoulder. The warm water softened the dried blood and ran red down his body, pooling on the floor. He peeled the sheet off his shoulder and exposed a gash an inch wide and very deep. He put his thumb and index finger on either side of it and spread it apart and it filled with fresh blood. He put his hand over it and held it there and looked at himself in the mirror. His face was swollen.

Holding his hand over the wound, he searched his apartment for the cause of it. He looked through all his knives, but none of them were bloody. There was no broken glass or pieces of metal lying around. He gave up looking and went back into the bathroom and went under the sink, where he had a bottle of isopropyl alcohol. It was half empty. He uncapped it, took a deep breath, and poured it over the wound. He screamed and gagged and breathed some deep breaths, and then he was okay. He found his first-aid kit in his storage closet and did a fairly good job at dressing the wound. He knew he should go for stitches, but he would need a few drinks first.

He got dressed and searched for his wallet. He could not find it, but he did find three crumpled twenties in a pair of jeans, which was enough. He straightened out the bills, stuck them in his back pocket, and went to put his coat on, but it was not in the closet or anywhere in the apartment. He put on two extra hoodies instead and went out to his car, but it was not in his parking spot. He walked around his apartment building twice, checking every row of every lot, but it was not there, so he walked the five blocks to the liquor store. He bought a forty of gin, two bottles of tonic water and a little bottle of lime juice. Back at his apartment he made a strong drink, sat on his couch, and drank. After three or four, he started feeling good.

After six or seven, he blacked out.

* * *

PART II

Chapter 14

"Soda water and lime," Hall told the waitress when she came to their table.

"A Coke for me," Hartford said.

"Get a beer," Hall said.

"I don't want a beer."

"You're not doing me any favors by not drinking in front of me. Actually, I think I find it more annoying that you don't drink around me. It's like you're accommodating some sort of disability of mine or something."

"Shut up," Hartford said.

"So that will be a coke?" the waitress asked.

"Get a goddamn beer," Hall said, "or a whiskey. A double rye and Coke."

"I'm paying for lunch, so I'll decide what I want to drink with it."

"You're not paying for lunch," Hall said.

"The hell I'm not."

"I got a job now so I can pay for it."

"Fuck off," Hartford said. "I'm buying lunch and I'm going to wash down the food I pay for with a goddamn Coke, and that's it." He smiled at the waitress. "I'll have a coke," he said to her, and she went away with their orders.

"Don't you think you should make it a Diet Coke?"

"The fuck does that mean?"

"Nothing," Hall said, and he looked at Hartford's gut.

Hartford's eyes went wide, and his mouth opened dramatically. "How fucking dare you!" he roared, and a few people turned their heads at them. "So the fucking Holocaust victim gains two pounds, and now he thinks he's tough shit. I could fold you in half if I wanted to. I'd pop your piece of shit liver like a zit."

Hall laughed. "Yeah, I bet you could. Hey, would you fuck our waitress?"

Hartford looked around the restaurant, spotted the waitress, and nodded solemnly. "Yes," he growled, "yes I would."

"Yeah, me too."

They finished their meals, Hartford drove Hall home, and they agreed to work out together the following day.

Inside, Hall opened the sliding glass balcony door and the bedroom windows, letting the warm spring air into his apartment. He took a shower, then sat on the couch and smoked cigarettes and read.

Later he thawed three chicken breasts in the microwave and cooked them in the oven and boiled some basmati rice. About ten minutes before both were done, he fried some asparagus with lots of pepper, and everything finished on time. He ate the chicken with hot sauce and the rice with soy sauce. After he did the dishes, he went back to the couch and looked through Facebook on his phone. He looked through his messages and contacts, but whenever he found someone he wanted to talk to, he could not think of anything to say.

He brought out his laptop and watched a recommended YouTube video about sinkholes. The video linked to another about earthquakes, and he watched a few of those, and then riots, and then prison riots and prison stabbings, and then police shootings. He watched videos of police shooting civilians, and then he watched civilians shooting police, and then he watched a long compilation video of all kinds of people killing all kinds of other people. After he had watched the compilation video, he tried to read again, but he kept losing focus.

It was getting late in the evening, but it was still bright out. Hall went out on the balcony and looked at the parking lot below. He looked at the houses beyond the parking lot and the trees and fences and power lines.

He got changed, put his apartment key in his sock, his headphones in his ears, and went outside into the street and started running, setting a moderate pace. His ankle locked up in the first hundred meters, but it worked itself out as his body warmed up. He panted sharply for the first ten minutes, but as he started to sweat, he got better control of his breathing. He ran diagonally across a school baseball field into a small copse of trees and bushes with a dog path cut through it. He ran on the path, which was paved with wood chips. When he came out of the trees and bushes, the path went on behind a row of houses.

He left the path and ran down a back alley. The houses on either side of him were old, their beige and brown paint long faded. A large tree was growing into the alley from someone's backyard. Its branches were long and thin, and the leaves were new and green. The alley reminded him of an alley he had patrolled through in a village in the desert, where a similar tree had grown. Near the tree, behind it, at the base of a mud wall, a massive IED had detonated. As he ran through the alley with his headphones in his ears and his apartment key in his sock he could smell the sweet, acrid smell of detonated explosives and smoke, feel the weight of a rucksack on his shoulders, the pressure of straps across his chest, hips, and legs, the strain in his forearms from carrying a weapon, the film of human grease on his gloves from searching the locals, and most of all, the dust collecting in the sweat on his face.

Chapter 15

yooooo wats up man?!?

Hall had gotten an apprenticeship as a pipefitter in a fabrication shop. He was sitting in the lunch trailer on his coffee break when he got the text message from an unknown number. He replied:

Who is this?

its laqua dude im out now got released last week wat u doing now?

Hall put his phone back in his pocket and finished eating. He drank a coffee, smoked a cigarette, and went back to work. He was cutting two-inch pipe into sections and beveling the ends to be welded. He wore coveralls and thick gloves and a face shield when he used the grinder. He cut and beveled three ends and smoked another cigarette.

Later, while he was standing at the urinal in the washroom, he took his phone out and texted Laqua back with his free hand:

Got a trade job. You?

Before he had finished washing his hands, Laqua replied:

moving back home next week!

He went to put his phone away, but it vibrated again:

theres a sick show at the shaw this fri u should come!

No thanks man, I'm partied out.

u quit drinkin???
Yeah man.
congrats dude!! well u dont have to drink im not.
You're going sober?
lol no just not drinking
What kind of show is it?
edm dude like i was telling u about come by my place fri night like 9 I have everything set up got a ticket for u n everything i need to no for sure tho if ur coming so I dont waste the ticket trust me dude it will be a blast i know u will love it!! tons of ass dude its unreal! i also have the most unreal m.

Hall stood up straight and stretched his back, squeezing his shoulders together. He closed the messages and pulled up the calendar on his phone. Friday was a payday. He looked at himself in the mirror. Something had been taped to the mirror and then ripped off. Some of the adhesive part of the tape had stayed on the mirror collecting dirt and grime in a square pattern that framed his reflection. He stretched his jaw and ran a hand through his hair. It stood up with sweat where his hand left it.

Chapter 16

The show was at the Shaw Conference Center on Jasper Ave. There was a line twenty metres long, which Laqua said was nothing, that an hour earlier it would have stretched over two city blocks.

The line was very colorful and seemed to consist mostly of teenagers. Their clothing made no sense to Hall. Some wore furry-looking hoods with dog ears attached to the top, some plain white or brown, others leopard print or tiger striped, others an obnoxious, vivid shade of pink, yellow, or blue. They were not attached to any jacket or sweater, as they should have been; they simply sat on the wearer's head and flowed in two strips down the chest, like the stole of a priest's uniform. Some of the females wore tutus, some multiple tutus, layered one on top of the other in different colors so that the frizzy material exploded out from their hips in all directions. Others wore fishnet leggings, tiny, skin-tight black shorts, or miniskirts, some black, some colorful. Almost all of them were adorned with colorful accessories, like glow stick bracelets and necklaces.

On the same city block on a weekday during business hours, one of those women would be a monstrous proclamation of female sexuality, but at night, together in that line, they were more digestible, though still wild looking.

"We're too fucking old for this," Hall told Laqua. "Jesus, man, look at what these kids are wearing."

"Relax," Laqua said, "just wait until we're inside. Here," and he pulled a water bottle out of his back pocket filled with blue liquid, "drink half of this."

"What is that?"

"It's M."

"That's MDMA? I thought it came in pills."

"It's crystalized, and it's best to mix it and drink it. Just trust me, dude."

"All right," Hall said, and he drank half the bottle. It was Gatorade but it tasted like rust. He handed the bottle back to Laqua, who drank the rest.

When their turn came, they showed their IDs at the front door and went inside to a wide set of stairs that followed the slope of the river valley down to the floors below. Hall heard the music, mostly the dull thump of the bass. Another line was at the bottom of the stairs, about as long as the first. They lined up behind a group of three young men, no older than twenty. One turned and smiled at them, raising his arms. He wore casual clothes except for a pair of pink glasses with no lenses.

"What's up, dudes?" the young man said.

"Hey, guys," Laqua said.

Hall glared at them, especially the one with the pink glasses. He did not like any of this. He was nervous, and he kept checking behind him.

"Are you ready for this?" Pink Glasses cried. He clapped his hands and started dancing for a moment, a bobbing kind of shuffle, and then he stopped and laughed with his friends.

"What the fuck have you gotten me into?" Hall asked Laqua.

Pink Glasses turned on Hall. "What's your deal, bro? Not having a good time or what?"

"Just please fuck off," Hall said.

"Whoa, what the fuck, bro?" Pink Glasses said.

His friends turned on Hall and Laqua.

"This was a stupid idea," Hall said to Laqua, "these people are fucking ridiculous." He kept his eyes on Pink Glasses.

Laqua laughed and put his arm around Hall's shoulder. "John," he said, "John, my man, just relax, please, dude. Just give it a chance, and you'll see. Wait until the M hits you, man. I promise you'll love it." He turned to the young men, "This is his first show and his first time doing M. It hasn't even hit him yet."

"Oh," Pink Glasses exclaimed, "no shit, bro. Oh, it's all good, fuck, man, you're going to have such a good time, dude. Your life's about to be changed forever. I hope I run into you later, bro. You're going to be, like, a different person, man."

Pink Glasses offered his hand. Hall looked at it and then at Laqua, who raised his eyebrows and grinned at him. Hall reluctantly shook the boy's hand. The boy's grip was firm, which surprised him. Pink Glasses introduced himself and his friends, and Hall forgot their names immediately. They all seemed genuinely excited for him, like he was about to be initiated into some kind of deeply personal circle of theirs, the implications of the initiation to remain totally incomprehensible until it was complete. Hall had no interest in it. He was only interested in what the MDMA would do to him. His vision was slightly hazy, and some colors might have been slightly brighter than they should have been, but otherwise he felt nothing of what Laqua had told him to expect.

"How much longer until it hits?" he asked Laqua.

"Any time now."

They were let onto the main floor, and they lined up again to have their tickets scanned and then again to be searched. The music was loud. Hall could feel it through the floor.

After they had been patted down, Hall met Laqua on the other side. The place was packed, and the same kind of people they had been in line with outside and on the stairs were everywhere on the main floor. There was even more skin now, as those who had been wearing coats had checked them, and many were now also shirtless. Some were moving around fast, others sat quietly in groups on the floor, others were shouting at each other and laughing, and some were dancing. The bass had gone quiet, and there was a high-pitched tune, some sort of stringed instrument, repeating a simple set of notes.

Laqua looked at Hall. "We have to get in there for this one, dude. Come on, quick!"

He broke into a run through the doors, and Hall ran after him. He liked that they were running. It gave him energy, and it suddenly felt like they were really doing something, charging into the concert hall, into the unknown, his legs feeling warm and full of energy and his motions very fluid.

The concert hall was massive and dark except for a soft purple glow being emitted from an arc of lights at the end of the hall. Between the lights and Hall was a dark mass of moving bodies: an untold number of people, only the tops of their heads and shoulders illuminated by the purple light. The mass was alive but calm, sedated, like they were clogged in a huge lineup, waiting for something from the purple lights.

They reached a large set of bleachers at the rear of the mass, and Laqua ran up the middle to the top. Hall followed him as a chanting started over the strings. They reached the top and turned around to view the purple mass from above.

A snare drum and a whistling joined the chanting and the strings, and the volume of it all continued to grow, approaching something, swelling, building pressure and suspense.

Hall's body was sweltering, pulsing heat, and everything around him was shimmering brightly. The music arced and finally fell silent, and from the silence, a deep, powerful voice, all bass, growled something, rumbled it so low that Hall could not understand it—one word that smashed into the mass of people with an explosion of lights of every color. For the first time, he saw the extent of the crowd: thousands of human beings, shimmering pink and blue and yellow and green. Simultaneously they erupted—jumping, dancing, screaming, and coming to life as one body. A monstrous, hammering bass carried on the pace, and the lights in the arc flashed with every beat like synchronized lightning.

"Pretty cool, eh?" Laqua said.

"Yeah," Hall said, "this is something." He was burning up. It was wonderful.

"You want to grab a seat and watch for a bit?" Laqua said.

"Sure." They sat down at the top of the bleachers and watched the crowd and the lights and listened to the music.

Hall looked around and saw a couple, roughly his age, maybe older, two rows down and a few seats away from them. The man was dressed casually, and the woman was wearing black leggings, a loose blouse, and had a few glow stick bracelets on her wrist. They were both moving to the music. Hall decided it was imperative that he spoke with them.

"I'll be back," he told Laqua.

"Sure man," Laqua said. He started moving to the music in his seat as Hall stood up and approached the couple.

He came from the row behind them and jumped over their row of seats, on the man's side, so as not to suggest any intentions toward his woman. He surprised them both, and they stopped their seated dance and stared at him questioningly.

"Hi," he said loudly, smiling at them, "I'm John."

"Hi," the man said.

"Hello," the woman said.

"I just had to come over here and talk to you guys, because you're the same age as me," Hall said, "or at least you look the same age as me. This is the first time I've been to a show like this."

As soon as he said this, a look of understanding grew in both of their faces, which made him feel very good. It connected him to them, and he wanted more of it.

"I've never done MDMA before," Hall continued. "This is my first time. Have you ever done it? Are you on M right now?"

They both laughed.

"Oh yeah, dude," the man said. "I'm fried."

"Yes!" the woman cried. "I feel so good right now!"

This made Hall nearly ecstatic. "Yes!" he said. "So you know exactly what I'm talking about. Oh, man, when I first got here, it hadn't hit me yet, and I was in line with all of these teenagers, these goddamn children, and I was thinking, 'What the fuck am I doing here? I don't belong here.' And then it hit me, and oh man, this is something, I'm just so happy to talk to someone my age. I'm John, by the way, did I say that? What are your names?"

He shook hands with both of them, and they told him their names, and he forgot them both immediately.

"It's all good, dude," the man said, "I know exactly what you mean. This is only my third show. I felt the exact same way you did when I went to my first show, but we're really not that old, man, if you really look around."

"Yeah," the woman said, leaning over the man to speak to Hall. "It was just your frame of mind when you came in here, like, all of this is new and probably pretty strange to you, and it's only natural that you were looking for the differences instead of the similarities, don't you think? Like, you feel good now, right? You're enjoying yourself now?"

"Yeah," Hall said, "I feel great. This is great, all of this."

"Well, look around now," she said, pointing. "Look, practically that whole row three down from us is our age or older, and look over there and there."

Hall looked at the people she was pointing out.

"See?" she said.

"Yeah," Hall said, "you're right. I'm so glad I came and talked to you guys, and I'm so sorry, but I forgot your names already. I think I'm really high."

They laughed and said it was okay and told him their names again, and he forgot them again. They turned and watched the lights and the crowd. Hall started moving to the music. It seemed horribly unnatural to sit still. Then he saw something four rows down.

"Hey!" he said to the man and tapped his shoulder, pointing. "Look at that! Look down there!"

"What? What is it?" the man said, trying to find what Hall was pointing at.

"Those two men just kissed! Holy shit! I need to speak with them, right now."

Hall stood up and went to climb down the row in front of them, but the woman leaped from her seat, stretching across the man, and grabbed Hall's arm.

"Hey!" she cried. He stopped and looked at her. "What are you going to do? Be nice!"

"Relax," Hall said, and he gave her a reassuring smile. "Of course I'll be nice. I couldn't be anything but nice right now."

Hall waved goodbye to them and continued his descent on the homosexuals. He leaped into the open seat to their right. The one closest to him had a high and tight haircut, except it was long at the top and combed back and to the side. He had a lip piercing and a softness to his face—a tenderness like that of a pregnant woman. The other one, sitting to the soft one's left, was more masculine. He had a beard and a short haircut.

The suddenness of Hall's approach surprised them both. The soft one looked worried, even scared, the bearded one defensive.

"Hi," Hall said.

"Hi," they both said cautiously.

"Okay, look, I just saw you two kiss a second ago."

"Okay?" said the soft one. "Does that bother you?" the bearded one asked.

"Not at all," Hall said. "I have nothing against you people. Now let me be honest: I've used the words 'fag' and 'queer' before. I actually used to use them quite a lot, but I never meant it in a way to purposefully demean you people, because I honestly have nothing against you. I don't believe it's a choice. I believe you're born that way, just like you people say you are."

"You people?"

"Yeah, gay people. I believe it's just like Down syndrome, right? I mean those people don't choose to be retarded, they're just born that that way, and I believe it's wrong to hate someone for the way they're born."

"So you're saying gay people are retarded?" The bearded one was starting to look angry, and the soft one still looked worried, which made Hall anxious. He had something important to say to these men, something he needed to say to them.

"Okay, maybe that came out wrong," he said hurriedly. "That's not what I meant. All I meant to say was that I believe in your right to fuck each other if you want to." He laughed as he said this but cut it short. They were starting to look utterly repulsed by him. "Okay, look, look, look, I'm going somewhere with this, I swear, I know I probably sound like an asshole, but I really do have good intentions. Okay, look, just answer me this. Do you two love each other?"

"Yes," the soft one said immediately, almost assertively, "we love each other."

"You see?" Hall said. "That's what's important. That's what I just realized when I saw you kiss, is how important it is that you love each other, how fucking important it is, because you loving each other exposes all our misconceptions of what love really is. It's a testament to the omnipotence of love."

He was shouting now and giving them the four-finger point, sweat pouring down his face. "It's a testament to the fucking greatness of it. I mean, we love our siblings and parents and our friends and even our pets, but true love has always been reserved for a man and a woman, has been sacred to a man and a woman, but if you two truly love each other—and do you? Do you really, truly love each other?"

"Yes," the soft one cried, "we do!"

The conviction in his voice made Hall happy and excited to carry on. "Do you know what that means? Do you know what that fucking means? That means you two are living proof that love is more than just a means to procreate; you are living proof that love is something without boundaries or limitations. You are living proof that love is something really, truly great."

He settled back in his chair and watched their reactions. The soft one look moved. His eyes were open wide, and he was smiling slightly. He had understood. The bearded one still looked angry, but that did not matter.

"All right, buddy," the bearded one said, "thanks for the speech, but you're obviously just high as a kite and looking for someone to run your mouth at."

"What?" Hall said. "You don't think I meant it?"

"No, I think that whatever drug you're on is doing the talking."

"Well, fine," Hall said, "but *you* believe I meant it." He pointed at the soft one. "You believe me, right?"

The soft one started to answer, but the bearded one interrupted, "Just ignore this guy. He's clearly just some douchebag."

"Did you just call me a douchebag?"

"Yes, you're a douchebag," the bearded one confirmed.

"Well, you're a cocksucker."

"Boys!" yelled the soft one. He whispered to his partner pleadingly, and then turned to Hall, his eyes shining. "I believe you meant every word of it," he said, "and thank you for coming over to speak with us, but we're going to go get a drink. Have a wonderful evening." He smiled once more at Hall, and the two went away down the aisle.

Satisfied, Hall wiped the sweat off his forehead with the back of his arm and turned back to the floor, where he saw a Middle Eastern man leaning against the railing of the bleachers. Something in him wanted to approach the man, he felt a need to get something across to him, to make another connection, the most important one yet, and it was almost strong enough. He stayed in his seat.

"Hey, you!" a quick, feminine voice said from his right. He turned and found a girl with bright pink hair sitting there smiling at him. She was tiny, maybe a hundred pounds, and she wore tight black athletic shorts and a pink sports bra. Around her neck was a bright yellow scarf of faux feathers or some other fluffy material, and little plastic jewels were glued to her face in various patterns and colours.

"Wow," Hall said, "how did I miss *you*?"

"I know, right?" she said. She giggled and threw her arms into the air and kicked her legs. It was a happy, energetic movement, and it made Hall laugh.

"What?" she whined. She stopped moving and stared at Hall seriously. Then she laughed and started moving her legs

again. She stopped and looked serious again and leaned in close. "I heard what you said to those gay guys."
"Oh yeah?" Hall said. "And what did you think?"
"I thought it was really nice. It was beautiful. Yeah, it was really, really, really, *really* beautiful."
"Yeah?"
"Yeah. I thought so. Well, you maybe could have said it a little better," she giggled, "but what you had to say was really beautiful. I was listening the whole time. You're a lover. Are you a lover? You have to be a lover to have said what you said to those guys. I'm a lover. It's the only way a person should be, I think. Are you high? Did you do any M?"
"Yeah," Hall said, and he smiled at her, "I'm really high. It's my first time doing MDMA."
"Oh my god!" she cried. "Really?" She clapped her hands. Hall laughed. He liked her. He had an urge to pick her up and kiss her, but he did not.
"Isn't it so wonderful?" she said. "Are you not just so in love with everything right now? That's why you said what you said, isn't it? Would you have said that if you weren't high?"
"No," Hall said, "I don't think I would have."
"You see? It was in you, because you're a lover. I know you are, but you never would have let it out if it wasn't for the M. Isn't it just so wonderful? Being high? That's why it's called being high: it's just so hiiigh." She giggled and started opening and closing her legs again. "Soooooo high!"
"You are so goddamn pretty and cute," Hall said. "You're exactly what I need right now. This is my first time at a show, and I think you should show me the ropes."
"Show you the ropes?" she said, unsure. "What does that mean?"
"It means teach me. It's like saying teach me the tricks of the trade."

"Ohhh," she said. "I thought it was a dirty sex thing." She laughed again, arms and legs moving. "Okay, so teach you what ropes? About raving?"

"Yeah, sure, about raving."

"Okay!" she cried. "It's easy! All you do is love and dance. Can you dance?"

"No," Hall said, "I don't dance."

"What? Yes, you do! Everyone dances! What do you mean you don't dance? I'm going to make you dance, and you'll see that you can dance. I promise you'll have fun. Come on, let's go right now. Come on!"

She grabbed his hand and tried to pull him up, but he did not move so she used both hands and leaned back with all her weight and started running backward on the spot.

Hall laughed. "Okay, okay, okay," he said, and he let her pull him up. She held on to three of his fingers and led him down the row past three young men, who stared at him, and he wondered if she was with them.

Off the bleachers and onto the dance floor, she took him into the crowd, not very deep, but far enough in so that they were fully enclosed. The people around them were moving, and she started moving too, taking a better grip of his hand so that she had all of his fingers. She smiled at him, and he started moving, and it felt very natural. He was still burning up, and the heat felt good—a warm pressure he pushed into and pulled away from as he moved to the music.

He took her hand with his thumb running along the back of it, holding her arm up, her coming in close, dancing under his arm and brushing up against him. Her hips and ass moved perfectly, the core of her dancing, where all her energy was, and he fit in behind her and fell in with her movements. He felt the heat of her and the vibrations of the bass running through them, and they glowed in the blues and pinks and yellows of the arc. All around them, glowing colours left trails through the air, glow stick tracers spinning and swinging from wrists and necks and hips, and he gave himself to all of it completely, and he thought of nothing.

They went on, dancing and sweating, and when the music slowed, they slowed down with it, saying a few things to each other, smiling, and then the music would pick up again, rising, building pressure, and he would take her hand again, and they would start moving faster, and when the music climaxed, they danced furiously to it.

"I should go see my friends for a bit," she said after a while, "but you should take my phone number, and we can dance again, okay?"

"Okay," Hall said. He took his phone out and took down her number. She leaned up on her toes, kissed him quickly, bounced away, smiled, and ran off through the crowd.

Hall found Laqua on the bleachers and sat beside him.

"Hey, buddy," Laqua said, "are you having a good time?"

"Yeah," Hall said, "yeah I am. This is amazing."

Laqua laughed and clapped him on the shoulder, smiling. "What did I tell you? I knew you'd like it. How are you feeling?"

"Good," Hall said, "but I think it's starting to wear off. I'm losing energy."

"Here," Laqua said. He handed him a water bottle. "Drink some of this."

Hall took the bottle from him and took a sip. It tasted like rust. Laqua started talking to a girl in a yellow tutu beside him. Hall took a few more good drinks, almost gagging on the last one. He screwed the cap back on, tapped Laqua on the shoulder with the bottle and Laqua took it from him. Laqua looked at the bottle and then at Hall, his eyes wide.

"Dude, you just fucking drank half of this."

"What?" Hall said. "How much was I supposed to drink?"

"Not half of it. Fuck, man, there's like two grams in here."

"Oh," Hall said. "Well, sorry."

"Oh, I don't care, man, but you need to be careful. You just took a fuck load of MDMA, man. It's a good thing you're not drinking. Just don't take any more, and make sure you get some water into you. Here." He passed him another water bottle. Hall took it from him and drank some.

"If you start really burning up," Laqua said, "just sit down and chill the fuck out, okay?"

"Okay," Hall said.

Laqua started laughing. "Man, you are about to get fucking bombed. Buckle up, dude, you're in for a ride. You want to go for a cigarette?"

"Oh yeah, I forgot about cigarettes. Yeah, a cigarette would be great right now."

"Okay, man, let's go."

After they finished smoking, they walked around the reception hall. It was crowded, congested near stands selling accessories, mostly things that glowed, and between these focal points a current of bodies flowed in and out of the main hall.

"I want to grab a drink and some gum," Laqua said.

"Okay."

They walked in between the stands and followed the flow of the current toward a concession stand. They got in line and waited.

Somewhere a woman screamed, and it caught everyone's attention, because it was sharp and uncontrolled, noticeably different from the ecstatic screams coming from the main hall. There was panic in it.

"Get the fuck out of the way! Move! I said get the fuck out of the way!"

The voice was deep, and the people walking between the stands jumped to the side. A path opened for two policemen carrying a young man through the parting crowd. The boy was barely conscious. One policeman had both his legs, and the other had one arm so that the boy hung sideways. His other arm dragged across the floor. A string of bile hung from his mouth and connected to his elbow, and when his elbow bounced off the floor, the carpet caught the bile and pulled it away from the boy's mouth. The boy vomited on his shoulder, his arm, and the floor. Another woman screamed, and the boy started moaning. Hall recognized him as the boy with the pink glasses, though he was no longer wearing them.

"You see that?" Laqua said. "They're carrying him in the recovery position. That's smart. You see how the puke came out of him? No choking."

"That's the kid we lined up behind on the stairs," Hall said. "I wonder what he took."

"Probably just some bad E and booze, man."

"Really? That's it?"

"Yeah, dude. Like I said, it's a good thing you're not drinking. That M will be hitting you soon, by the way."

"Good."

They went back into the main hall and sat down on a lower row of bleachers. The crowd was massive in front of them, and the music might have been hitting its climax. People everywhere screamed, jumped, and danced, but none of it meant much to Hall anymore. The bass felt good, and the lights were nice to watch, but there was no real power in it like there had been before. He was no longer gripped by it or lost in it. The music and the lights were just there, and they were what they appeared to be, nothing more. He was tired, especially in his legs.

Two arms wrapped around his neck from behind. He grabbed the attacking wrists and stood up, jerking his torso around, keeping a firm grip on the wrists, pulling the person across the back of his seat, and twisting the arms, which were small and thin. He heard a squeal of pain, and some pink hair brushed across his face.

"Oh, fuck."

He let go of the girl with pink hair, and she lay across the back of the seat beside him, her feet in the air, her hands searching for support.

"Shit," Hall said, "I'm so sorry." He picked her up and turned her so that his arms were under her knees and shoulders and he had her cradled. He sat down in his seat while holding her like that. "Are you okay?"

"You hurt me!" she cried.

"Fuck, I'm so sorry. Where did I hurt you? What hurts?"

She made no reply. She swept her hair behind her ears and to one side, down her front, and ran a hand through it several times to smooth it out. She adjusted her bra, rewrapped the feathery yellow thing around her neck, and wiggled around a bit in his lap so that she was sitting more erect and more comfortably. When she was all finished, she looked at Hall.

"I'm okay."

"Are you sure?"

"Yeah, I'm fine. Holy cow, I just wanted to surprise you."

"Well, you did."

"I know I did. So, who's your friend?"

Hall introduced her to Laqua and learned that her name was Amber. None of them said much. They were all tired. She leaned back against him, fitting her head under and to the right of his. He put his arm around her waist. She took his hand and moved it slightly to the music as they watched the crowd and the lights.

"You're very beautiful," Hall said after a while.

She hummed in response.

"No, really," he said. "Look at me. I said look at me."

She turned in his lap and looked at him. He kissed her, and her mouth was hot, and their tongues swam in the heat together, and he held her tightly as he kissed her. The pleasure of it all started exploding locally, filling his limbs, his chest, and his groin with powerful, euphoric heat.

"Oh my god," she said. "Look how much you're sweating."

* * *

Amber had aged ten years and her pink hair had darkened. It was purple now, and she looked very serious, but still very beautiful.

"Amber," Hall said.

She did not acknowledge him. His shirt was bunched up in his lap, and he put it back on.

"Amber," Hall said again.

She turned and looked at him, and suddenly he felt uncertain and uncomfortable and became aware of a pins-and-needles sensation in his legs, feet, and hands.

"Not this again," she said. Her voice was soft but commanding.

"Not what again?" Hall said.

"You know what. This Amber thing."

"It's just that you look exactly like her," Hall said, "but older. She was sitting with me just a minute ago, and now you're here. It's like—"

"Just a minute ago?" she said.

"Yeah, just a minute ago. I was just sitting with her. It's like she just, or you... It's like... Never mind. Excuse me. I'm not thinking straight."

"That's all right," she said. She angled her body toward Hall, relaxed her brow and smiled, all very slightly. She opened a black purse and took out a small metallic bottle. She unscrewed the cap and carefully dumped a small pile of white powder onto the underside of her pinky nail, which was longer than her other nails. "Take this," she said.

"What is that?"

"Cocaine."

Hall looked around and saw a security man standing on the floor near the bleachers. Hall made eye contact with him.

"Don't worry about him," she said. "I sold him some earlier."

The security man grinned at Hall and turned around to face away from the bleachers. Hall snorted the cocaine and felt it coat the back of his throat, and it tasted faintly like gasoline. A light, euphoric feeling took him. The woman put the bottle away in her purse.

"So, John," she said, "I'm assuming you don't remember anything we talked about in the last hour?"

"Hour?" Hall said. "We've been talking for an hour?"

"Yes, John. We have been."

"Really?"

"Yes, really. Do you know what time it is?"

He took his phone out of his pocket, but it was dead. "No," he said, "I guess I don't."

"It's five in the morning."

"Really?"

"Really."

"Fuck."

He looked around. The lights and the music and the crowd all continued, but there were fewer people than he remembered, and they were making less noise. Many stood idly, watching the lights in a daze at the rear of the crowd. The bleachers around them were full. "I need to find my friend," Hall said.

"No, you don't," the woman said. "You're leaving with me."

"I am?"

"Yes. We talked all about it. The fact that you don't remember talking about it doesn't change anything."

He did not need to think about it for long. She was beautiful.

"Sure," he said. "And I hate to ask, but I'm being serious, I don't remember us talking at all, and—"

"Courtney," she said. "My name is Courtney. Are you ready to leave?"

"Sure," he said. "Why not?"

They stood up and walked down the bleachers. She was wearing a black mini-skirt and a black tank top. Her calves were toned, and he could see the muscles working as she walked. Hall followed her off the bleachers and across the main hall, into the reception area. They passed security and a no re-entry sign, and she started up the stairs.

Before he followed her, he looked back, and on the other side of security, Amber stood watching him. When he saw her, she waved goodbye to him, the yellow feathers of her scarf wrapped around her neck and up her arm so that it trailed her wide, slow wave. He waved back at her and smiled. She twirled around and ran to someone, and he turned to the stairs. Courtney was standing close to him, smiling, but only slightly, as seemed to be the only way she could.

Chapter 17

Courtney brought him to a house in a developing neighborhood. He offered to pay the cab fare, but she ignored him and handed the driver two twenties. The sun was coming up, and the sky glowed orange and the streets blue.

Inside the house, he heard the low bass of electronic music coming from down the hall, darker and calmer than what had played at the show—more ambient.

Courtney took off her shoes and looked at him. "Her name is Kitty," she said.

"Who?"

"Who we talked about."

"I told you, I don't remember—"

"It doesn't matter. Come."

Hall took his shoes off and followed her down the hall into the living room. A woman and a man were lying on opposite ends of a large, U-shaped leather couch wrapped around a glass coffee table. On the opposite wall was a flat-screen TV, the largest Hall had ever seen, hooked up to an expensive-looking stereo system. The woman had long blonde hair she had swept around her neck and down her chest. She was thin, and her legs were long. She was wearing wide, wrap-around sunglasses, and she might have been asleep.

The man wore a wife-beater and had a goatee. He was wiry, and Hall saw veins and tendons in his arms and neck. The skin under his eyes was dark and lined. He sat up straight when they came in and put his elbows on his knees. Courtney walked over to the couch and laid down so that the only place for Hall to sit was at the feet of the blonde woman. He sat down there, and the man stared at him, and he stared back. The man's leg started bouncing up and down on his toes.

"Who the fuck is this?" he asked.

Hall looked at his bouncing leg and back up at him. "I'm John."

They went on staring at each other, neither of their heads moving, both of them concentrated on what they had started. The man's leg continued to bounce. All of Hall's focus went to the muscles in his face. He commanded them not to move, not before the other man looked away. His bottom lip started to twitch, so he bit it carefully without opening his mouth. The music slowed, and a voice started talking, but he did not register anything it said, only the change of sound. In his peripheral vision, he saw Courtney sit up, and he might have seen the woman lying beside him stir. Everything was begging for his attention, demanding that he look away from the other man.

"Stop it," Courtney said, breaking it for him.

Hall looked at her and then back at the man, who was still staring at him. The man smiled and looked at Courtney. She stood up and walked over to him and touched his head. "Come."

The man stood up and followed her up a flight of stairs beside the hallway.

Hall looked at the woman beside him. She was facing him, but her sunglasses were too dark to see if she was looking at him or if she was even awake. He settled in deeper into the couch and looked around the living room and then back at her.

"Are you Kitty?" Hall asked.

She did not respond. She was wearing black leggings that stopped at her calves, which were slender and white.

Hall reached under her left leg and touched the bottom of her right calf. "Hey."

She lifted her legs in the air and crossed them so that the calf he had touched rested on the shin of her other leg.

"Are you Kitty?"

"Mhmm. . . .."

"I'm John."

"I know."

"So you were awake."

"I was." Her voice was small and light and did not seem to cost her anything.

"Do you live here?"

"No."

"Does Courtney?"

"Sometimes."

"What about that guy?"

"He lives here."

"Who is he?"

"Just some guy."

"He seems like an asshole."

"That's what some people say."

"So, what's Kitty short for? And why are you wearing sunglasses?"

"It's not short for anything."

"Okay, well, why are you wearing sunglasses?"

"Because I'm on drugs." She left her lips apart, not quite smiling, but in a way that showed she wanted to.

"You're on drugs?" Hall said.

"Aren't you?"

"I guess so. What kind of drugs are you on?"

"Good ones."

Hall smiled. "That's good."

"Yes," she said, "it is good." She smiled.

"You have a nice smile," Hall said.

"Thank you."

He looked at her legs again and then looked forward and rubbed his chin with the tops of his fingers. He looked back at her sunglasses. "I think Courtney brought me here to meet you, but I'm not entirely sure."

"She did."

"She did? So you know about this?"

"Yes," she said, "she's been texting me." She looked away from him and smiled again and brought her hand up to her head and took some of her blonde hair between her fingers. "She told me what you talked about at the show. All the things you forgot you told her."

"What did I tell her?"

"Wouldn't you like to know?"

"I would," Hall said.

"But isn't it more fun this way?"

"For you, maybe."

"Oh, please," she said. "Don't be a baby."

"A baby?"

"A baby."

"Goddamn it."

"Baby . . . ."

Hall moved around a bit so that he was facing her better. "Can you give me a hint at least?"

"Okay." She brought the hair in her fingers to her mouth and pressed it against her lips. "A hint . . . A hint . . . I don't know what kind of hint I could give you. I don't want to give away too much, or I'll ruin it. A hint . . . No, I don't think I'm going to give you a hint."

"Oh, don't be a tease. Well, if you can't give me a hint about what I said, can you tell me what you thought of it?"

"It certainly caught my attention."

"Why don't you take off your sunglasses?"

"I don't want to."

"Please?"

"Baby...."

"You like calling me that."

"I do."

"What else do you like?"

"Lots of things."

"Like being a tease."

"Yes, like being a tease."

"I'm tired," Hall said. "I don't feel like being teased."

"Baby...."

"Tease."

"Yes?"

"Nothing. I'm tired."

"Go home then, baby."

"Are you kicking me out?"

"No," she said, "I like you here. I like teasing you. But if you're tired, go home. It's six in the morning."

"Yeah," Hall said, "It's been a long night."

"Good though?"

"Very good."

"That's good."

"Do you have a boyfriend?"

"No."

"Let me take you out sometime. You can tease me all you want."

"Baby...."

"Legs."

"These legs?" She raised them and re-crossed them.

"Those legs."

"It was nice to meet you, John."

"You, too."

Hall stood up, pulled his shoulders back in a light stretch, and looked around the room. Blood rushed to his head, and he felt slightly dizzy for a moment, but it passed. He put his hands in his pockets and looked at Kitty. She was twirling her blonde hair in her fingers, under her chin. He smiled at her. She smiled back and pressed her hair to her lips again. Hall walked around to the foot of the couch and faced her with his hands in his pockets. He looked at her legs and her sunglasses. She was still smiling. He laughed softly, and her smile widened, but she did not laugh.

"Tease," he said.

"Baby."

"Goodbye, Kitty."

"Goodbye, John."

Hall went out into the daylight, lit a cigarette, and started walking. He walked several blocks and smoked three cigarettes before he found a payphone and called a cab.

Chapter 18

It was the middle of the week, and Hall was cutting and bevelling pipe in the shop when she texted him:

Baby . . .

He was not supposed to have his phone while he worked, so he put it back in his pocket after he read the message, pulled his face shield down, and took the zip cutter back to the pipe. Sparks shot out ahead of him and into the front of his coveralls, and the cutter screamed and wailed as he dug it into the steel, not too forcefully, letting the machine do the work to not wear down the disc. The vibrations were strong but small, a pins-and-needles sensation. He made six cuts and switched the zip disc to a grinder disc and started beveling the edges. He finished three and took off his face shield, wiped the sweat off his forehead, and checked the time. It was coffee break. He went to the lunch trailer and texted her back.

Tease . . .

After break, he went back to the shop, but the foreman came and got him and a journeyman to help a picker truck lift a load of steel off a trailer that had just pulled into the yard. They formed into a group by the load. There was the journeyman, the foreman, the picker operator, the truck driver, and Hall. The foreman handed out an FLRA for all of them to sign and gave the safety brief, which reminded Hall of a range-safety brief in the army. The process and significance of the two kinds of briefings were very similar. Men in uniform, either combats or coveralls, gathered together, because something important needed to be done—something big and dangerous, and though the purpose of the brief was to be educational, it was more of a ritual than a learning experience. They had all done, if not the exact task, a similar task before, and all the safety points could be gathered from common sense. What was important was the indoctrination of the group into a serious mindset, because what they were about to do was dangerous and serious. By coming together in a group and formally acknowledging the danger, they all became serious.

The lift took nearly an hour, and when they were finished, they had moved 20,000 pounds of steel from a trailer to the ground, where it was picked up in sections by a forklift. Hall went back to the shop and checked his phone, but he had no new messages. He continued beveling the pipe and wondered if he should have sent something else. Maybe he should not have called her a tease. He could have thought of something better to say, something with more of an opening. Not necessarily anything witty or amusing, but something. He could have asked her how her day was going or how the rest of her weekend was or any question, really, because he really did not know anything about her. He should have stayed at that house longer. He had left too early; he had not made enough of an impression.

No, he thought, "Tease" was enough. That was a good thing to text her. But it's been over an hour now. You should send something else. No, you shouldn't, you goddamn child, stop this. Stop this and just grind the fucking pipe.

He finished beveling two more ends. While he was working on the last one, he felt his phone vibrate in his pocket. He shut off the grinder immediately and checked his messages:

Would you like to come to my apartment tonight?

He read the text over three times.

"Hey, John."

He looked up and saw the journeyman pointing at his phone.

"You know you're not supposed to have that on you."

"Yeah, sorry." He put the phone back in his pocket. "I have to piss."

He walked out of the shop to the wash car and took his phone out. He started to text her, but he deleted what he wrote three times. Finally, he just said,

Yeah. I'd like that.

Her next message was her address.

Chapter 19

He did 200 push-ups, the first 100 in sets of 50, the second in sets of 25, and he curled a 50-pound bar to failure three times. He flexed his chest and arms in front of the bathroom mirror, took a shower, and put on his best pair of jeans and his second-best shirt. He had worn his best shirt the night he had met her.

He left early and had some time to kill, so he stopped by a grocery store on a whim. Across the street was a Liquor Barn. He sat in his car and looked through the car window and the Liquor Barn windows. The ceilings inside were high, the walls painted dark burgundy. There were four rows of wine racks, and the hard alcohol lined the walls. He could not see the walk-in cooler from where he was looking, but he knew where it was, because he had been in that store many times. It always smelled slightly of bleach, and the floors were always clean, except for once when he had walked in to buy some beer, and several bottles of white wine had smashed on the floor. The pool of wine had spread under two rows of wine racks, and the sweet smell of the wine had mixed with the sour smell of the bleach. It was a sharp smell, and he could smell it clearly as he sat in his car looking through the car and the store windows.

He got out of the car, walked into the grocery store, and picked up a bouquet of flowers, the most expensive one, which was thirty-five dollars. The lady at the counter explained to him what each flower represented. He thanked her when she was finished and forgot everything she had told him.

He parked on the street near Kitty's building. He still had ten minutes, so he rechecked the address and stared at himself in the rear-view mirror. With five minutes remaining, he got out of the car with the flowers and walked up to her building but turned around, went back to the car, and threw the flowers in the passenger seat. He returned to the building.

He entered her buzzer number. His hand was shaking slightly, and he shifted his weight back and forth between his feet. His knees were also shaking. He took a deep breath, then another, and then her voice came over the intercom.

"Hello?"

"It's John," he said. His voice cracked, and he recoiled from the speaker, releasing the button, swearing at himself, hoping the static of the speaker had covered the nervousness in his voice. His heart beat furiously, and he felt ill, his hands cold and clammy and shaking.

I could just say I forgot something in the car, he thought. *I could go for a quick drive. I could come back. I could always quit drinking again. I've gone this far, and I could do it again. Just enough to get me through the door, and I'll pick up a couple bottles of wine, because that's very normal, to bring a bottle of wine or two to a first date, which this is, a first date, and she thinks you're confident and sociable and put together, because that's how you were when you met her, because you were high, but you're a fucking wreck now. What is she going to think of you now? You can always quit drinking again. You've made it this far, John, and drinking didn't kill you before, and now it can help you. Just enough to get you through the door. Say you'll be right back. It will take ten minutes at most. The Liquor Barn is just around the corner, all you—*

"Come on up," she said. The buzzer sounded, and the door unlocked. He opened it and walked inside. He got into the elevator. It had mirrors on every wall. He rubbed his chin, studied his reflection, shifted his weight back and forth between his feet, and wiped his cold, sweaty hands on the back of his jeans.

She was on the eighteenth floor, and her apartment number was 1807. He breathed in through his nose and out through his mouth and knocked on her door.

Her eyes were pale blue—Siberian Husky eyes. He breathed in through his nose and out through his mouth. He said something, and she opened the door wider. She smiled at him and said something back. She stepped aside to let him in. He walked inside. His knees shook, and he kept moving to hide it, shifting his weight. He leaned against the wall and moved away from it. She said something else, and he responded. Her eyes went over him, and he knew she could see how nervous he was. She smiled again and went away somewhere. He breathed in through his nose and out through his mouth, and the worst of it was over. The world carried on.

"Take a seat on the couch if you like," she said.

She was in the kitchen to the left. Ahead of him, down a short hallway, was the living room. One wall was a window that overlooked the river valley. The floors were hardwood, and the couch and chair were white leather. A white rug was spread across the living room, and the coffee table was stainless steel and glass, as was the entertainment stand and end tables. Everything was very clean, and several pieces of art hung from the walls, mostly paintings done in dark colors. The hardwood floors were a shade between the furniture and the paintings and brought everything together.

"You have a nice place," Hall said, pleased to hear that his voice was steady. He wiped the cold sweat off his hands onto his jeans again.

"Thank you," she said from the kitchen.

"You don't have any 'Live, Love, Laugh' shit anywhere," Hall said. His voice almost cracked that time. He clenched his jaw.

"What?"

"Nothing."

She stepped out of the kitchen. "No, what did you say?"

"It was nothing."

"Would you like a drink?"

"I don't drink."

"I know you don't." She smiled. "I didn't mean alcohol."

"Oh. Well, what do you have?"

"Lots of things."

"I have to work in the morning," Hall said.

"Don't worry, baby, I'll make sure you get some sleep tonight. I'll take good care of you. I promise."

"I don't know," he said, trying to sound playful, "I don't even know you."

"Yet here you are in my apartment."

"Well, yeah, but you—"

"I'm going to make you a non-alcoholic drink, okay?"

"Okay," he said, and she disappeared back into the kitchen.

His jeans were riding into his crotch, so he stood up, adjusted them the best he could, and sat back down. He rubbed his hands on his knees and looked around again. There was an easel he had not noticed before sitting by the window with a half-finished painting of a woman with her hands raised, her head lowered, and her eyes closed, like she was surrendering at gunpoint, but her face was calm and happy. The woman was naked.

Kitty came back into the living room with two short glasses with something red in them. She sat down beside him and handed him one.

"Best to drink it all at once."

They did, and it tasted like rust.

"That was MDMA," he said.

She nodded. "Yes, but it's very good. It's very clean. I think everyone should try this kind at least once."

"What's it called?"

"Oh, it has some silly name, but I don't remember it. It makes no difference." She took his glass but stayed on the couch.

"You're an artist," Hall said.

"I paint, yes."

"That woman you're painting, she's beautiful."

"Thank you."

"You're welcome."

She hummed and smiled at him again, stood up, and disappeared back into the kitchen. When she came back, she sat close to him, facing him, with her arm on the backrest of the couch. He could not feel the MDMA, but that he had consumed it, that it was only a matter of time until it took effect reassured him, calmed him, and made looking into her pale blue eyes a little easier.

"So, what do you do?" he asked.

"I go to school," Kitty said. "For art. I don't work. My father supports me."

"That's nice of him. You have a nice place here. He must really love you."

"He does," she said, "and this is the only way he's genuinely capable of showing it. He wasn't around much while I grew up, and when he was, he still wasn't really present, or at least not as you'd expect a father to be. All of this is compensation, I suppose. I'm very comfortable for it."

"Well, you seem at peace with it."

"It is what it is. I like this apartment, and I like going to school, and I like not working. I'm comfortable and happy here because of my father. I have no resentments. I think it's selfish to accost a person for loving you in their way and not yours. He loves me, and that's all that should matter. Love is love. And besides, isn't this apartment wonderful?"

"Yes, it's very nice," Hall said. "And you don't have any 'Live, Love, Laugh' shit anywhere. I like that."

She raised an eyebrow and smiled. "Is that what you said before?"

"What?"

"When you first came in, you said something, and I didn't quite hear you. Is that what you said?"

"It was."

"You really don't like that phrase, do you?"

"It's terrible."

"Oh, how dark and manly of you."

Hall laughed without having to force it.

"So, are you still going to travel?" Kitty asked.

"Did I tell Courtney I was going to travel?"

"You told her lots of things."

"Well, it's good to finally hear some of them. That was the plan for a while, yeah, but now I'm not so sure."

"Would you still go to Brazil?"

"Did I say Brazil?"

"That's what I heard."

"I don't know. I've thought of Australia."

"Do you surf?"

"No."

"Hmm . . . ."

"Why were you at that house the other night?" Hall asked.

"I went to pick up one of my paintings."

"What was that guy's name?"

"Jason," Kitty said, "and yes, I used to be his girlfriend."

"So you went over there to pick up your painting but you—"

"I got caught up in his bullshit."

"Ah," Hall said. "I still think he's an asshole."

"He is, but there's more to it than that."

"There always is. How old are you?"

"Twenty-seven."

"You're a little bit older than me."

"I know."

Kitty hummed, and they continued talking until the MDMA hit them. They were facing each other on the couch, his right arm and her left arm on the backrest. He reached forward and took her hand, looking fearlessly into her eyes now, into their paleness and their blackness, and she held his hand and his eyes.

She stretched her fingers through his, brought them out, ran them up and down his arm, back to his fingers, and through them again. They fell into it so easily, so naturally, as if they had been doing it for years, like everything was falling into place exactly as they always knew it would.

"Let's listen to some music," Kitty said. She stood up and went to the entertainment stand and picked up two sets of headphones. One was white and one was black. Both were wireless. Kitty flicked a switch on both sets and handed him the black pair. She went into her room and came back out with an mp3 player. She put on her headphones, he put on his, and she stood in front of him, close to him, her leg touching his, and went through the mp3 player. Music started playing in the headphones: a piano accompanied by a woman singing softly. Kitty looked at him and smiled, sat down on the couch, and put her legs across his lap.

He ran his hand up her leg. She took it and put her fingers through his again. A bass started in the headphones, and they looked at each other and smiled. He stretched. Kitty closed her eyes, laid her head back, and he moved his hand up her leg again. When he came close, she took it again and held it up. He kept stretching and yawning, each time sending ripples of pleasure through his body. She moved around so her head was on his lap. He ran his hand through her long blonde hair, and she reached up, cupped the back of his neck, and the music carried them through it. She closed her eyes, and he looked her over, looked at the slenderness and the fineness of her, at her lips, the gentle angle of her jaw, the thinness of her neck.

Suddenly, her eyes snapped open, wide and awake and focused, and a current of electricity shot from his skull down through his spine, raising his hair and tightening his skin.

The music was gaining energy. She came up from his lap and the couch, turning as she stood, facing him, and her hips started dipping deeply on either side, a careful sway starting, her arms raising, her head tilted down, held at gunpoint, smiling, calm, beautiful. He brought his feet up on the couch while Kitty danced in the living room. She danced for a long time with the headphones connecting and muting them simultaneously.

Chapter 20

Wright stabbed at three steaks on his barbecue, and blood leaked out of them, sizzling on the grill. Flames rose up and licked the meat.

"I'll tell you what I'd like to do," he said. "I'd like to stick their hands in this fucking grill. Get their hands in there and pin them down. Most people couldn't do that shit, you know, hold another human being down and cook him, but I could do it. I wouldn't mind it. Jundies smell better burnt and dead than they do alive."

He talked between clenched teeth, the muscles in his jaw bulging like bunched-up pieces of rope. He poured more Grey Goose vodka into a tall glass full of ice, took a long drink, hissed through his teeth, and coughed into his arm.

"Fuck."

It was a Saturday, and the day was hot.

Hall and Hartford were sitting on lawn chairs on Wright's deck, smoking cigarettes. Hartford was drinking a beer, and Hall was drinking a ginger ale. He had been seeing Kitty for over a month now, and they had stayed up most of the previous night doing cocaine and talking in her apartment. He had gotten about two hours of sleep before Wright called and invited him over. He had not felt good and said he could not make it, but Kitty gave him two pills to swallow and three smaller ones to dissolve under his tongue that made him feel better, and he decided to make the drive to Wright's house. Kitty had given him another dozen of the small pills, nine of which he still had in his pocket. He felt relaxed as he sat in a lawn chair on Wright's balcony.

Hartford took back the rest of his beer, burped, and wiped his mouth with the back of his hand. "Man," he said, "you already beat the cocksuckers half to death. What more do you want?"

Wright had gotten cut off in traffic by a pickup truck a week before. He had followed the vehicle, laying on the horn for several kilometers until it pulled over. When two Middle-Eastern men in their mid-twenties got out of the vehicle, he immediately attacked them.

He knocked the first man down with his first strike, and with time to work on the second one, he beat him viciously. While he was on top of him, attacking his face and throat with his fists and palms, the first man regained consciousness and stood up. Wright returned to the first man and put him back on the ground. The second man managed to crawl back into the truck, lock the doors, and call the police. After he had beaten the first man unconscious again, Wright saw the second man on his phone and that two vehicles had stopped and parked behind them. Both drivers were also on their phones. Wright came out of it and returned to his car. He sat and smoked cigarettes as he waited for the police to arrive. It helped that there were two of them and one of him, that he was in uniform, that they were Middle Eastern, and that one of the policemen was ex-military, but both men were charging him with assault. He had spent a few hours in the city jail and a few nights at the military police station.

"You guys planning on having kids?" Wright asked.

"I don't know," Hall said.

"Yeah," Hartford said.

"Well, here's what you have to do if you have girls," Wright said, "because both of you are going to be shit fathers."

"Hey."

"Fuck off."

"It's true, you will be," Wright said, and he took another long drink, hissed, and coughed into his arm. "Especially if you have girls. Your daughters are guaranteed cases of daddy issues, so as soon as their little axe wounds start to bleed, they're going to try and fuck you off by getting fucked, so that's why you have to start early and condition them."

"Man, what the fuck are you talking about?"

Wright finished the glass of vodka, dry heaved for a moment, spit, and filled the glass again. "I'm talking about this fucking filth. Sand niggers. You have to be careful about how you speak of sand niggers around your daughters, because if they figure out you hate them, they'll use it against you after you fuck them up enough. So what you have to do is condition them."

He spat on his deck again and stabbed at the steaks. They sizzled on the grill. "You have to start early and teach them that jundies aren't something you hate. They're simply something foul, something to be avoided, like a piece of dog shit on the side walk. You see what I'm saying? You have to teach your daughters that they're something to laugh off, that they're something only to be tolerated, like a stomach flu, and you have to put them in the habit of avoiding them, just like you'd teach them not to step in a pile of shit. Never humanize them. You see what I'm saying? Charge me with assault, you fucking cowards, the both of them. I should have gotten my tire iron. I should have dragged the smaller one, that one I had on the pavement, I should have dragged him back to my fucking car and crushed his head in my fucking door. The cocksuckers, the fucking cowards, man, fuck. Then I'd gore the second one. Smash his windows and pull him out by his hair and gore him with that fucking tire iron." Sweat poured down his face. He drank more vodka, spat, stabbed at the meat on the grill. "Charge me with assault? I should have cut their fucking eyes out."

"Jesus Christ, man . . .."

"Jesus Christ what? What, Hall, what the fuck do you have to say?"

"How're those steaks?"

"What?"

"How are the steaks?"

"They're done. Go get some plates."

Hall went inside and got plates and cutlery, and they sat around on the deck and ate from their laps. The steaks were overcooked. Hartford took long drinks of his beer, finishing a quarter can with every pull, and Wright took mouthfuls of vodka, hissing and coughing after every drink. Hall could not eat more than half his steak. He felt uneasy and started sweating. He went inside and threw the rest of the meat in the garbage, poured a cold glass of water, added some ice, and drank it all. He put another three pills under his tongue, and as soon as he could taste them dissolving, he started feeling better. He held the cold glass to his forehead and closed his eyes. His ears started ringing softly. He listened to the noise, and it did not last long.

He went back outside. Wright and Hartford had put their plates down on the deck and were smoking. Hall lit a cigarette and sat down in his chair. Hartford pulled the tab off his beer can. Wright stood up and walked into his house. Hartford and Hall finished their cigarettes, Hartford opened another beer, and Hall opened another ginger ale.

"What's your girl's name again?" Hartford asked.

"Kitty."

"Kitty?"

"Yeah, Kitty."

"Is that short for Catherine?"

"It's not short for anything."

"Huh."

"Yeah."

"So you're dating now?"

"Yeah, man, we're dating. I'm into her. Fuck, I might even move in with her. We just started talking about it last night."

"Good, man. Good."

"Yeah, man, it's pretty good. It's been a long time since I've had a girlfriend."

"Yeah, no shit," Hartford said. "I'm proud of you."

"Thanks, man."

"Hey, what was the name of that dude who blew his head off last winter?"

"I don't remember."

"I think it started with an S. Like a Sal-something. Or a Sor . . . Soli . . . Fuck, it was bugging me the other day. Whatever. Fuck it. You know what I did last weekend?"

"What?"

"I shotgunned a beer," Hartford said proudly.

"You shotgunned a beer?"

"Yeah, I shotgunned a fuckin' beer. I haven't done that in forever. I crushed the fuckin' thing. We should shotgun a fuckin' beer. Right now."

"I'm drinking ginger ale," Hall said.

"Oh yeah, I forgot. Fuck, sorry. Never mind."

"No, you shotgun a beer. I'll shotgun a ginger ale."

"That's fuckin' stupid."

"Have you ever shotgunned a pop?"

"No."

"Then how the fuck would you know?"

Hartford laughed. "All right."

He finished off the rest of his beer and pulled another one and a ginger ale from the cooler. He took his keys from his pocket and stabbed a hole in the cans, and they dug their thumbs into the holes to widen them.

"One, two, three, go!" Hartford said.

They put the holes to their mouths and opened the cans and had them empty in a few seconds. They slammed the empty cans onto the deck. Hartford grinned. Hall burped, and a bit of froth came up. He burped again, and more came up. He leaned over the side of his chair and let it pour out of his mouth and nose. They both laughed. Air kept coming up as Hall laughed.

"Fucking retard," Hartford said.

"Fuck you," Hall said.

They smoked a few more cigarettes and talked for a while longer and eventually agreed to leave. They tidied up the deck, said their goodbyes, and Hartford went around the side of the house to his truck while Hall took the plates and cutlery back inside. He put them in the dishwasher and threw away the garbage. He wiped the counters off and stood at the island and listened for a moment. He walked into the living room and found Wright on the couch. He had a wet cloth folded over his eyes, his arm hanging off the side of the couch. The bottle of vodka had fallen on the hardwood floor and spilled, but not much, as Wright had already drunk most of it. Hall picked it up and put it on the island in the kitchen and found some paper towel to clean up the spill. He sat on the coffee table for a moment and looked at the demon whispering into Wright's ear. It was on his side, and the wet cloth was covering the head. Hall carefully picked up a corner of the cloth and folded it back on itself so he could see the expression on the black demon's face.

Chapter 21

Hall turned left when he should have turned right and drove down 118th Ave. He put the last three pills in his mouth, and they dissolved into a chalky paste. He spread it over his gums and cheeks with his tongue, and the wonderful softness took him again, wrapped itself around him and released him from all the small discomforts he endlessly endured but never noticed until they were gone.

He came to a stop light. He lit a cigarette and watched three homeless people who had set themselves up on the sidewalk in front of a liquor store. One was leaning against a wall. With the sun beating down on him, he had a sleeping bag pulled up to his neck. Another was stumbling, looking up at the sky, trying to stay in one spot long enough to find whatever he was looking for above him. His face was swollen and pitted and dark with dirt. The third was a massively obese woman, her head shaved. As the light turned green and Hall pulled away, she vomited on the sidewalk. Hall turned the radio up and lit another cigarette as his car glided smoothly across the pavement.

He turned the air conditioning up, and it blew coldly across his face and destroyed the smoke he exhaled. His phone vibrated in his pocket. He took it out and saw that Kitty had texted him:

When are you coming back to me, baby?
Now, babe.

He stopped at another red light beside another liquor store and a bus stop. On the bench was a man wearing three filthy jackets. He had an arm around a garbage bag full of empty bottles and cans and a wine bottle wrapped in a plastic bag between his legs. On his neck was a massive swelling that bulged out to his shoulder and warped his jaw on one side so that his mouth hung open. It was grey and pink in blotches. The man looked at Hall, and Hall looked down at his phone. Kitty had texted him again:

Good. I love you, baby.
I love you, too.

Chapter 22

Hall used the key Kitty had given him to get into the apartment. She was sitting in front of the easel, painting with the blinds open to let the sunlight in. She was wearing her wraparound sunglasses and her wireless headphones. Her blonde hair fell straight down and hung in the space the arch of her back made.

Hall approached her quietly, as he had many times before while she was painting. He used to worry he would startle her, but she always seemed to know when he was there, and when he wrapped his arms around her, she never jumped. When her brush was a safe distance from the canvas, he put his arms around her then and kissed her cheek. She squeezed his arm and hummed. He came away from her and brushed her hair to the side and kissed her neck. She continued painting. He sat on the couch and picked up one of her books he had been reading. His fingers left wet marks on the pages. He put the book down and rubbed his hands on his jeans. He tried to read again, but an uneasiness had settled into his stomach and legs, and he could not stay focused. He put the book down and watched Kitty paint. She was still painting the naked woman with her head down and her arms up. She had painted bruises on her ribs and her throat as she had continued developing the rest of her. The painting held him, at first because of the bruises, then because of her nakedness and her beauty, and then he was not sure why it held him.

He wondered how she had been moved to paint that woman, and he wondered about the painting at Jason's house, and then about Jason.

Kitty stopped painting and sat quietly staring at her work. After a while, she cleaned her brushes and put her paints away. She took her headphones and sunglasses off and sat down on the couch with him, put a hand up his shirt, and touched his chest. She put her legs across his lap.

"I feel like doing more blow," Hall said.

"Baby . . . ."

"Do you?"

"I don't know."

"It's Saturday."

"We did some last night," Kitty said.

"But there's some left."

"We don't have to do it just because it's there."

"Well, do you want to do it?"

"I guess we could."

"We don't have to," Hall said.

"But you want to."

"Yeah, I want to. Do you?"

"I said we could."

"But do you want to?"

"I can take it or leave it," Kitty said.

"So you want it to be my decision?"

"That's not what I'm trying to say."

"I know, babe. I just don't want to feel like I'm pressuring you into it."

"You're not pressuring me into it. I can make up my own mind."

"I know you can," Hall said. "You know what I mean though. Okay, well, I'm going to do some, because I want to. You do whatever you want, okay?"

"Okay. I want to do some. Maybe we can do some MDMA tonight, too. We haven't done it together in a little while. I love doing it with you."

"Me too, babe. Yeah, that sounds good. So, where is it?"

"I'll get it."

She took her legs back from his lap, stood up, and went into her room. Hall stretched his back and rubbed his hands on his jeans. He looked at his phone. It was after six. He thought about being high. He thought about the MDMA taking over the cocaine and holding Kitty on the couch and running his hands over her.

She came out with two little baggies on a glass picture frame with no picture in it and set it down on the coffee table. Hall took the baggie of cocaine and poured it onto the picture frame. He took his driver's license and another card out of his wallet and pressed one card flat over the clumps of cocaine and crushed it up, moving it in a circular motion. He used the other card to scrape the cocaine off the first and chopped the pile up with both cards, running their edges along each other in opposite directions.

When most of the clumps were gone, he separated the pile into eight lines, but Kitty said they were too big for her. They were big lines, but that was how Hall wanted them, so he turned her four lines into six and left his the same. He had an old twenty and two new tens in his wallet. He took one of the new bills, which worked very well for snorting drugs, and rolled it up. He gave the bill to Kitty. She swept her hair to one side and let it fall beside the coffee table so that it was held away from her face and the picture frame. She put one end of the bill into her nose and guided the other end slowly and smoothly across her first line, making no sound at all. She handed the bill to Hall, and he bent over and railed his line fast and loud. He looked at her and smiled. She smiled back. He touched her leg. She rubbed her nose. They fell back into the couch.

"So," Kitty said, "how was the barbecue?"

He did not want to talk about the barbecue. He wanted to talk, but not about that. He was not sure why, but the question irritated him. He rubbed his hands on his jeans.

"It was okay."

"Was it at Hartford's house?"

"No, at Wright's house. Hartford was there though."

"Were there lots of people there?"

"No, it was just the three of us. We should get your painting back from Jason."

"Sure," she said. "We can go this week. I'd like that."

"How long were you dating him?"

"Almost a year."

"Why? Because he was a drug dealer?"

She brought her legs up and crossed them underneath her and looked away from him. "That was one reason, I suppose. A very silly reason, but I can't say it had nothing to do with it."

"How did you meet him?"

"Courtney knew one of his friends. We went to his house after a show. He was having an after party."

Hall saw it perfectly. He saw the house, the sectional couch, the type of people there, the music, Kitty and Courtney walking in, Kitty talking to Jason, them getting high together, laughing, touching.

"Did you fuck him that night?"

"Excuse me?"

She had. Hall could see it. He pictured it happening in a bathroom—her bent over the sink, him pushing into her. Hall was the mirror. He saw them both, saw her mouth open, her grab the sink, saw Jason's hands on her hips, his brow furrowed. Hall's heart started beating quickly. He rubbed his hands on his jeans. He focused on his breathing, took a breath in through his nose and blew it out through his mouth.

This is irrational, he thought. *This is stupid and it should not matter. It does not matter.*

"Did you hook up with him?"

"Why would you ask me that?"

"I don't know. I'm making conversation."

"Well, this conversation has no point. You're mad now, I can see it. Baby, don't do that to yourself, please?"

"Okay, you're right, I'm sorry," Hall said. "It's the cocaine. I'm going to do another one."

"You just did one."

"I feel like getting nice and high. I don't like dragging it out. No point." He took the bill and did another line. He sat back on the couch and felt his hands start to shake. "Let's take that MDMA now. Then it'll hit us right about when we finish the cocaine."

"It won't take that long to hit us. Less than an hour. You want to finish the coke by then?"

"I'm already done half of mine."

"But those were big lines."

"Yeah, but I want to finish sooner than later, babe. I don't want to be up all night. I want to be on somewhat of a normal sleeping schedule for work Monday morning."

"Okay. I guess so. I'll get it."

She stood up and went into her room and then into the kitchen. She came back with two glasses and handed him one. They drank the drinks and put the empty glasses on the coffee table. They sat back, and he put a hand on her leg. She swept her hair to one side.

He saw her skin ripple from the force of Jason's hips. She knocked over the soap dispenser by the sink. She put one hand on the mirror and the other gripped the edge of the counter. He pulled her hair, and her head jerked back, and she whined and squeezed her eyes shut.

Hall rubbed his hands on his jeans. His heart was pounding, and he was sweating. He wanted to bring it up. He had to bring it up.

"So, how are Hartford and Wright?" she asked.

"They're all right," Hall said. "Well, Wright was wasted. I think he's starting to lose it. He spent a few days in jail last week."

"In jail? What did he do?"

"He beat the shit out of a couple of sand niggers, which isn't unusual for him, but it sounded pretty bad this time. It sounded like he tried to kill them. He put them both in the hospital."

"Excuse me?"

"Yeah, he put them both in the hospital."

"He put who in the hospital?"

"The sand niggers."

"Sand niggers?"

"Yeah. Jundies."

She took her legs away from his lap. He looked at her. Her brow was furrowed, her mouth slightly open, her nose and eyes tight.

"John, that's disgusting."

"What?"

"Those names are appalling. Do you know how ignorant you sound when you use names like that?"

"What the fuck do you know about—"

"Do not swear at me, John."

He took a moment and a breath. "I'm sorry for swearing at you, but I'm not sorry for saying sand nigger or jundie. They're only names, Kitty, and fitting ones. I know where you're going with this, that they're not all the same, that I can't discriminate against an entire race based on a few, but why not? I can only speak of things based on my personal experiences, and in my experience, those people are rotten. They're the worst people on Earth. Look where they come from; look at their homeland. They're thousands of years behind us, and they're like that for a reason, because of the way they are, which is just plain savage. They live in mud and spend their lives tearing themselves and everything around them apart. And all in the name of some pathetic, barbaric religion. The way they are is just disgusting. There are exceptions, I know, but as a rule, they're shit. They hold the rest of the world back, and we try to help them, and a few of them can be helped, but most of them just bring their filth to our country and spread it like an infection, and now they're rotting us from the inside out. You know, I wish more than anything I could have killed at least one of them when I was over there. I dream about it. All the time I dream about killing them, but then I wake up, and I'm crushed, because I know I'll never get another chance. It wouldn't have bothered me; I would have been proud of myself. They're only jundies, Kitty. They're sand niggers."

He had not been paying attention to her while he talked, and when he looked at her he saw that she was crying. She stood up and sobbed and put a hand over her mouth and walked to the bedroom without looking back at him and swung the door closed behind her.

His palms and feet were sweating, and his legs itched. He rubbed his nose and rubbed his hands on his jeans. There were dark spots on his jeans where he had been rubbing each hand.

He listened carefully, and he heard her crying through the closed door.

He stood up and stretched and swung his arms back and forth at his sides. He rubbed his chin and looked down at the cocaine on the coffee table. He got away from it, went into the kitchen, opened the fridge, and closed it without looking inside. He thought about Wright lying on the couch with the wet cloth over his eyes and the bottle of vodka on the floor beside him. He took out his phone and called him, but there was no answer. He thought of calling Hartford but decided against it. He would not understand like Wright would. But understand what?

What the fuck are you doing? he thought. *You have this woman, this beautiful woman you love and who loves you, who you respect and who you understand, who you really, truly love, and this is how you conduct yourself? She sees right through you. She's more intelligent than you, but she'd never lay it on you, because she's also kinder than you. But you both damn well know how small you're being right now. But that was not really you. You're not really like that. You are not a bad person. No, you are not a bad person.*

He sat back down on the couch and picked up the cards and started swiping the cocaine back and forth across the picture frame, forming one large line and then two, and then three, and then two again. He rerolled the bill and snorted one of the lines. He stood up and snorted again and felt it coat the back of his throat. *You are not a bad person.* He sat back down and stood up again. He walked to the kitchen and back to the living room and looked out the window. He looked at the brown river, the buildings, and the trees on the slope of the valley. He went to her bedroom door and listened but could not hear anything. He knocked on the door and waited, but there was no answer, so he knocked again and let himself in. She was not in her bedroom, and the bathroom door was closed. As he came into the room, he heard the shower start. He went back to the living room and went through his phone. He started texting people, all of it nonsense.

He split the last line in two and did one as the MDMA hit him. Kitty came back into the living room. Her eyes were dull, and she seemed calm and relaxed. She walked slowly into the room and did not look at him.

"Hey, babe," he said.

"Hi."

"Can I talk to you?"

"Okay."

"Can you come here, please?"

"Okay."

She came over to the couch, sat on the opposite end from him, settled into the corner, and leaned her head on her hand, her elbow on the armrest. She looked at him with a neutrality he had never seen in her before. She did not look sad or disappointed or angry or anything negative. She looked empty. He wanted to ask her what she had been doing in the bathroom, but it would not help. He needed to explain himself. He was burning up. He felt very good and he knew he needed to connect with her.

Make her feel good, too, he thought. *Bring her close to you again. But don't betray yourself. That outburst, that very small moment you had, was wrong, but it had a reason. There is truth in everything you say, because even if your words are false, they come from a part of you that is very real, and not the words but the part must always be respected.*

"Look, babe, that probably sounded like some pretty heavy shit, but I—"

"Pretty heavy shit? You sounded sadistic, John. You sounded evil."

What she said should have held some emotion, but there was none. Her tone was flat, and her eyes stayed dull.

"Okay, yeah, I can see how it might have sounded that way, but you know I'm not sadistic, and you know I'm not evil. I was expressing something to you that I've never expressed before. I've never said anything like that to anyone, ever, and I was fucking high. I am high, and I didn't know how to do it, how to say it, because I've never said it before. I know what I said was wrong, but once it started coming out, I just had to get it all out, because I've been holding it in for so long."

"So what, you want to kill people? That's what you had to get out? That you want to murder other human beings? Other people?"

"That's a normal thing, Kitty. Human beings have been killing other human beings since the beginning. You can't argue the importance of it, it's very natural, and to keep things moving forward, to protect, or to enforce, we have to—"

"I know it has to be done, John, but the way you talked about it . . . You made it sound like you want to kill someone for pleasure."

"Well, shit, Kitty, I spent two years being trained to kill people, and then I went overseas, and I didn't fire a single fucking shot. All we did was walk and drive around for seven months. Seven months of shit blowing up—vehicles, buildings, people, all kinds of shit—and that's all there was. Walking and driving around and shit blowing up. Sometimes it was like there was no enemy, like we were just doing it to ourselves, like it was a game where we tried to get as far as possible or go as many days without something or someone blowing up. So, not only did I never fire a shot, I also can't even be sure I ever saw whoever the fuck it was we were supposed to be fighting. So, yeah, it was pretty frustrating, and I came back with some pretty fucked-up thoughts, but it doesn't mean I'm evil or sadistic. I know I went a little far with what I said, but I've been holding that in for so long, and I think I just got carried away in letting it out. That's not how I really feel, Kitty. You know that's not how I am."

"What about those names you used? Do you always say things like that?"

"Not always."

"But you do."

"I do."

"I never took you for such a hateful person. Do you understand what you're doing when you use names like that? I know you've had experiences that most people will never have, and I'll never understand how frustrating it was for you over there, but do you think it's fair to condemn an entire people because of your experiences in a war-torn country on the other side of the planet? You just . . . You . . . ."

It was growing; her face was changing. He felt the things in her expression. Anger, sadness, and something stronger, something like despair. Hopelessness. His legs and feet were pulsing with wonderful, euphoric heat, the ecstasy of it driving him to meet the things she was feeling head-on, to make her feelings his, to feel them with her and for her.

"Oh, god," she said, "it's just that you sounded so much like my father. He could be such a hateful person. He could be so cruel sometimes. Never to me but around me, because of me, or maybe, as he saw it, *for* me, like he was protecting me from the world with his hatred or something. But just being exposed to it, seeing how awful he could be, it hurt me, because he was supposed to love me. He was my father who told me he loved me, but how could a person who acted so vile know anything about love?"

"What did he do?" Hall asked. "You told me he was distant, but you've never talked about this before. Was he violent?"

"Sometimes, but not very often. He was much more . . . much more effective with his words. When I was a little girl, we were at the grocery store, and he let me buy a pack of gum, and I took a piece out of the pack before we paid for it, and the middle-aged woman at the till scolded me for it. Not in a cruel way; just how your mother would scold you for swearing, and my father just . . . attacked her. He never lost control. He talked so quietly and calmly. He called the woman a snide cunt and said she should be ashamed of herself for interfering in the personal business of people above her class. He said that a woman her age working a teenager's job should not press her worthless values on other people's children. He kept going on like that. He saw what things hurt the woman the most, and he pursued them and kept carving into her until she ran away crying. Then a manager came over, but the woman was so upset she couldn't speak. Since my father seemed so calm, the manager assumed she had just had some sort of random breakdown, and he actually apologized to my father and finished running us through the till.

"There was another time when we were walking on the sidewalk, and a brown man bumped into me, and my father attacked him the same way he attacked that woman. He used the same kind of words that you just used, and . . . I don't know, John . . . I just . . . I love you; I love you so much, and for you to say things like that, you must have so much hate in your heart that I knew nothing about, and it scares me, John. It really scares me."

"Kitty, you know I'm not like that. Yeah, there's some hate in me, but not like that. It's not vicious, senseless hate like that."

"All hate is vicious and senseless, John."

"No, I don't think that's true. Hate isn't a good thing, you're right, but it's important. You need hate to fight hate."

"No, John, you don't. Hate is only a reason to fight, and there are better reasons. You should fight for the things you love, not fight against things because you hate them."

"Kitty, you've never seen what those people can—"

"Don't say that, John. Don't even say 'those people.' You can't paint an entire race with one brush based on your isolated experiences. When you use the words you used, you refer to all of them: to their families, their children, all of them. What about the ones here in Canada? What about the ones who live in this building or who went to school with you or the families who take their kids to the park or walk their dogs in your neighborhood? They're people like you and me, John. How could you possibly hate them for being the same colour or having the same religion as the men you fought in a whole other world? They struggle and learn and love and hurt and grow just like us, John." Her face was tense, and there were tears in her eyes.

He touched her leg. "Come here, please." She came closer to him on the couch, and he wrapped his arms around her and held her. "I love you so much, Kitty. You're such a beautiful person, and I know if I make you feel like this, then I'm doing something wrong. I'll figure this out, babe. I can't ignore it; I can't say it isn't there, because it is, but I know it's wrong, and I want to fix it, because I love you."

She pulled away from him again. "I don't want you to fix anything for me. I want you to do it for yourself. I can understand why you hate those men over there, John, but when you use words like that, it says you hate them all. And you're too smart and too strong and too good to hate them all. Somewhere close by, probably in this building, there's a man with brown skin, and he's holding a brown-skinned woman, and he's loving her in the same way you love me. You can't hate that, John. I know you can't."

"Okay, Kitty, I won't use those words again."

"And when you talked about killing one of them, you—"

"Stop it, Kitty. I told you that what I said was wrong. I can't unsay it now, so it will always be there, but it was wrong, and I'm sorry for it. But now I just want you to feel loved."

"I feel loved."

"Good."

"I love you, too," she said. "So much."

"I know you do. You are so goddamn beautiful, you know that?"

"No I'm not. I'm a mess."

"Are you calling me a liar?"

She laughed, wiped her eyes, and he laughed with her.

"No," she said. "I'd never call you a liar."

"Good." He ran his hand through her hair and cupped the side of her neck, and his thumb came up to her cheek. He kissed her. The warmth of her mouth and the softness of her hair and the wetness in her eyes was perfect.

Hall laid on the couch, and Kitty laid her head on his chest. He ran his hand over her arm and shoulder.

"Can I ask you something?" she said.

"Of course."

"Did you drink because of what happened over there?"

"Not much really happened."

"Don't do that, John. You can't let me in and then shut me out. What about the explosions you talked about?"

"Yeah, there was that."

"It must have been scary."

"Not really at the time. When it happened, it just happened. You were in it, and there was nothing you could do about it. You just acted the best you could, and then it was over, and that was it. But after was worse. Once you knew how it happened, you always looked for it, which you did anyway, because that was what you were trained to do, but after it happened, you also waited for it, and that was where the fear was: in the waiting. It was almost a relief when it happened again, because then the fear was gone, and again all you had to do was act. But then it would be over, and you would have more ideas of how it could happen, and you would look for it harder and expect it more, and the waiting would be all the worse. And then when it happened enough times, you knew it could always happen, and you still looked for it and expected it, but you didn't care as much if it happened anymore, and you stopped waiting for it, which made it easier."

"What was it like when Hartford got hurt?"

"I don't want to talk about that."

"Okay. I'm sorry."

"No, it's okay. It's not because it's hard; it's just that it's very personal to Hartford."

"That's fair. But you didn't answer my question. Do you think you drank because of what happened over there?"

"Maybe. It's hard to say."

"We don't have to talk about it if you don't want to."

"I don't want to."

"Okay. I guess it doesn't matter anyway. All that matters is that you don't drink now. I'm proud of you for that. You know, I . . . Sometimes . . . ."

"What?"

"It's, well . . . It's not something I want to talk about."

"Because it's hard?"

"Yes."

"Babe . . . ."

"I know."

"Is it about your father?"

"No. Well, in a way, maybe."

"Can you tell me more about him?"

"I don't want to, baby. Not right now."

"After I told you everything I just told you?"

"No, it's not like that. I don't want it to be like we have to trade. I want tonight to be about you, because I love you. You can help me, baby, and one day I'll tell you everything, and you'll help me, because you love me, but not tonight. Do you think it helped to talk about everything you talked about?"

"Of course it did, babe. I told you a lot of stuff I've never told anyone before. I feel much better, actually, and now I'm also nice and high. I love you so much."

"Baby, I love you more than anything," she said, "and I'm happy you feel better. I feel good, too. I feel so good."

Chapter 23

The drugs were finished, and they were in bed, him on his back, her spread across him, her head on his chest, her hand running over him. She had given him some pills but had not taken any for herself. His mind was quiet, and he was comfortable.

"What a night," she said.

He ran his hand up and down her arm, barely touching her. Her skin stiffened, and she hummed and smiled, and he knew the sensation he was sending through her. They came down gracefully together, assuring each other there were still good things, good feelings—that where they had been together was not the only way to feel good, though there really was no other way to feel like that.

"I still want to talk about your father sometime," he said.

"We will, baby, but not now. It won't do any good now. Just keep doing that with your hand."

He kept his fingers running up and down her arm. She hummed.

"I think I want to take a break," she said.

"A break from what?"

"Drugs."

"Yeah?"

"Yeah. I think it's time for one."

"Why do you think that?"

"It's just time," she said.

"Fair enough."

"Are you happy?"

"Yeah," Hall said, "sure."

"Are you really?" She lifted her head and looked at him.

He looked at the ceiling. "Yes, I really am."

"Will you be sober with me?"

"Yeah, I think it's a good idea. For how long?"

"I think a month would be good," she said. "Maybe we can go a little longer if we want to, but we'll start with a month."

"Okay then, one month, starting now."

"Well, not just yet," she said, and she tapped her fingers on his chest.

"No?"

"No. I want you to try something first."

"What?"

"Just wait."

She got out of bed and went to her dresser and took something out of the top drawer. He watched her naked body as she prepared it on the top of the dresser. She shifted her weight back and forth between her feet, and her shadows extended and retracted across her back and up and down her legs. It sounded like she was crushing and cutting up lines of cocaine.

"Come here," she said.

He got out of the bed and came up behind her, wrapped his arms around her, and looked over her shoulder.

"You want to do more blow?" he said. The idea suddenly seemed very good to him. She had set up two large lines.

"That's not blow," she said. "It's ketamine."

"What the fuck is ketamine?"

"It's nice. It lets you dream while you're awake. Just try it, baby; you'll like it. I promise. And then no more for one month."

"For one month?"

"For one month."

They snorted the lines of ketamine and got back into bed. They talked for a while, and the shift started slowly. It was odd, but it was good. He closed his eyes. White flashes and outlines of shapes appeared in the darkness. They transformed and danced for him, expanding, circling, twisting, and exploding in a pseudo-visual display. He heard Kitty say "Baby . . .," and he thought about the desert.

He thought about the people with desert-born skin. A boy came to mind, the only one he could remember clearly. That was why everything he had said was so wrong; why Kitty had been right, because the day he met that boy, he truly cared for him as only one human being can care for another, and it was completely regardless of the colour of his skin, which was dark from birth and the sun and the layer of dust that covered him.

The boy was maybe ten years old and had short black hair and a determined face. They had been halted in a ruined courtyard for hours, and Hall was sitting on a mud wall that had almost completely crumbled into a pile of dirt and dust. Earlier that morning they had been walking down a path between a grape field and an opium field, which was being harvested by two farmers. The farmers dug their thin curved knives into the pale-green pods that were already bursting in bright reds.

As they walked by the farmers, there was a blast ahead of Hall in the patrol. A machine gunner had stepped on an IED. One of his legs had been blown away, the other mutilated, and his pelvis had been ripped in half. The men closest to him went to work on him, and Hall took up arcs with his fire-team partner. He could see the blood from where he was as the medic and two others worked frantically in a tight circle around the casualty. They looked more like feral animals surrounding a kill than men trying to save another man. They did not have to work for long.

The patrol was delayed while the process for this kind of thing was carried out. One section returned to the forward operating base with the body while Hall's section formed back up to carry on with the patrol. A pack of children followed them as they continued down the path between the grape and opium fields. The children laughed and squealed and threw stones at them.

They reached their objective, and Hall sat on the crumbling mud wall, staring at the boy. He was a good-looking boy, which was not a good thing to be in Afghanistan. He had heard the stories about the Afghan police—how they picked what they wanted right off the streets in the middle of the day, and how they discussed it openly over their radios. Once their platoon interpreter had translated one of these conversations, and explained how one policeman invited another to the cellar of a compound to share what he had acquired. It was not a unanimous practice in the country, and the Afghan interpreter had spit in the dirt after he had translated the conversation between the two Afghan policemen. Hall wondered if it might have happened to this boy, and he started feeling ill in his stomach and congested behind his eyes and nose as he sat on the crumbling wall under the sun.

The boy started throwing rocks at him. Hall let him get a few in, trying to not let anything show on his face. One bounced off his tac vest, another off his leg, and then a larger one hit him on the mouth.

"You stupid little fuck," Hall snarled. He picked up a rock the size of his fist and threw it at the boy. It hit him in the chest, and he squealed and crumpled to the ground.

Hall flinched. "Shit." He ran over to him. The boy was doubled over and holding his chest. The rock had winded him, and he was wheezing.

Hall knelt over him and touched his shoulder. "Breathe. Just breathe, you little fucker. You'll be fine."

The boy was crying, and once he started getting air into his lungs again, he let out a sob. He looked at Hall, looked him right in the eyes, and he jumped up and took a few steps back, breathing hard, taking a fighting stance. He wiped the tears and snot away from his face with a sleeve. Hall stood up as well.

The boy picked up another rock.

"You little bastard," Hall said. "Do it. I fucking dare you."

The boy threw the rock, and it bounced off Hall's helmet.

Hall laughed. "You could not be any dumber, could you?" He found a rock larger than his fist. He held it up so the boy could see it.

They boy spat and said something in his language, something nasty.

"You're really something," Hall said. He dropped the rock and took a pen out of his pocket and threw it to him. It landed in the dust near the boy's feet, and he pounced on it. He picked it up and turned it over in his hands, curious. He pressed the spring a few times and looked back up at Hall. He held out his hand and said something else.

"No more," Hall said. The boy took a step closer and thrust his hand out again.

Hall picked up the rock again and held it up as if to throw it, and the boy turned and sprinted away, kicking up dust as he went.

As Hall watched the boy run, he hoped he would live long enough to have a rifle put in his hands, but he hoped it for the boy's sake, because he seemed like the type of boy who would grow into the type of man who would feel good, if not do any good, with a rifle in his hands.

The shower was running. Hall stretched out on the bed, and his hand found the warm spot where Kitty had been. He waited in the dark until the shower stopped and she came back into the bedroom and onto the bed. He pressed himself against her. She was dry.
"You didn't shower?"
"No, baby."
"Then why was it running?"
"Not now, baby, please."

Chapter 24

"Jason lives near here," Kitty said.

"Where?"

"Further down and left."

"Do you want to get your painting?"

"Do you mind?"

"Of course not."

It was early in the afternoon on a Saturday. They had gone out for lunch and were going to buy groceries. He had moved into Kitty's apartment, and since her father took care of her rent, Hall always bought the groceries, and they always bought good food. Kitty had been going to all of her classes, and Hall had been going to the gym and was in a good routine. They had stayed sober for three months but had started talking about it again earlier that morning.

"If Courtney's home, we can get some MDMA while we're there," Kitty said.

"Does she live there now?"

"I think so. I'll text her."

He scratched at a callous on his hand with the thumb of the same hand. He lit a cigarette and rolled the window down a little. It was cool outside.

Kitty looked up. "Left here."

He turned left. "Have you talked to him lately?"

"Baby, you know I haven't."

"I know."

The neighborhood started to look familiar to Hall. He drove on and waited for further direction. He finished his cigarette, flicked it out the window, and rolled the window up. He was wearing a black windbreaker, and Kitty was wearing a light grey pea coat.

"Is there anything else there except the painting?"

"No, just the painting. There it is." She pointed to the house.

He parked in front of it. They got out of the car and walked to the front door. Kitty knocked and stepped back. He stood close behind her. He heard music playing inside. He put his hands in his pockets but took them out again.

Jason answered the door. He looked thinner than Hall remembered him, and he had a full beard. He looked at Kitty, at Hall, and then back at Kitty.

"Hi, Jason," Kitty said.

Hall heard voices over the music coming from the living room.

"Hi," he said.

"How are you?"

"Fucking great."

"I'm here for my painting."

"Your painting?"

"Yes, my painting. You still have it, don't you?"

He did not respond right away. "Yeah, I still have it. Come in."

Jason turned and walked into the house, and they followed him. Hall closed the door behind them. Three other men were in the living room. Two were Hall's height but much heavier and in bad shape. The third was short and skinny. The bigger ones were sitting on the edge of the couch, leaning over the coffee table. The skinny one was slouched back and might have been asleep. The coffee table was covered with garbage: little baggies and wrappers, empty beer cans, burnt pieces of tinfoil, rolled-up bills and pieces of paper, lighters, and different kinds of pipes. One of the big men kept rubbing his hand with the other in a quick, jerky motion. His head was shaved, and he was breaking out badly on his cheeks and forehead. The one beside him wore a hat. The skinny one was clean-cut but unhealthy looking.

Jason rolled his jaw. Hall's heart was beating fast.

The big one rubbing his hand stared at Kitty. "Hey, Kitty," he said.

"Hi," Kitty said, and she said his name.

"It's in the basement," Jason said. "You'll have to find it."

"Okay."

Kitty walked to the basement door, and Hall followed her.

"Why don't you stay up here, John?" Jason said. "It's John, right?"

Hall looked at Jason. He was wearing a black T-shirt and a backwards black hat. Hall looked at the back of his hat and the bags under his eyes, and then he looked at Kitty and nodded. "You go ahead."

Kitty stalled for a moment, like she wanted to say something, but whatever it was, she pushed it aside. "Okay," she said and she went through the basement door.

Hall walked over to the wall where the TV was and leaned against it. He was facing all four of them, and his legs felt weak.

Jason stayed standing. "You two are dating now, aren't you?"

"Yeah," Hall said. "Yeah, we are."

Jason kept staring at him, but Hall did not hold it. He looked around the room. It was a mess compared to when he had first been there and met Kitty. Jason took a step back and leaned over and picked up some things off the coffee table. He put something in one of the pipes and held it up to Hall. The

pipe was made of glass with a large, bulb-like bowl and a thin stem coming off the bulb near the opening. "You party?"
"Not with that," Hall said.
"You're a good boy," Jason said.
Hall did not reply.
"Kitty's a good girl, for the most part," Jason said. He looked at the pipe, at the men on the couch, and back at Hall. "I really loved her, and she really loved me." He lit a torch lighter, held the bowl at an angle, and started heating the bottom. Smoke started rising from the bowl. He put his mouth to the stem and inhaled it all. He held it in his lungs, passed the pipe to the man wearing the hat, sat down hard on the armrest of the couch, and blew the smoke out toward Hall. The man he had passed the pipe to had already refilled it and was heating it up.
"She really loved me," Jason said again.
Hall looked at the other big man, the one with bad skin. He was staring at him intently, his spotted brow a large lump. Hall turned back at Jason.
"She loved me so much," Jason said, "she even let me fuck her in the ass a few times."
The big man wearing the hat blew out a stream of smoke and started laughing and coughing.
"Have you fucked her in the ass yet?"
Hall's knees were shaking. They felt weak. A great pressure formed in his throat, and he knew he would not be able to speak. His heart pounded, and he felt it in his chest, his arms, his legs, and he heard it in his head. He held Jason's stare now.
"No?" Jason said. "That's a shame. She's got such a tight little ass. I'll tell you what, I'll be a good guy and give you a few tips, you know, because you can't have such a wonderful girl like that and not fuck her in the ass. The secret," he held his hands up and flexed them, grabbing the air, "is not to ask her.

You just have to hold her down and jam it into her. She'll fight it. She'll pretend she doesn't want it, but she does."

Hall came away from the wall carefully. He brought his fingers into the palms of his hands and flexed them into fists.

"They all do."

Hall shifted his weight slightly. *Start with your legs,* he thought. *Start with your legs, and make it go all the way through you. Make it wide and make it fast and make it count.*

Both of the big men on the couch were laughing.

"It's in a woman's nature to be dominated. And there is nothing more dominating than being fucked in the ass. That's why they enjoy it. Kitty cried every time. She cried, but she still took—"

Hall took the step and swung wide, but it was not enough. He only clipped Jason's nose, but he heard and felt the cartilage. Jason's head snapped to the side, and he brought his arms across his face. Hall hit him in the ribs, and Jason crumpled. Hall hit him in the head, where he was exposed. He kept swinging into him, into any part of him, it did not matter.

Then someone hit Hall in the ribs. He came away from Jason, and the one wearing the hat was on him. Hall dropped his head and swung low. The other big man started hitting him as well. Hall fell to the floor. A great weight pressed down on him, and the blows came hard and fast. He put his arms over his head.

He heard Kitty scream, and the blows stopped, but the weight stayed on him. His right eye was starting to swell shut, and blood was running from his mouth and nose. He looked out from under his arms and saw Jason grab Kitty and hold her. Kitty screamed and moved frantically to get away from him. She was sobbing, and her face was wet with tears. Some of her hair stuck to her cheek and her mouth. The man pinning Hall down was watching Kitty and Jason. Hall attacked him and took him by surprise and started to get up. He put a hand on the floor, got to one knee, and then something hard and dull struck the side of his head.

* * *

They were pinning him down again. His face was pressed against the floor, and a knee was pressed against the back of his neck. A small pool of blood had formed around his mouth. When he inhaled, the blood crawled into his mouth, and when he exhaled, it spattered out, and the pool grew.

He was facing the sectional. Jason and Kitty were sitting on the couch closest to him. She was on Jason's lap, and he had his arms wrapped around her. When Hall opened his eyes, she cried out to him and tried to stand, but Jason held her tight.

"Please, let him up, please, please," she said, sobbing.

"Shh . . .." Jason said, "Shh . . . shh . . . shh . . .. It's okay, Kitty. It's okay, just calm down, and everything will be okay. I still love you, Kitty. You know I love you, and I'd never do anything to hurt you. You know that, don't you? Don't you? That's how all of this started. I told him I still loved you, and he hit me. That's all I did. All I said was, 'Man, I'm still in love with that girl,' and he fucking attacked me."

"Just let us leave, Jason. Please, just let us leave."

"Kitty," Hall said, and the pressure on his neck increased.

"Get off of him," she said, "now!"

"Kitty," Jason said, "you—"

"No!" she snarled. She wrenched herself around so that she could see his eyes. "You're pathetic," she said. "You're pathetic, and you disgust me. You were a man once, but now you're nothing. You're only pathetic and vile and disgusting."

"That's not going to—"

"Let us go!" Kitty screamed.

Her voice took him by surprise, and he released her. She jumped up and ran over to Hall and started pushing the man on top of him. He made no fight against her. Hall stood up slowly. Kitty put her arm around him and pulled him to the hallway. Hall stopped and looked back. Jason was standing and watching them.

"Come on, baby, please," Kitty said.

"Go ahead, baby," Jason said.

Hall turned back to the hallway, and they walked to the front door. Kitty picked up their shoes, opened the door, and they left without her painting.

Chapter 25

They stayed sober after that, or at least Hall did. Kitty was on and off something, some kind pharmaceutical drug, he guessed. She had a collection of different pill bottles, but he did not know what any of them were. He tried bringing it up once, but it went nowhere. She got mad at him. She asked him what had really happened while she had been in the basement looking for her painting. He got mad at her. They stopped sleeping together. And then he was driving home from work one day, and he saw Jason standing outside a bar near Jasper Ave. He was with the skinny one and the big one who had held Hall down. Hall's hands started to tremble, and everything left his mind except for what was happening in that moment.

He turned right and parked on the street. He got out of his car and slammed the door and started walking. He made it to the corner but stopped, took off the black windbreaker he was wearing, went back to the car, and threw the jacket in the passenger seat.

The bar was on the next block, slightly downhill, so he could see it well. They had gone back inside. The bar had a large overhang and a black iron fence wrapped around a patio area, which was empty. He passed a laundromat and a convenience store. Attached to the convenience store was a liquor store. When he saw it, he went for it and walked through the door. A short, mean-looking Indian man eyed him from behind the counter. There was a fridge beside the counter. He took a bottle of ginger ale and asked for a mickey of vodka. The Indian man took one down from the shelves behind him and looked up at Hall when he saw his hands shaking as he handed him a twenty.

Hall opened the vodka as he walked out the door and took a pull from it. The first one went down easy. He took another one and got three swallows down, but it made him gag, and his stomach throbbed and poised itself, and his mouth started pouring saliva. He stopped and leaned against a stop sign. The feeling passed, and he drank some ginger ale and kept walking. He took another small shot of vodka and crossed the street. The bar was close now, only half a block away. He took one more from the mickey. It was almost empty, and he threw it on the sidewalk. He washed the vodka down with the ginger ale and threw that away, too. He came up to the corner of the black iron gate and looked at the bar. The windows were tinted, and only faint shadows of people sitting and standing inside showed through. He opened the door and walked inside.

The entrance hallway led straight to the bar. The lighting was dim, and there was a mirror on the wall behind the counter. Hall walked up to the bar and looked at the seating areas through the mirror. Two groups of men were on the right side and one group of men and a group of older women were on the left. A few singles were on both sides, and two men were on stools at the bar. On the right side, Hall's view of one of the groups of men was cut off by the wall of the entrance hallway, but he could see the back of the big man, and also the side of the skinny one. Hall listened carefully for Jason's voice.

"How ya doing?" the bartender said.

Hall looked at him for the first time. He was balding and staring at him impatiently.

"Good," Hall said.

"That's good. What you having?"

"Triple rye and ginger."

"Triple?"

"Yeah, triple."

"Good man." He made the drink while Hall watched the parts of the men he could see.

"Here you go," the bartender said, putting the drink on the counter.

Hall paid him and walked to the seating area on the left and sat down next to the hallway wall, which was sectioned in tinted windows. He could see the group fully now, though dimly. They were only shapes, but he could make out the shape of the big one, the skinny one, and Jason.

He watched the shapes, and eventually a waitress came over to his table. He ordered a double. When she went away, he looked at the group of men on his side of the hallway. There were three of them. They were roughly his age and in good shape. One of them was looking at him. He had broad shoulders, a thick neck, and his arms were covered in tattoos. Hall held his stare for a moment, but he let him have it and turned back to the shapes of Jason and his friends.

The waitress brought him the drink. He paid for it and moved seats so he could still see the shapes through the entrance hallway and also see the entrance through the mirror behind the bar.

After he finished the double, he saw Jason move up to the bar. He had a direct line of sight to him. Jason said something to the big man and walked down the hallway to the entrance. The big man headed for the restroom, and the skinny one stood at the bar talking to the bartender. Hall stood up and walked to the entrance. The skinny one saw him, and when he did, he ran to the restroom after the big man. Hall walked down the entrance hallway after Jason. It was all happening fast now.

    When he got outside, Jason was past the black iron fence with his head down, lighting a cigarette. Hall came up behind him, took a good stance, and tapped him on the shoulder. Jason turned around. His cigarette was in his mouth, and he was pulling on it, and the ember was bright. Hall hit him in the mouth, and the ember exploded into orange and yellow sparks. Jason stumbled, and Hall pushed him hard, sending him sprawling onto the cement. Hall got on top of him and started hitting him. Jason tried to protect himself, and sometimes Hall hit his arms and hands, sometimes his head, other times his nose, his eyes, his temples. Jason's head bounced back against the pavement and made a dry popping sound, and Hall knew he had him. Jason was still conscious—his arms were still up—but he was stupid now. He was limp and unaware and weak.

    Hall gave him everything in that moment. The skin came away from the edge of his knuckles, and their blood mixed together. When Jason went unconscious, Hall picked his head up by his hair and continued with his fist so that when his head snapped back, it made that same dry popping sound against the cement. Jason's face was red, and blood was coming out of him everywhere, was being squeezed out of him as it had been squeezed out of Hartford when he was on his back in the sand with a hole in his cheek so that Hall could see his shattered teeth through it, with blood pouring from his mouth, with his throat making wet sucking sounds and with another hole close to his ear and another under his eye and a thousand tiny ones that did not gush like the large ones did but bled in their own right so that whenever the medic pressed something against his face to cover the holes, to cover Hartford's two mouths, the blood kept soaking through.

Hall took a kick to the ribs and rolled off Jason. His lungs stopped working. He made a small, high gasping sound and took another kick, this time to the face, and everything became very simple. He tried to stand, tried to fight, but he took another kick to the side of the head and another in the spine, and the blows became dull sensations. He tucked his legs in and wrapped his arms around his head. The blows kept coming, but it was all dull now. He had given everything to the man who lay still and bleeding beside him. He was empty, and it did not matter that he was being beaten. And then the beating stopped.

Everything stayed dull for a moment, and then he heard his gasps, each one louder than the last. There were other sounds: grunting, swearing, panting, and dull blows. He got onto his hands and knees and then sat down. The big man was curled up against the black iron fence, and two men were kicking and stomping on him. The skinny one was lying next to Jason and appeared to be unconscious.

A man appeared by Hall's side and put an arm around his shoulders. "Hey buddy," he said. He was the one who had been staring at him in the bar, the one with the broad shoulders, thick neck, and tattoos.

"Hey," Hall said.

"Think you can stand?"

"Yeah."

As the man helped him up, Hall felt a sharp pain in his side. He took a few steps and found he could walk if he stayed hunched over to that side, where the pain was.

"Come on boys, let's fucking go!" the man helping him yelled at the other two.

They stopped kicking the big man, and one of them spit on him. They kicked the skinny one in the stomach once more as they walked by him.

"Hold on," one said when they passed Jason, who was still on his back and unconscious. "I want a picture of this." He took out his phone and held it close to Jason's face. The blood was brilliant red in the flash, and his eyes were slightly open, but only the whites showed.

They got into a black Jeep, and the one with the tattoos drove them away from the bar with the black iron fence.

Everyone in the Jeep was excited, and there was much yelling and laughing for the first few blocks they drove down. Hall was in the back seat behind the driver. He moved around to find the pain in his side. It was not so bad, probably only a fractured rib or two. He felt his face, and it was tender under his right eye and bleeding a little.

"Check this out," the man sitting beside him said. He showed Hall his phone and the picture of Jason. Hall looked at the whites of Jason's eyes, at the blood, and the swelling, and then the screen dimmed and went black.

"You really fucked that dude up, man. What's the story there?"

Hall recognized the man. He was slightly shorter than him, well-built, and clean-shaven. He also recognized the driver, the one with the tattoos. He was also clean-shaven. They all were, and their hair was high and tight.

"They kicked the shit out of me a few weeks ago. You guys are army, aren't you?"

"Yeah, dude," the driver said, "you were on my fifty cal course. I remember you, because you showed up wasted one time before a range, and the warrant jacked you the fuck up in front of everyone. It was great."

"No shit, I remember that," Hall said. "I did gate duty all fuckin' day for that. So you guys are infantry? I don't remember seeing you around the lines."

"We're para, dude."

"You're paratroopers? Of course you are. Well, fuck, you guys really saved my ass. Those guys were fucking junkies, man. That big sack of shit would've kicked me to death if it wasn't for you guys."

"What's your name?"

"John."

"What's your last name?"

"Hall."

"So, what now? Drinks?"

"Fucking of course drinks."

"Let me see that picture."

"Let's do it again!"

"Oh fuck yeah, let's fucking do it again!"

"Oh fuck yeah!"

"All fucking junkies will fucking bleed!"

"Fuck yeah!"

"Oh fuck yeah!"

"But let's drink first."

Chapter 26

"Jesus, look at the tits on that thing."

"She wants your cock."

"Oh, fuck yeah."

"I'd like to pin her down and—"

"Shut the fuck up. Here she comes. Hi there. My god, you're beautiful. What's your name again? That's such a pretty name. Marry me. Yeah, you heard me. I'll buy you a house. Fine, get lost. Okay, let's do these."

"What are these again?"

"Hand grenades."

"Here we go."

"Ugh."

"Fuck."

"Goddamn it."

"Awesome. Let's do another one."

"Fuck yeah."

"Oh fuck yeah!"

"Hey! Yeah, us again. Another one, okay? No, Jager bombs this time. That's right."

"So, did you ice any jundies on tour?"

"Fuck off with that shit, man."

"No, it's fine. No, I didn't. We just got blown up the whole tour without a single firefight."

"Jesus."
"Fuck, man."
"Yeah, it was frustrating."
"I fucking bet. That's too bad, dude. Firefights are fuckin' fun."
"Just the best."
"Fuck yeah. I wish I could have shot one up close, though."
"I'd like to kill one with the twenty-five."
"What about the M203?"
"The M203 would be good. Or the fifty."
"Yeah, the fifty."
"Fuck yeah."
"Didn't what's his name kill a dude with the fifty?"
"Who's what's his name?"
"The dude with the fucked-up back now."
"Cullner? No, he never killed anyone. Are you talking about Davis? Davis killed three dudes with the cannon, not the fifty."
"Wasn't it Davis who blew that jundie in half and then the torso crawled like ten feet with its guts hanging out?"
"I remember that! Yeah, that fuckin' dude was literally cut in half, and he just kept crawling away like the undead, man. That was fucked up."
"You were there for that?"
"Yeah, dude, I was in Davis's platoon."
"Did you see it happen?"
"Well, no, but I was there."
"How were you there if you didn't see it happen?"
"I was on the other side of the village."
"So you weren't there."
"Fuck you, man, I was fuckin' there. I saw the body."
"But you didn't see it happen."
"Fuck you, what have you seen?"
"I've seen some shit."

"Uh oh, look out, this guy's seen some shit. What the fuck have you seen, bad boy?"

"He was there when Price died, dude."

"Oh, shit, yeah, I forgot about that."

"Yeah."

"Well, that sucks, Price was fuckin' awesome, but you still don't need to be calling me out and shit."

"I was just fucking with you."

"It didn't fucking sound like—"

"Shut up, you two. The lady's back. Did I tell you how beautiful you are? I did? Well, did I tell you that I'm single? Hey, where the fuck you going?"

"I thought you had a wife."

"I do, but I hate her."

"You hate her or she hates you?"

"Both."

"Let's do these."

"To Price."

"Price."

"Price."

"Price."

"Goddamn it."

"Ugh. Fuck."

"Fuckin' eh."

"Oh, and perfect timing. Let's do these ones, too."

"Who the fuck ordered these ones?"

"He did."

"Yeah, I did while you two were arguing."

"Fuck's sake."

"Hey, get me a double vodka water, please."

"Yeah, and a double rye and ginger for me."

"Same for me."

"I'll have a water."

"Get fucked."

"What?"

"Fuck off."

"He'll have a double rye and ginger."

"All right, fuck, yeah, a double rye and ginger. You guys know we have PT tomorrow morning, right?"

"Fuck off."

"Stop being a pussy."

"Wait until you're my age."

"Your age?"

"How old are you?"

"He's not old; he's just a pussy."

"Okay, let's do these shots. Who are these ones for?"

"How about Watson?"

"Yeah, to Watson."

"Watson."

"Watson."

"Ugh."

"Jesus."

"What the fuck was that?"

"Vodka."

"Vodka? What the fuck is wrong with you?"

"Ugh, Watson, you son of a bitch."

"Don't blame Watson; blame this asshole."

"Yeah, who the fuck orders vodka?"

"I like vodka."

"I miss Watson, that funny motherfucker."

"Yeah, well, so it goes."

"So it goes."

"The fuck is that dude looking at? Hey you. Yeah, you, cunt. What the fuck are you looking at? Oh, you're just trying to have a good time? Well, so are we, and now you're ruining it.

Don't ignore me. I said don't ignore me, you fucking cunt, or I will smash your fucking face—"

"Hey, hey, dude, forget about it."

"Yeah, man, don't get us kicked out."

"By who? There's no bouncers here. You think that fucking jundie bartender is going to kick us out? I'd kill that motherfucker."

"He makes good drinks."

"He's a fucking jundie."

"Yeah, but that's Chris, dude. Chris is awesome."

"Is he?"

"Yeah, he's cool."

"Oh. Okay."

"Fuck, man, I want another tour."

"Afghanistan is done, dude."

"The jundies aren't though. Those people are still doped right up on religion, and they are fucking breeding, man."

"Think something big is coming?"

"Something will happen."

"Like World War Three?"

"Maybe something at home."

"You think so?"

"I don't think so."

"You never know."

"Something better fucking happen. What the fuck are we going to do if we don't go anywhere or nothing happens? Get drunk and do PT for the rest of our fucking lives?"

"There's always peacekeeping."

"Fuck peacekeeping."

"What are you doing, Hall?"

"Trade work."

"You like it?"

"It's work."

"Would you get back in if something went down?"
"In a heartbeat."
"Good man."
"Sweet Home Alabama."
"Oh boy."
"Is that a new watch?"
"That cunt is looking at me again. Hey! I fuckin' saw that, motherfucker. Why don't you take your pan-faced girlfriend and fuck off, huh?"
"Here we go."
"Yes I'm talking about your girlfriend. She's a fat, ugly cunt, and you should be ashamed to be in public with her."
"He's going to get another assault charge tonight. Hey, idiot, you're going to get charged again."
"No I'm not; they're leaving. Yeah, have a good night, faggot. Fuck you."
"I can't believe they haven't kicked us out yet."
"I told you, Chris is cool."
"Let's do some more shots."
"Hey! Over here. Yes, ma'am. What are we getting? More Jager?"
"I liked those hand grenades."
"How about some Irish Car Bombs?"
"Rum. Let's get some rum."
"Yeah, I like rum."
"All right, four shots of Captain Morgan."
"Let me see that picture again. Man, you fucked that dude up good."
"Let's do it again."
"Fuck yeah, let's do it again."
"Oh fuck yeah!"
"All junkies will fucking bleed!"
"And jundies."

"All junkies and jundies will fucking bleed!"
"Except for Chris."
"Fine, except for Chris."
"I am fucking drunk."
"Look at that slut in the far corner there."
"What about her?"
"Yes or no?"
"Yes."
"Yes."
"No."
"No? Why not?"
"Too fat."
"Seriously? You like them anorexic?"
"Ah, here we go. Thank you, darling."
"Okay, who are these for?"
"Ross."
"Who's Ross?"
"Ross is dead."
"Fair enough."
"To Ross."
"Ross."
"Ross."
"Ross."
"Oh man."
"Ugh."
"I think I'm going to be sick."
"Oh god."
"There is no god," John Hall said.

Chapter 27

A cold wind was blowing. Hall walked down Jasper with a bottle of whiskey in a paper bag in one hand and a cigarette in the other. He was thinking about Kitty. He came to their building, threw his cigarette into the street, and walked through the door.

In the elevator, he took the whiskey out of the bag and looked at the bottle. He crumpled up the bag, stuffed it into his back pocket, and looked at himself in the mirror. He had a bit of dried blood on his chin. He wiped it off.

The elevator stopped at the eighteenth floor. The bell rang, the doors opened, and he walked out. A woman with purple hair passed him and walked into the elevator. She was wearing sunglasses. He turned and looked at her as she pressed a button. The woman stared back at him, her purple hair tied into a bun high on the back of her head. The sunglasses looked like the wrap-arounds Kitty had been wearing the morning he met her.

"Courtney? What are you doing here?"

She tilted her head slightly and smiled as the elevator doors closed between them. He stood there for a moment, staring at the closed doors. He walked to the apartment, unlocked the door, and walked inside. Something was happening, or there was something in the apartment. Something about how

Courtney was, how the apartment was. It was quiet, but he knew Kitty was home. He left his shoes on and hurried inside.

He put the bottle of whiskey on the floor. She was not in the living room. He walked into the bedroom. The light was off, and he saw the shape of her on the bed, and he knew it was there, that this was it. This was the feeling, her shape on the bed: her.

He turned on the light, and she was lying on her back, her legs dangling over the side of the bed. An empty needle was on the bed near her hand. A long strip of blue rubber hung loosely from her bicep. He saw the mark where it had been tightened on her arm before it had been released.

Hall went to her, put a knee on the bed, and leaned over her. He looked at her face. He touched her, listened for her breath. He looked at her chest.

Listen for it, he thought. *No, look for it. Listen for her breath, and look at her chest. That's what you were taught. Remember what you were taught. Look and listen first.*

He put his ear close to her mouth, her nose touching him, and watched her chest. He waited. Time screamed and moaned and crawled, and he did not breathe so that he would not mistake his breath for hers.

Her chest lifted slightly, barely, but he could not hear the breath. It was shallow. He looked at her face again. "Oh, God, fuck, Kitty, please. Kitty, open your eyes, babe. Open your eyes. Please, God. Please, Kitty, babe, please, please."

He touched her cheek. He looked and listened again.

He took his phone out, but before he dialed, he saw her chest move again, higher this time. Should he do CPR? Would CPR work if she was barely breathing or only if she was not breathing? It only worked half the time, or was it a quarter of the time? He would probably break her ribs. He would have to break her ribs to do it properly.

He dialed 911 and put the phone to his ear. He put his other hand on her chest and tried to feel it rise, willed it to rise. It rose and fell again.

"Baby...." she whispered. Her eyes opened slightly.

Hall stood up, backed up, hit the wall behind him, and slid down to the floor. He looked at the phone. He had forgotten to press dial. He shut it off and threw it across the room. He stood up and leaned over her. She was looking at him. He wrapped his hand around her head and put his face against her neck.

"Oh god, Kitty. Oh god . . . Fuck...."

He stood up and saw that she was more awake. "Say something, babe. Please say something. Tell me you're okay."

"I'm okay, baby."

"Kitty...."

He started pacing at the end of the bed. He was breathing fast, and his eyes were wet. "Fuck, Kitty. Fuck...."

He hit the wall, and the drywall caved to his fist. He hit it again and again. He clenched his hair with his fists and paced back and forth a little longer, and then he was okay. He breathed in through his nose and out through his mouth.

He went over to the bed again and leaned over her and gently pressed his head against her stomach.

She ran her fingers through his hair, and said, "Baby...."

PART III

Chapter 28

The first snow was falling. It was early in the afternoon, and Hall was smashed on gin and cocaine, and Kitty had been smoking heroin for the past two or three days. They were in the parkade, and he opened the car door for her.

"Darling."

"Oh," she said, "why thank you, sir," and she smiled at him.

When he closed the door, she blew him a kiss through the window. He punched the glass lightly, and she jumped. He laughed, and she pointed her finger at him, feigning anger, but she was still smiling.

He went around to the driver's side and got in. He had a bottle of gin with him. It was full, but half of it was tonic water with lime juice. He tossed it into the back seat and started the car. Kitty reached over and cupped his cheek with her hand. Her hand was cold. He looked at her.

"Baby . . .."

"What?"

"You're so handsome."

"What?" he said again.

"You heard me, my handsome man."

"Come here." Hall stretched his arm out, grabbed the back of her head, and pulled her to him, kissing her hard. Her lips were cold, but her tongue was warm and wet. He ran his other hand along her neck, down to her stomach, and up her shirt.

"Oh!" she cried. "Baby, your hands are cold!"

He pressed the back of his hand, which was colder, against her skin.

She squealed and slapped him. "Stop it!"

He kissed her again and took his hand away from her skin and dug it underneath her and grabbed her ass.

"Oh, you think so?" she said.

"I know so."

"Oh, really?"

"Really." He brought his hand around to her front, squeezed her leg, and rubbed between her thighs.

"Well, I don't think so, sir."

"Think what you want." He rubbed her harder.

"Stop it!" she cried and took his hand away. "Not in public. You're a wild animal."

He took his hands back and started the car. "Where should we go?"

"I don't know," she said. "This was your idea."

"Fuck it," Hall said. "Let's just drive."

"Baby, promise me one more time you're okay to drive."

"I promise, babe. I'm nice and high."

"You've drank a lot of gin, though," she said.

"Well, I'll do some more blow then. That will clear me up."

"You should have done it in the apartment before we left. You'll make a mess in here."

"I'll be careful."

She handed him the bag of cocaine, and he took the driver's manual out of the glove compartment and used it as a platform to bust the cocaine on. Kitty took her bag and a piece of tinfoil out of her pocket. He crushed and chopped the cocaine into a large line. She dumped a bit of heroin into the tinfoil she had formed into a spoon shape. He rolled up a bill, and she heated up the bottom of the tinfoil. He railed the cocaine to the back of his throat, and she sucked the smoke through an empty Bic pen.

"I fucking love you so much," Hall said.

"I love you more," she replied.

"Impossible."

He kissed her once more, put the car in drive, and they spiraled down the parkade and onto the street. Kitty took her mp3 player out of her coat pocket and plugged it into the stereo. She played some good music with a strong bass and a woman's voice singing. The snow fell slowly and heavily.

They drove with nowhere to go, keeping to quiet streets. They enjoyed the heat inside the car and the music. On most streets they drove down, they were the first to leave tracks.

They pulled into an empty church parking lot. The snow was undisturbed, and they circled the church once, carving a ring around it, and parked on the side opposite the road. Kitty smoked more heroin, and Hall snorted more cocaine. He brought the bottle of gin up front and drank it from the bottle. Kitty did not drink any of it. He talked fast, and she kept touching his leg and his arm, smiling at him and humming softly. He stuck his hand outside and watched the snowflakes melt in his palm as he talked and she hummed. The music filled everything in between.

He brought his hand back inside the car, wiped it on his jeans, and rolled the window up. He poured some more cocaine on the armrest between them and started busting it up with two cards. Kitty emptied a baggie into a fresh piece of tinfoil. She heated it up with her Zippo lighter. Hall carefully rolled up a ten, pinching the ends tightly between his thumb and index finger. The heroin started smoking, and she breathed it in through the tube of the pen. He stuck the bill in his nose and snorted the line of cocaine hard and fast. She held the smoke in for a moment and then rolled her window down slightly and blew it outside in one smooth, even stream. He snorted again, and it coated the back of his throat and tasted like gasoline. They kissed.

"Baby, I'm all out," she said.

"What do you want to do?"

"Baby...."

"Okay."

"I love you."

He put the car in drive and put his hand in her lap. She took it with both of hers.

"I love you too," he said. The gin was sitting between his legs. He took his hand away from her, took a long drink, put the bottle in the back seat, and gave his hand back to her. He drove a little faster, heading west.

"How much are you getting?" he asked.

"Enough for today and tomorrow."

"And then you'll kick it?"

"Yes."

"Okay."

His phone rang, and he took his hand away from her and answered it. He did not recognize the number.

"Hello?"

"Hello, can I speak with John Hall, please?"

"Speaking."

"Hi, Mr. Hall. My name is Emily, and I'm calling from Cash Money about your account with us."

"Okay, sure, but can you hold on one second?"

"Of course."

He took the phone away from his ear and hung up.

"Was it them again?"

"Yeah. Fucking sharks."

"Are you doing okay for—"

"I'm fine."

"Okay."

Kitty took his right hand from the steering wheel and put it back in her lap as they drove across the city. When they were a few blocks from their destination, in a residential neighbourhood, Kitty suddenly shouted, "Oh my god! Stop! John, stop!"

Hall stopped in the middle of the road. "What? What is it?"

She was already getting out of the car. He put it in park and got out. Kitty ran to a pickup truck parked two cars behind them and knelt down by the driver's side door. He came up behind her.

"Oh you poor little thing. You poor baby. Come here. Come on, little baby. Come here, please."

Hall knelt down beside her and saw a small white cat creeping forward, but when it saw his face, it backed up and started crying.

"Give it some space," Kitty said, her eyes on the cat. Hall stood up and took a few steps back.

Kitty kept talking to it, coaxing it to her, and eventually the cat came out from under the truck. She picked it up and put it inside her coat and held it with one hand, cupping its small head with the other as she rubbed the fur around its ears with her thumb. "You poor little baby. You poor little thing."

They got back in the car, and he parked on the side of the street. Only the cat's head poked out of her coat. She kept talking to it and petting it. The cat was crying, but it made no attempt to get out of her coat.

"Babe, it's wearing a collar," Hall said. "That's somebody's cat. They're probably looking for it right now."

"It's not a cat," she said, "it's a baby. Look at her, John, she's just a kitten. Poor little baby."

The cat was tiny. He did not know much about cats, but it was obviously too young to be out alone, especially with the weather the way it was.

"Either way," Hall said, "it belongs to someone."

"If they let her out in this weather, they don't deserve her," she said sharply, glaring at him.

"Are you sure?"

"Yes, I'm sure. Can we go please?"

"All right."

He put the car in drive and steered back into the street and into the snow. The cat cried, and Kitty held it, talking softly to it and rubbing its head.

They arrived at a brown-and-grey townhouse on a street of brown-and-grey townhouses and apartment buildings. Hall parked on the street and left the car running. As soon as they stopped, the cat stopped crying and tried to climb out of Kitty's coat. It was a very attractive cat, as they all are when they are young, unless they are deformed or have been mutilated. Its coat was completely white except for two grey smudges between its ears. It dug its claws into Kitty's pea coat and stuck its head out and looked around the car and cried excitedly. It was hard not to like this cat.

"I don't know about this fucking thing," Hall said.

"She's not a thing!" Kitty cried, and the cat cried with her. "Oh, poor little thing."

He laughed. "You're ridiculous." He had not done any cocaine in a while, and he was starting to feel uneasy. He did not have much left, maybe a line or two.

"Don't laugh at us," Kitty said. The cat cried again. Kitty laughed and kissed it on the grey smudges. "Oh, you have such a pretty voice, you pretty baby."

"Babe, are we going in or not?"

"I can't take her outside yet! We're going to stay in here where it's warm. You go get it."

"What?"

"You go get it. I'll text him and tell him it's just you coming. You were with me last time; he'll recognize you. It's fine, baby. Here's some money." She cradled the cat with one hand and handed him her purse with the other. He held it for her, and she took out some money and her cellphone. She gave him the money and sent a text on her phone.

"He always gets back to me quick. It won't take long. Buy some blow, too. My treat."

"No, it's fine," Hall said. He took his wallet out of his back pocket. He had $60, enough for a bag. He put Kitty's $200 in his wallet with his $60, and Kitty went back to the cat. He went into his phone and went on Facebook.

He tapped on an article titled, "Mullah rapes eleven-year old girl, family plans . . .." It featured a picture of a Muslim man with large, yellow teeth and a thin collection of neck hair, screaming into the camera. A mullah, a religious figure in Afghanistan, had raped an eleven-year-old girl, had torn her body in the act, and left her unconscious in the street. In wake of the attack, the girl's father had decided that the honorable thing to do was to kill her. Hall told Kitty about the story.

"And what about us?" she said.

"What about us?"

"Can't we be just as disgusting? How many children in our country are raped every year? How many are murdered? This is your narrow mind focusing in on your favorite prejudice. How many times do we have to go over this?"

"It was just something on my news feed," Hall said.

"Your news feed? John, I've seen all the groups you're subscribed to on Facebook. It's no wonder you're so hateful when you're being fed one-sided stories all day long. Do you ever look for solutions instead of just getting mad about the problems?" She looked at her phone. "He texted me back. You can go now."

The cat whined and tried to claw its way out of her coat, but she held it in.

"I can go now?"

"Yes," she said. "Would you go? Please?"

"Yeah, I'll go," Hall said. "I'll go get your fuckin' heroin."

He got out of the car and started walking to the townhouse but stopped and went back to the car on Kitty's side. She rolled down her window.

"What one is it?" he asked.

"Seventeen."

He turned back and headed to the townhouses but stopped and returned to the car again.

"What now?" Kitty asked.

He ignored her and went into the back seat. He found his bottle of gin, took three good drinks in the street, and threw it back in the car and slammed the door.

Chapter 29

The drug dealer's name was also John. They were the same height, but the drug dealer was bigger, more muscular. He had a receding hairline, and he was sweating.

"I like meeting other guys named John," he said.

They were standing on either side of an island in the dealer's kitchen. A picture frame covered in cocaine and other drugs sat on the countertop, a mortar and pestle beside it. The dealer took a pill out of a prescription bottle and crushed it up in the mortar, shifting his weight constantly between his legs.

"It makes first impressions much clearer," the dealer said. "Know what I mean? Like when you meet a dude named John, a dude with the same name as you, you're either happy or upset that his name is John. Like if some tiny hipster faggot came in here and told me his name was John, I'd say, 'Fuck no, you little hipster faggot, John is *my* name. John is a strong, manly name for strong, manly men.'" He held the pestle out like a club. "It's like anything. Like when you see some dude on your team making a fool of himself in front of the other team. It's like, 'Smarten the fuck up, you little prick. You're supposed to be on my team. You're supposed to be on the winning team.' So anyway, I'm happy—"

"Johnny," a shrill, broken voice said from the living room. A thin girl leaned over the couch holding her head up with her hands. She wore dark, heavy makeup. "Johnny, where's the down?"

"Would you shut the fuck up?" The dealer pointed the pestle at her. "I'm trying to have a conversation with my friend here."

"Ugh." She collapsed back on to the couch, out of sight.

"Unbelievable," the dealer said. "Junkie twat." He went on crushing the pill. "Anyway, what I was saying is that I'm happy your name is John, so I know you've made a good impression on me and that I'll probably like you."

"Well, I'm happy your name is John as well," Hall said.

"Good," the dealer replied. "You juice?"

"Do I juice?"

"Yeah, juice. Testosterone, steroids, juice. No? You should juice. You have a good frame on you. You clearly work out, but you should be bigger. You got a big, strong name. It would only be fitting. I got a great steroid guy. Great juice, great four hundred, fuckin' great tren, too. Amazing tren. You don't want to start on that though. You should start on four hundred. Two shots a week. Some guys say to start small on your first cycle, but I say, fuck it. If you're going to do it, do it right. D-bol, too. Pop those things like fuckin' Tic Tacs. You'll get huge, bro. It'll be fuckin' cool. Way cool. Here, you want a line? Sorry, bro, I've been talkin' your fuckin' ear off. Here, dig in."

The dealer organized two massive lines of cocaine and handed Hall a small brass tube. He snorted a line, the biggest line of cocaine he had ever done, and it burned far and high behind his nose, a chemical taste exploding in his mouth, almost making him gag, but he fought it off, and he was instantly high. It was the relieving kind of high particular to cocaine when you have been doing it but have stopped and have been wanting—needing—to do more, and then finally you do. Hall handed the tube back to the dealer.

"Like a champ," the dealer said. He bent down and snorted his line.

Hall sat down on a stool at the island. He snorted hard, felt it coat the back of his throat, and he went higher still.

"So, where's Kitty?"

"In the car. She found this little cat in the street and thinks she's going to adopt it. She's fine. That thing could occupy her for hours."

"A cat? She just grabbed it off the street?"

"It's a kitten," Hall said. "It's tiny. It shouldn't have been out in weather like this. She's in love with it; there's no splitting them up now."

"Kitty's a good girl," the dealer said. He crossed his arms and stepped back and leaned against the counter, suddenly solemn. "I've known her for a while now, met her through her ex-boyfriend, a guy named Jason. You ever meet him?" The words were heavy—they carried more than the question they asked.

"Yeah," Hall said, "I've met him."

"Oh yeah?"

"Yeah."

"More than once?"

"A few times."

"Huh."

"Yeah."

Hall was still sitting on the stool, but he could stand before the dealer reached him if necessary. The dealer had about twenty pounds on him. Hall could hear him breathing through his nose, snorting, his chest rising against his folded arms. Then the dealer smiled.

"I heard you beat the piss out of him."

Hall exhaled. He had been holding his breath. Otherwise, he did not move. "Where'd you hear that?"

"It's all good, man," the dealer said. He came away from the fridge and uncrossed his arms. "I fuckin' hate that little bitch. We used to be good buddies. He was a good dude once, but now he's just another fuckin' junkie speed pusher who thinks he's all that. He's a piece of shit, dude, a fuckin' goof. Yeah, I heard you fucked him up pretty good. Well, I heard a few things, actually. I'd like to hear your side of the story, though. So, what happened? He and his boys knocked you around in front of Kitty, so you found him on the street? That's what I heard."

"Yeah, that's basically it."

"You put him in the hospital, I heard."

"I heard that, too," Hall said.

"You had some pretty mean boys with you when it went down, eh?"

"Yeah, those guys saved my ass. Jason's buddies were kicking the shit out of me, and they came out and took care of them. They recognized me from the army. Fuck, if it wasn't for those guys—"

"The army?"

"Yeah."

"You were in the army?"

"Yeah. I just got out last winter."

"No shit, dude. Did you go over there?"

Hall nodded. "Yeah. I went over there."

"No shit, dude! No fucking shit. That's fuckin' cool, man. So did you see any shit? Did you leave the wire or whatever?"

"Yeah, I was in the infantry."

"No shit, dude, no fucking shit. Here, bro, let me cut you another line. That is fucking awesome, bro." He organized two more lines on the picture frame and handed Hall the brass tube. Hall snorted his and gave the tube back to him.

"Fuck, that is some cool shit, bro. I'll tell you right now I have nothing but respect for what you boys did, bro, nothing but respect."

He stretched his arm across the island and offered his hand, and Hall took it. He went into it firmly, and he was right to do so, as the dealer squeezed his hand just as hard, and they shook. The dealer took his hand back, bent over the picture frame, fired back the cocaine, and stood up with his eyes closed, head angled up, and started laughing.

"Jason got fucked up by a couple of fuckin' army guys, man. That is fucking beautiful—fucking beautiful! I fuckin' knew that fuckin' goof would get what's comin' to him sooner or later. He's always running his fuckin' mouth. It was only a matter of time. Yes, that makes me so fuckin' happy, man, yes!"

"What are you screaming about?" the girl on the couch said, leaning over the back of it again.

"Shut the fuck up!" the dealer screamed at her.

She disappeared into the couch again, and the dealer laughed. The dealer looked at Hall and stopped laughing. He glanced back at the girl.

"I'm only kidding, sweetie," the dealer said. "Come over here and meet my new friend."

The girl from the couch approached the island cautiously. She was skinny and pale, and she had spots on her cheeks and neck. Her eyes darted between the dealer and Hall and then to the picture frame covered in drugs and stayed there.

"John, this is Abby. Abby, John."

"Your name is John, too?" she said. "That's cool."

"Real fuckin' cool," the dealer said. "So, you have any close calls over there? Got any stories?"

"I got a few," Hall said, "but they're not the kind of stories you'd expect."

"Oh yeah? What do you mean?"

"Well, we didn't get into any firefights. By the time I got there, we were fighting a small guerrilla force, so we weren't really fighting at all. We were mostly just looking. Sometimes we found suspects, other times we found traps, but most of the time we didn't find anything at all."

"Traps? What do you mean?"

"IEDs."

"IEDs?"

"Improvised explosive devices."

"You mean, like, roadside bombs?"

"Exactly."

"No shit. So you had some close calls with those? You seen some shit blow up?"

"Yeah, I've seen some shit blow up." Hall talked quickly and enthusiastically as the cocaine dripped down the back of his throat, and he knew he was trying to impress the drug dealer. He told him how the world shook if you were close enough and the blast was strong enough—how up and down got mixed up and there was only colours and heat. He told him how dirt and debris showered down on you, tapping on your helmet, and how for a moment it sounded and felt like rain. He told him about the few seconds of silence that followed, but then the apartment buzzer rang, and he instantly remembered her, waiting outside for him and the heroin.

The dealer answered the buzzer and let Kitty inside. She came in with her arms wrapped around the cat and snow in her hair.

"Sorry, babe," Hall said. "We got caught up in conversation."

"Yeah, your boyfriend was telling me some badass war stories," the dealer said.

"War stories?" Kitty said. "John never tells war stories."

"He got me in the mood," Hall said.

"Oh my god, she's so cute!" Abby cried. She came around the island to Kitty and the cat in her arms. Abby came alive when the cat made a noise.

"Isn't she adorable?" Kitty said. "I found the poor thing under a truck on our way here. Can you imagine leaving this poor little baby out in a snowstorm like that?"

"Oh my god, that's terrible," Abby said. "It's so good that you found her."

Abby stroked the cat in Kitty's arm, and it cried and tried to climb up Kitty's coat. Kitty looked up at Hall and the dealer.

"Did you get it?" she asked.

"No, not yet," Hall said. He took his wallet out of his back pocket. "So yeah," he said to the dealer, "can I grab everything now?"

"Of course. What you need?"

"I've got two sixty here." Hall put the money on the countertop between them. "Just one bag of that blow for me. The rest for Kitty."

"Down?" the dealer asked Kitty.

"Yes, please, John," she said.

She looked at Hall again, and the look was full of everything he knew she wanted to say to him, but he did not care. He just wanted more cocaine. And a drink.

The dealer went away somewhere and came back with several baggies. He tossed them on the counter and went over to a stereo system in the living room near the TV and turned some music on.

"You guys should stay awhile and hang out," the dealer said. "I won't start getting busy for another few hours."

Hall looked at Kitty and was about to answer, but Kitty spoke first.

"Sure," she said, "sounds like fun."

"Oh, yay," Abby said. "We can play with this little sweetie for a bit. Let's let her run around over here."

"Okay," Kitty said, "but can you take her for a second?"

She handed the cat to Abby. She asked the dealer for some tinfoil, and he gave her some, along with a lighter and an empty pen. She took her first hit in the kitchen. She was standing at the end of the counter. Hall watched her go through the ritual he had become so familiar with. She caught all of the smoke with the pen except a small trail at the end that floated up and dissipated in her hair and around her face as she raised her head and closed her eyes. When she released it, she let her head down and looked at Hall. Her eyes were dull, relaxed, and satisfied. She came over to him, stroked his arm lightly, and kissed his neck.

"Hey, baby."

"Hey, you," he said. "Feel better now?"

"Yes. I'm sorry if I was being short with you earlier."

"It's okay," he said. "Sorry I took so long in here."

"It's okay. Abby, would you like some?"

"Oh, yes please," Abby said. She thrust the cat back into Kitty's arms, but Kitty did not get a hold of it before Abby let go, and the cat fell between Abby's hands and onto the hardwood floor with a soft, dull thud. Kitty whimpered and dropped to her knees and picked up the cat. It was crying incessantly now.

"Oh my god!" Abby cried. "Oh my god, I'm so sorry! I'm so sorry! Oh my god!"

"Jesus Christ," the dealer said. "Good fucking job, you dumb cunt."

"John!" Kitty cried. "Don't say that; that's terrible. It wasn't her fault." She stood up with the cat cradled in her arms. "Poor little baby. Oh, you're okay, baby, you're fine." The cat seemed unharmed, only rattled.

"I'm so sorry," Abby went on. "Is it still okay if I take a hit?"

The dealer laughed. "'Is it still okay if I take a hit?'" he said, mocking her. "Jesus Christ, you're such a fucking junkie, you know that?"

"Yes, it's fine, Abby, go ahead," Kitty said. "And what's the matter with you, John? Why are you being so mean to her?" She walked over to the living room with the cat. "Bring it over here on the couch, Abby. We'll leave the boys alone if they're going to be mean."

Abby collected the bag of heroin and all the kit, avoiding the dealer's eyes, which stared at her viciously. When she was out of the kitchen, the dealer looked at Hall and shook his head. "Un-fuckin'-believable," he said.

"Hey, I got a bottle of gin in the car I'm gonna go get," Hall said. "I need a drink."

"Fuck man, why didn't you say so? I've got gin here. I've got it all here. What you want? Gin and tonic?"

"Yeah, that would be perfect."

"You got it, dude. I'll have one too." He went through his cupboard and fridge and made the drinks. "To new friends," the dealer said.

They tapped their glasses, Hall tapped his on the counter top, and they put them back. The dealer made another round and found a lime, cut it up and put a slice in each glass.

They carried on like that, the women playing with the cat and smoking heroin in the living room, and the men drinking gin and snorting cocaine in the kitchen. Hall and the dealer drank at the same pace and got along better and better the more they talked. Hall told him a few more war stories and a few different things about the army.

The dealer was thrilled with everything he heard. After a pause in the conversation to do more cocaine, he started telling Hall about his business.

"I sell fuckin' everything," he said. "I'm a one-stop shop. Most of the profit comes from the heavy hitters like down and soft, and I sell to a few party people like you and Kitty, but mostly to addicts. Especially opiate addicts. Opiate addicts are the best customers. They're always on time, and they always need more. Down can still be cool, though. I barely touch it. I'll do a couple lines to level me out after a coke bender like this, but I don't need that shit, because I'm too fucking cool for that. Being cool is about being in control."

He picked up a card and swiped the cocaine back and forth on the picture frame. "That's why doing this coke is so fuckin' cool, because we don't need it."

The dealer looked at Kitty and Abby in the living room. Kitty was playing with the cat on the floor, and Abby was taking a hit of heroin, sitting cross legged and slouched over.

"You see that?" he said. "Look at her suck that shit back. Does that look cool? Fuck no. It's not cool, because she needs it. It fucking owns her. But this," he pointed at the cocaine in front of them, "this is cool, because we could stop right now if we wanted to. We don't need this shit. We do it because it feels good, because we want it, not because we need it. Fuck it."

"Fuck it?" Hall said.

"Yeah," the dealer said. "We don't need it. Fuck it."

"Yeah all right," Hall said. "Sure, fuck it."

The dealer picked up a card again and started organizing the cocaine into two lines. "That's what I like to hear," he said. "We don't need it. But we're going to do it because we want to."

He laughed, and Hall let out a quiet breath of relief. They both snorted a line, and the dealer made more drinks.

"Fucking good times," the dealer said.

"Yeah," Hall said. "It's a snow day."

The dealer laughed. "Yeah, fuckin' eh, it's a snow day. School's cancelled; it's a snow day! I'm having a good time. You having a good time?"

"Yeah," Hall said. "I feel great. I didn't really know what to expect when I came in here—I had only met you briefly the last time—but I'm really glad I came in." "Yeah, me, too, dude. It's good to meet you, John."

"You too, John." They turned and looked at Kitty and Abby.

"You got a good girl there, dude," the dealer said. "There's not too many girls like Kitty in this lifestyle. She's a rare one. She's cool."

"Yeah," Hall said, "she is. I don't know about cool though, at least not the way you described it. Not lately."

"Yeah? She been hittin' it pretty hard or what? I haven't sold her too much lately, just what I gave her today and what I gave her the last time I saw you. That's nothing too bad."

"Yeah, usually she gets it from one of her girlfriends."

"Who?"

"Courtney."

"Courtney? As in Jason and Courtney?"

"Yeah, I guess so. So you know her?"

"Yeah, I fucking know that cunt. You watch yourself around that one, dude. She's an evil fucking bitch. She's put two of my buddies in jail and got another one jumped. Jason's her latest little play toy, and it's only a matter of time before she gets bored of fucking him and fucks him over. I'm telling you, dude, that woman is straight fucked. She deals, but not for the money. She gets people hooked on the down, usually guys who want to fuck her, and once they're on it hard, she hands them over to Jason. As far as I know, Jason doesn't even cut her in on it. She gets these guys just drooling all over her at shows and clubs, and then she takes them home and tells them she'll only fuck them if they get high together, and then she'll rig the dude up and push him over the edge. She'll knock him right on his ass so there's no way he can fuck, but she'll give him the best high he's ever had in his life, and then that's it. She'll give him Jason's number, and sure as shit, as soon as the next fucking day, the dude is texting Jason. Jason gives her the best dope to do it with. I get it once in a while for close friends. It's fucking strong, man. If you can take a hit of that shit and call it quits, then that's fucking cool. There's nothing cooler than that."

Hall watched Kitty. She was tossing a piece of balled-up tinfoil around the floor, and the cat was chasing it, sometimes tripping on its own feet. She and Abby were laughing and looked happy.

"Courtney was the one who introduced me to Kitty," Hall said. "She picked me up from a show and brought me to Jason's house."

"And she didn't try to push any dope on you?"

Hall shook his head. "No. And I wasn't really trying to fuck her. That was the first time I had ever tried M. I was pretty fucked up."

"Really? Huh . . . Well, maybe she was bringing you home for Kitty."

"Yeah, she was," Hall said. "Courtney was texting her about me at the show. Kitty must have asked her to bring me back. Kitty and I hit it off pretty well right away."

"And Jason was there?"

"Yeah, he was there, not for long though. He went upstairs with Courtney pretty soon after I got there. I didn't stay too long. Long enough to make a first impression, I guess."

The dealer laughed. "Fuckin' midnight cowboy, eh? I like your style. I bet if you had stayed longer and tried to fuck her, you'd never have gotten a shot with Kitty."

"Yeah, you're probably right," Hall said. "So, the heroin Courtney gets is pretty strong?"

"I've never tried anything better. It's the best. Or it is around here, at least."

"Yeah, I believe it," Hall said. "I found Kitty nearly dead in our apartment once. I saw Courtney leaving as I was coming in, and when I came into the bedroom, Kitty was passed out on the bed with a needle in her hand. Fuck, man, she scared the shit out of me. I didn't know what to do, I hadn't even known she used that shit before then. I was drunk, too. Fuck, did it scare me. Fuck. . . .."

"You really love her, don't you?"

"I do," Hall said.

"I'm happy for you."

"Thanks."

"Well, if you think about it, Kitty might've saved your ass from the dope. Kitty's the only girlfriend Courtney has, as far as I know. If she didn't bring you back for Kitty, she would've brought you back for the down."

"I wouldn't have tried it," Hall said. "That's one thing I don't ever want to try. Even when Kitty does it right beside me, I have no desire whatsoever, probably because of that night I found her all fucked up on it."

"Yeah, you say that now," the dealer said, "but you'd be surprised at how fucking conniving that cunt can be. She got me to try it for the first time. She didn't get me hooked though, the cunt, because I'm too fuckin' cool for that."

Hall laughed. "Oh yeah? How'd she get you to do it?"

"It was when I met her for the first time. I knew who she was, and I knew she had a thing going with Jason, so naturally I wanted to fuck her. That was last year. I wasn't even selling shit yet, and I wasn't partying too hard, you know? Just M and blow and some G here and there. Anyway, we get back here, and she's acting all fuckin' slutty, being a real tease, you know, like rubbing up against me and grabbing my cock, but every time I'd go to kiss her, she'd laugh and pull away and then come right back and start rubbing me again. The kind of shit that drives a guy fucking mental, you know? She plays a good game. Anyway, we're doing lines, and she busts some dope out, and says 'Try this, darling,' and I don't even think about it, I just fucking do it. I don't even know what it is, and next thing I know we're on the couch smoking the shit, and I'm just fucking gone, man, just fucked. It was the best high I've ever had in my life. Fuck, man, I just remember lying on the couch, staring at the ceiling, and she put some music on, and she kept touching me with her hands all over, and it was like her hands were made of electricity or something, man, and I felt like I was floating, like I was suspended, and everything was so warm, and it was just . . . It was just so fucking good. Unreal, bro, it was fucking unreal. Anyway, at some point I blacked out, and when I came to the next morning, she had put her number in my phone and taken off. I texted her to come over and bring some more, but she just gave me Jason's number, so I told her to go fuck herself."

"So that's all she does? She gets guys hooked on heroin and hands them over to Jason?"

"That's pretty much it, dude. She's had a few guys overdose on her too, and she just leaves them to fucking die in their apartment or their hotel room or whatever. Apparently, one guy did. Can't say for sure, but it was in the news and everything, and I heard she had been with him earlier in the night."

"She killed someone? She gave him too much?"

"Gave him too much and left him for dead. That's the rumor anyway. That cunt is vicious, dude. You be careful with her."

"Kitty never told me any of this shit. I can't believe she's friends with her. She seems so out of place in all this, you know? It doesn't make sense to me."

"It's because she sees the good in people. Even if there barely is any, she still sees it."

"Yeah, I guess so. I don't think it will ever sit well with me though. I still can't get my head around the fact that she dated Jason, that piece of shit."

"Well, you took care of him, didn't you? You beat the fuck out of him, so you don't need to get your head around it. You took care of it, because you're fuckin' cool."

"I'm glad you think so," Hall said.

The dealer poured them another round. "I'm getting a little edgy," he said.

"Yeah, me too," Hall said.

"Fuckin' cocaine. You ever do oxy?"

"No."

"It's great with coke. Levels you right out. I'd love to sell it if I could get a good connection, but it's hard to come by these days. I got a couple oxy originals though. They're not abuse proof, so you can snort them. They'll sort you right out, dude. They take the edge right off the coke, get you nice and fucked up, too. Want to try some?"

"Sure," Hall said, "why not."

"My man," the dealer said. "Okay, sit tight."

He disappeared into a room somewhere. Kitty looked up from the cat and smiled at Hall. He smiled back and winked. The dealer came back out with two pills. He put them in the mortar and crushed them up with the pestle. When he was finished, he poured the powder onto the picture frame and organized it into a pile and two small lines.

"These are eighties, so you don't need much. You gotta be really careful with this combo. Better to cut off the booze from here on out. People die mixing this shit all the time, but they die for a reason."

"What's that?"

"Because it's fuckin' awesome," the dealer said. He smiled at Hall and bent over the picture frame and snorted his line through the brass tube. He came up and snorted again and handed the tube to Hall. Hall leaned over his line and snorted it and came up and put the tube down on the table. He waited for it, waited for a rush, but he felt nothing new.

"You feel it?" the dealer asked.

"I don't know," Hall said.

"Well, give it a bit. Trust me, you don't want to overdo this shit."

"Okay."

They snorted more cocaine and then more OxyContin, and then some MDMA. The dealer went over to the stereo and turned the volume up. He found a specific song, and it was when the song started that Hall realized how high he was and how good he felt. He was utterly relaxed and energetic simultaneously, overcome by euphoria, totally content, but also awake, sharply aware of everything around him, the ecstasy swelling in his chest, his legs, his face, and his hands.

"Oh my god, I love this song!" Abby cried.

A low, warped sound of a scratched record reverberated back and forth across the room, swinging from side to side, gaining speed, rising higher and higher. Some chimes started in the background, and the boomeranging sound fell into a beat. A higher sound joined, and another sound, a bass, and Hall came across the room to Kitty and took her hand and brought her up so she was standing, leaving the cat with Abby. Hall looked her in her eyes, and she looked in his. He kissed her, and the back of his neck exploded, stabbed by millions of needles of pleasure. She came away from him and smiled. Her eyes were dull and happy. She came in close to him, and he wrapped his arms around her. She wrapped her arms around him, and they started swaying slowly back and forth. She put her face against his cheek and closed her eyes. He brought one of his hands up and held the back of her neck, and his mind was empty.

The power of life varies with time. At its weakest, it provides nothing more than a place for us to dwell, but at its strongest, it builds the pillars that become the foundation of our human experience. There had been no greater pillar for John Hall than when the world was only colours and heat, and for so long he had been wandering lost in the place between the pillars, but now he had Kitty, and they swayed gently back and forth in nothingness together.

Chapter 30

Hall was bent over the toilet dry heaving. His body itched terribly, and he scratched at himself as his stomach muscles contracted and he drooled into the bowl. He was slick with thick, greasy sweat. He stayed there for a while, letting his guts work away until the feeling passed. He stood up, went to the sink, washed his face with cold water, and looked at himself in the mirror. He was pale, and little red blemishes and pimples stood out clearly against his skin. He ran his hand through his hair a few times, and his sweat kept it in place where his hand left it. He brushed his teeth and splashed some more cold water on his face.

He still felt something, still had the numbness, but the euphoric heat was gone. His chest felt empty, and the fear was nipping at his heels. He itched everywhere and continued to scratch himself and left red marks all over his body. He left the bathroom, checked the front door, made sure it was locked, and went back to the bedroom. Kitty was on the bed, curled up around the cat, stroking its head softly and slowly with her thumb. It seemed to be asleep.

Hall stood in the doorway and watched her. Kitty had e-transferred more money to the dealer before they left, and they had gotten more drugs. What was left was sitting on the bedside table, everything mixed together: a pile of cocaine,

OxyContin, and MDMA. Kitty had put the heroin away somewhere else. Hall went over to the pile and swiped it back and forth and cut out a small line and snorted it through a five-dollar bill.

"I don't think you need any more of that," Kitty said.

"You're probably right," Hall said. He sat down on the bed with his back to her. He reached out behind him, found her hips, put his hand there, bent over, and put his head in his other hand. "I don't feel so bad," he said. "Just empty."

"OxyContin is a serious drug," Kitty said. "You need to be careful with that one, baby."

"I will." He looked at the pile. Only four or five small lines were left. "Do you want any more?"

"I'm okay."

"Okay."

"Well, maybe a bit," she said.

"Okay." He looked at his watch. It was six in the morning. He had to be at work in two hours. Kitty got up, being careful not to disturb the cat and came to the night table and snorted a line.

"Let's go sit on the couch for a bit," she said. "I want to let her sleep."

"Okay."

Kitty made a small pen out of pillows around the sleeping cat.

"She could easily get out of there," Hall said.

"It's not to keep her in," Kitty said. "It's to make her feel safe."

They took the drugs into the living room and put them on the coffee table. Hall turned on the TV but left the volume off. He continued scratching himself.

"Stop that," Kitty said.

"I can't help it."

"Do you still feel good?"

"I'm okay. You?"

"I'm okay."

"Good."

They sat there, not talking, staring at the silent TV. An hour later, the drugs were gone, and Hall phoned in sick to work.

"Again?" his boss said.

"Yeah."

"John, you know we're going to have to have a chat about this, right?"

"Sure."

"You doing okay though?"

"Yeah, I'm fine," Hall said.

"Will you be in tomorrow?"

"Yeah."

"All right. I'll see you tomorrow morning then. Come straight into my office."

"Okay."

He went through the fridge and the cupboards and found some rum but nothing to mix with it. He poured it into a glass with lots of ice and some water and tried to drink it, but he threw it up into the kitchen sink. After it was out, he kept dry heaving, but there was nothing else to bring up. When it was over, he tried a second time and got a few sips down. He poured the rest of the drink out and went back to Kitty and sat on the edge of the couch next to her and continued scratching himself. Sweat and grease collected under his fingernails. Suddenly, he felt light-headed. He sat back and put his hands on the couch to steady himself. He focused on his breathing, and every breath made him anxious. He breathed faster and deeper.

"Are you okay?" Kitty asked.

"Sure," he said. "I'm fine."

"Do you want some Seroquel?"

"Sure."

Kitty went into the bedroom and came back with two little brown pills. She gave them to him with a glass of water.

"Just two?"

"You shouldn't take too much of that if you've been taking oxy. It's dangerous."

"Babe, I can—"

"John, please, just trust me."

"Okay."

He swallowed the pills and washed them down with a small sip of water, and it all stayed down. He sat back on the couch, and Kitty wrapped a blanket around him.

"I'll get it all sweaty," he said.

"I don't care." She got up and checked on the cat and then came back with another blanket and wrapped it around them both and put her head on his shoulder. Half an hour later, he felt slightly drowsy but better. He went through his phone, through his e-mail, Facebook, and his internet banking.

"Holy shit," he said, leaning forward on the couch.

"What's wrong?"

"There's fifteen grand in my bank account."

"What?"

"There's fifteen grand in my bank account."

"Really? Where did it come from?"

"From the army. It's the payout I've been waiting for."

"Really? Baby, that's awesome!"

"Yeah. Yeah, holy shit."

"See? Everything's going to be okay."

"Yeah," Hall said, "everything's going to be okay."

Chapter 31

They were in the bird section of a pet shop. Kitty held the cat in her arms as it quietly eyed two yellow canaries in a cage. One of the birds started singing and the cat raised its head.

"She likes them," Kitty said.

"She's hungry."

"No, that's not what she's thinking. She's too young for that."

"Look at her tail flick."

"It's because she's happy."

"And hungry," Hall said.

"Stop it."

"Have you thought of a name for her yet?"

"I have a few ideas," Kitty said.

"Like what?"

"I don't want to say yet."

"Tease."

"Can you take her while I find someone that works here?"

"Sure," Hall said. Kitty gave him the cat and she went away somewhere. Hall could hold it easily with one hand, but it started squirming so he held it with two.

"What's wrong with you, Cat?" he said. He stroked its head with his thumb but it continued to squirm and started to cry. Hall looked around the store and there was no one near by so he held the cat up close to the bird cage. It went quiet and raised its head again. The birds stopped singing and started chirping and jumping back and forth between the bars.

Hall took one of the cat's paws and put it through the cage. The birds chirped louder and fluttered their wings and the cat cried and withdrew its paw.

"You'll learn one day," Hall said. "It's in your nature."

He left the bird section and walked down the isle of reptiles, stopping at the largest aquarium, which held a dark brown ball python. There was a fake skull in the tank, and the python was coiled up behind it. Hall put the cat near the glass to see the snake, but the reptile stayed frozen and the cat had no interest in it. He brought the cat back to his chest and stared at the wet black eyes of the snake. He could not tell if it was watching him or not.

A child cried near by and Hall turned and saw a woman in black coming down the isle toward him. She wore a full burka, with only a slit for her eyes to see through, and she held a small child to her hip with black gloved hands. The child was not covered, and it stared at the cat in Hall's arms.

Hall looked back to the aquarium. He saw the muscles of the snake contract and expand. It did not move its position; it only seemed to flex, keeping its small, heart shaped head perfectly in place.

Out of the corners of his eyes, Hall watched the woman come closer down the isle, a black shadow in his peripheral vision. She was looking at the different tanks and the child continued looking at the cat. She stopped next to him in the isle, and Hall looked at the child in her arms. It stretched a small brown hand out toward the cat, its fingers grabbing at empty air.

Hall held the cat out and the child touched its head. The cat cried and the child giggled. The woman turned her head and looked at Hall and he saw that her eyes were bright green. She looked at her child. Hall held the cat out a little more and it rolled upside down as the child reached for it again. The cat swatted at the child's hand with its claws retracted. The child was laughing. Hall looked at the woman again, and by the way her eyes were squinting he could tell that she was smiling beneath the burka.

The woman said something to her child, looked at Hall once more, and walked back the way she had come. Hall looked at the snake and saw that it was still again.

"Baby," Kitty said from behind him. He turned and faced her. She wrapped her arms around him and kissed his cheek. "You're so wonderful," she said, and she kissed his other cheek and then his lips. "I love you so much."

Chapter 32

"Well, fuck you guys, I'm getting another round. Give me another Charlie Sheen and a double rye and ginger."

The waitress laughed. "You got it."

They were in their usual bar on Whyte Ave, and it was snowing outside. Hartford was drinking a beer, and Wright was drinking water.

"You're really off the sauce?" Hall asked.

Wright nodded. "Really."

"Grow up," Hall said.

"Yeah, you're being a real grown up," Hartford said.

"So, what else is new? I feel like I haven't seen you guys in forever. What's going on at the battalion?"

"Same old shit," Wright said.

"What happened with those two guys you put in the hospital?"

"Still don't have a court date."

"What are they saying at the lines?"

"Half the brass wants to hang me. The other half wants to promote me."

"Promote you?"

"Yeah. They might put me on the course to hide me away. Or I might get pulled back into recce and put on sniper, but I could still get dishonorably discharged. As long as the media doesn't catch onto it, I should be fine."

Hartford turned to Hall. "So, what are you doing? I heard you lost your job."

"I got laid off," Hall lied. "I got paid out though, so I'm just going to take some time to chill the fuck out for a bit. I need a break."

"So you're going to get drunk for a month?"

"No, fuck that. I don't drink too much anymore. I just thought we'd all be getting on it for old time's sake."

"Eh, some other time," Hartford said.

The waitress brought over Hall's drinks. He put the Charlie Sheen back and took a sip of the double rye and ginger.

Hartford laughed. "Don't drink too much anymore, huh?"

"You should order three more," Wright said.

"I should," Hall replied.

"No, you fucking shouldn't, you retard," Hartford said.

"Fuck off," Hall said. "If you're so responsible and in control all of a sudden, why aren't you in better shape?"

Wright laughed loudly.

"My power comes from my size," Hartford said, patting his stomach. "This is a power gut."

They continued talking, Hall drank a few more doubles, and Hartford drank another beer. After they agreed to leave they paid their bills and went outside for one last cigarette. It was snowing lightly, and the smoke they exhaled was thick. Hartford left first and gave Hall a hug.

"Fuck, it was good to see you, man," Hall said.

"You, too. You fucking take care of yourself, all right?"

"Yeah, all right," Hall said.

Hartford walked away to his truck.

"I'm going to take off, too," Wright said. "But listen, I have a buddy who works a few hours up north delivering firewood to this little cabin community. Not much money in it, but the guy is sober. You'd live with him in his cabin while you worked. He was on my second tour. He's a good guy. It could be a good gig for you for a month before you get another job. Just keep it in mind."

"Yeah, all right, thanks," Hall said, and they shook hands.

"Take care, Hall."

"You too."

Hall stood under the overhang of the bar and finished his cigarette. When it was done, he put his hands in his pockets and looked up and down Whyte Ave. Vehicles moved slowly across the street, and people walked quickly on the sidewalks, their shoulders hunched, their hands in their pockets.

He walked to his car, got inside, and let it heat up, but he did not drive anywhere. He listened to music and smoked another cigarette and went through his phone. He found the dealer's number, started to send him a message but changed his mind and found Kitty's number instead. She had gone to one of her art classes. He could not think of anything to text her, so he put his phone back in his pocket, shut the car off, and went back outside.

He went to a liquor store across the street. It was small, and there was cheap tiling on the floor and a layer of slush and mud at the entrance. He asked the girl behind the counter for a mickey of vodka and took two bottles of juice from the fridge. He walked back across the street to his car, made a screwdriver, took two large drinks of it, then refilled what he had drank with more vodka. He got out, lit another cigarette, and walked down Whyte Ave.

He walked to Kitty's favorite art shop and found a painting she had pointed out to him once. The painting featured a woman in a kitchen. She was wearing a long dress, and she had collapsed on the floor with one hand still holding onto the edge of the counter. It was an oil painting, and the colours bled into each other slightly. The woman was painted in a realist style. Looking at her was like looking at a photograph through old panes of glass. The kitchen window in the painting stood in sharp contrast to the rest of the style: it was done in abstract, and the world outside the window was a swirl of colors splattered by other colors, mostly blues and reds. The painting was titled "Evening View of Oblivion."

Chapter 33

"Give me an eight ball."

"You got it," the dealer said, and he left for a room somewhere.

Hall was sitting at the island. He took his keys, wallet, and phone out of his pocket, put them on the counter, took some money out of his wallet, and put that down, too. The dealer came back with the picture frame, the brass tube, a bag of cocaine, and a couple of cards. He slid it all over to Hall, who undid the bag, poured some out, used the cards to crush it up and form two lines, did one, and slid the frame over to the dealer.

"No thanks, dude, I'm all good," the dealer said.

"Yeah?"

"Yeah. I'm getting back into the fuckin' gym finally. I was getting small. I just fired three CCs into my fuckin' leg right before you got here. I popped a couple DBols, too, so I'm gonna have to fly outta here and get under some weights in the next hour or so."

"Good for you," Hall said. He leaned over the picture frame and snorted the line he had cut for the dealer.

"So, what's good, man?" the dealer said.

"Same old shit," Hall said. "Got my payout from the army finally."

"Your payout? What do you mean?"

"It's a piece of your pension they let you at."

"Oh yeah? How much?"

"Fifteen grand."

The dealer laughed. "Oh man, that is not something you want to be telling your fuckin' drug dealer."

"Oh, yeah?"

"Yeah. Don't worry about it though. And you know what? Forget the gym right now. I'm gonna stay here and be your bartender. What'll you have, sir? Would you like a fuckin' menu? Have I ever told you that you're my finest customer?"

They both laughed.

"Well, you got any oxy?" Hall asked.

"No oxy, sir. I got some percs though."

"Those aren't very strong, are they? Can you snort them?"

"Sure can. Not much bang for your buck, so they'll plug you up pretty quick if you do a lot of 'em, but I'll give you a good price so you can just keep swallowing them."

"Yeah okay," Hall said. "And what about M? You got any M? And I need some shit for Kitty."

"Yes, sir, coming right up."

The dealer left, and Hall did another line. The dealer came back with various little bags, and he laid everything out on the counter. "I'll give you twenty-five percs for two hundred dollars, if you want. I normally sell them for ten a piece. How much M and down you want?"

"Okay, cool. Yeah, I'll get twenty-five percs then, two bags of M, and give me five hundred worth of down."

"Five hundred? You're treatin' the girl. That's romantic. Okay, man, here you go." The dealer handed Hall a bag of Percocet and two bags of MDMA. "Just let me weigh out the down. I'll give you a good deal."

He went away and came back again with a scale, measured out the heroin, and bagged it. "There you go, my man."

"Great, thanks. So, how many of these should I pop at a time?" Hall asked, looking at the pills.

"Have you been drinking?"

"A bit."

"A bit? I know what that means. Start with two."

"All right." Hall put two of the pills in his mouth, stood up, went to the sink, and drank some water from his hand.

"So, what're you going to come down with?"

"Kitty might have a few Seroquel left."

"Yeah? You ever try G?"

"What's G?"

"GHB. I take a shot of it every night. A lot of bodybuilders do. Gets you right into REM sleep. It's fuckin' great. Goes good with coke, too, you know. Takes the edge off. You want to try a little bottle?"

"Sure," Hall said. "Why not?"

The dealer went away again and came back with a little 5-Hour Energy drink bottle. "But if I sell you this, you gotta promise me something."

"What's that?"

"Don't drink on it. Alcohol and GHB is a bad fuckin' mix, man. It's dangerous for you and everyone and everything around you. You'll black out and turn into a wild animal. That mix is some fear and loathing shit, except it's not cool, it's not funny, and you won't remember any of it."

"Yeah, all right," Hall said. "I won't do any tonight then. How much is it?"

"Sixty bucks."

Chapter 34

"Oh, baby, it's the one I wanted. It's wonderful. Thank you, John."

Kitty put the painting down on the coffee table and hugged him. It was a long hug. He never let go first; he always let her have it as long as she wanted.

He gave her the heroin next, and then he took her out to dinner. They went to a nice place downtown with high ceilings, dim lighting, and a massive shelf of expensive-looking liquor bottles behind the bar. They split an appetizer but did not finish it. Neither of them could eat. He drank four gin and tonics, and Kitty had a glass of wine. He got her talking about her art class.

When they got home, they got right into it. Kitty started cutting up pieces of tinfoil into neat little squares, and he brought Kitty's empty picture frame out and mixed the cocaine with a bag of MDMA. He poured a drink, a rye and ginger with lots of ice, and used it to chase down a couple of percs.

"Babe!" he screamed at her.

He had never raised his voice at her before, and it made her jump. She looked at him. "What?" she said quietly.

"I love you."

"I love you, too," she said and she turned back to what she was doing. Then she looked up at him again and smiled. "You're an asshole."

He smiled back at her and snorted a line. After she had smoked, she came over to the couch with him and did a line of MDMA. They put some music on, and she settled in close to him on the couch.

"I heard what you and John were talking about the other day," she said. "About Courtney."

"Oh, yeah?"

"Yeah."

"Well? Is it true?"

"It's not true that she killed someone."

"What about the other stuff?"

"About her getting guys hooked on heroin and handing them over to Jason?"

"Yeah."

"That's exactly what she does."

"Well, good for her," Hall said. "Sounds like a good career plan."

"John, there are things about everyone you meet that you will disapprove of or not agree with, but part of being a friend is looking past what others won't. It's probably why you're still friends with someone like Wright. She does the same for me."

"I don't think anything you do or have ever done is comparable to what she does."

"Are you sure?"

"Don't make me start imagining things."

She moved away from him. "Do you know how much pressure you put on me by doing that?"

"By doing what?"

"Holding me up to such a high standard. I'm not some perfect, ideal woman like you make me out to be."

"Really? What's going on, babe? You're being pretty defensive here. I didn't say a damn thing about Courtney. You brought this up."

"I know. Okay, I'm sorry, I just get questioned about our friendship a lot. I should've known you wouldn't question it."

"Well, I don't like it," Hall said, "but I love you, and I trust you, so I leave it up to you. Unless you need my help."

"What would I need your help with?"

"With anything."

"Oh, I see," she said. "Yes, there's a few things I need your help with. Occasionally I have some things in high places to reach and some heavy things to pick up. Maybe some spiders to kill or some jars to open. I'll call you right away."

He laughed and squeezed her. "I love you so fucking much. Come here."

He picked her up and carried her to the bedroom. He laid her down carefully on the bed and got on top of her. She arched her back when he kissed her, he slid his arm under the small of her back and pulled her up into him, and they pulsed together, drowning in their pleasures, their own and the ones they had manufactured.

He had never needed any pills to function with Kitty. It always came naturally with her, even when he was drunk and high. When it was over, they went straight back to the cocaine and the heroin.

He was using an old bill, and he asked Kitty if she had a new one. She said she had one in her purse. He got up, went into her purse, and found a pack of needles. He took them out and threw the purse on the floor.

"What the fuck is this?" he said, holding up the needles.

She said nothing. She was frozen.

"Kitty, why the fuck are these in your purse?"

She turned away from him, and he saw tears forming in her eyes. He went over and sat down on the couch next to her. He threw the needles across the room.

"You fucking promised me you'd never shoot it again. You fucking promised me."

Tears rolled down her face. She put her hand over her mouth.

"No, you're not crying your way out of this one. Do you know how selfish you're being? Do you know what last time did to me? Do you not understand how much I fucking love you and what it did to me when I found you nearly dead with a fucking empty needle in your hand?"

"I know, baby. I'm sorry."

"No, I don't think so. I don't think you know what it did to me. Either you don't know or you do know and you don't give a shit. Here, watch, this is what it feels like." He took the bill, rolled it up, stuck one end in his nose, the other in the pile of cocaine and MDMA, and snorted deeply. A large chunk of the pile disappeared.

"John, what are you doing?"

"Watch. Watch me finish this pile, because it will make me feel good, and that's worth it, even if it might fucking kill me." He put the bill back in the pile again. More disappeared. He felt it fill his nose and slide down the back of his throat.

"John, stop it! John, don't do anymore! You're being stupid."

"I'm sorry, am I scaring you? Are you worried about me, Kitty?"

He stuck the bill back in the pile and snorted again, but he choked on it and gagged a bit. He took a drink of his rye and ginger, and he felt better. He put the bill back in the pile and snorted again.

"John, stop it! Please!"

She grabbed his arm. He looked at her. The world was on fire. He leaned forward to the pile again, but she leaped up, swiped her forearm across the table, and his drink and her picture frame and everything on it smashed on the hardwood floor. He sat back and looked at her, and she looked at him.

"I wanted to do that cocaine," he said.

"You're such a fucking asshole," she said. She stood up, really crying now, heaving, and ran to the bedroom. He picked up a few Percocet off the floor, went over to the sink, and washed them down. He stood in the kitchen. The music was still playing.

He picked up his coat, looking for his pack of cigarettes, and found the 5-Hour Energy drink bottle. He took it out and threw his jacket on the floor. He opened the cap and poured half the bottle into his mouth. It tasted like sweat and he gagged and spit it out on the floor and over his chest. He went to the sink and dry heaved a few times.

When it was over, he drank some water, made himself another rye and ginger with no ice, poured the second half of the 5-Hour Energy drink bottle into his mouth, and washed it down with the rye.

He went back to the couch and turned on the TV.

* * *

Hall was sprawled out naked on the floor. He was still high, but he was nervous. Something had happened. His jeans were lying next to him, and he got up and put them on. The TV was on, but it was muted, and the music was off. The cat was on the floor in the living room. It cried, and that was all he heard, until he heard the two flicks of Kitty's Zippo lighter from the bedroom. The door was open slightly, and he saw that the lights were on inside.

He opened the door all the way and saw her on the bed, facing him, the empty pen in her mouth, sucking the smoke rising from the tinfoil. One of her eyes was dark. A purple bruise had formed below it. He caught his breath and put his arm on the door and leaned forward. "Oh, god, Kitty. . .."

He went over to her carefully, slowly, and she looked up at him when he was close to her. He came down onto the bed next to her, slowly, and she did not move.

"I'm so sorry, babe. Kitty, I'm so fucking sorry."

"It's okay," she said. "It wasn't you."

"What?" He came away from her and looked at her black eye.

"I mean it wasn't *you*, John. You were in a trance. You didn't know what you were doing. I'm guessing you've never taken GHB before?"

"No, I haven't," he said. "But how could I have done that?"

"You didn't do it. It wasn't you. It was like you were sleepwalking. So stop worrying about it."

"I don't understand."

"It's called G-ing out. When you take too much GHB, you G out. Some people sleepwalk, some tense up and moan, some have seizures, and some just die. You were sleepwalking, and you were still mad, so you were being aggressive, but it wasn't you. It wasn't John. So let's stop talking about it."

He stood up and looked at her. She was not angry or upset or really anything. She put the empty pen back in her mouth and lit the Zippo lighter.

Chapter 35

A week later, when the money was almost gone, Hall went over to the dealer's house. He had been spending a lot of time and money there.

"Well, fuck, bro," the dealer said. He came away from the island, leaned against the stove, and crossed his arms. "I'm gonna miss ya."

"I'll be back."

"So, what exactly are you doing again?"

"Chopping wood for a bunch of cabins up north."

The dealer laughed. "Oh yeah? That's great. John's gonna go chop some wood and get his life together. Good for John."

"Yeah, it sounds pretty funny, eh? I think it'll be good for me though."

"Sure, sure. So, what about Kitty?"

"She's staying here."

"She's staying here . . .."

"Yeah," Hall said, "she's staying here. I fuckin' smacked her, man."

"You smacked her?"

"Yeah. I was all fucked up, and I didn't know what I was doing. I don't remember any of it. She said it was like I was sleepwalking."

"You drank on the G, didn't you?"

"Yeah."

"Man, I told you—"

"Yeah, I know. I know, okay?"

"Okay, sorry. Fuck."

"Yeah, fuck."

"Whatever, bro. Good people do bad things. Yeah, you fucked up, but if she really loves you, then she'll get over it. Don't worry, man. It's all gonna be fine. Shit is gonna be all good."

"Yeah, all right," Hall said. "I'm leaving today though. I want to go on a good final rip, you know what I mean?"

"Well, I just happen to have all the ingredients for the John Hall special," the dealer said. "Coke, oxy, and MDMA. I'll tell ya what, I'll fuckin' mix it up for you and everything."

He left and came back again with some bags, the picture frame, his cards, and the brass tube. He set everything up and gave it to Hall for no charge.

Hall had already said goodbye to Kitty, but he went back to the apartment and knocked on the door.

"Did you forget something?"

"No," he said, "I didn't forget anything."

"Well, there's not much more to say," she said. "Go take care of yourself, John. Go figure things out. Come back, and maybe we can figure some more things out together."

"Kitty," Hall said, "Kitty, please, babe, just...."

"Just what?" she said. She started crying.

"Come here." He took hold of her and held her for a long time. "I love you."

"I love you, too," she said. It was the first time she had said it since that night.

Chapter 36

The lights were on, and smoke was coming from the chimney. It was a small cabin, and an old blue GMC pickup truck was parked in the driveway. Hall parked beside it and turned his car off. He felt uneasy and wished he had saved a bit, or at least had something to drink to ease the transition a little, but he had nothing, only his nerves.

He got out of his car, went up to the cabin, and knocked on the door. He heard some banging around and some heavy steps, and the door opened. The man was slightly shorter than him but barrel chested with a shaved head and a dark, thick handlebar moustache. He was not the kind of man who was easy to meet while strung out.

"You John?" he asked. His voice was deep and raspy, like Hartford's.

"Yeah," Hall said, "I'm John."

"I'm Will," the man said. He held out his hand and Hall took it. They did not shake hard, only firmly. "Come on in," he said. "You look like fuckin' shit."

"Thanks," Hall said, and he followed him inside.

The living room and kitchen were all one room. The floors were dirty. Two old reclining chairs faced a tube TV near a fireplace. It was warm inside, and Hall began to sweat. A meal was cooking. He could not remember the last time he had smelled a meal cooking.

"Leave your shoes on," Will said. "You can hang your coat up right there. Where's the rest of your shit?"

"In the car."

"Grab it later. Food's almost done. You hungry?"

Hall took his coat off and hung it on the hook. "Not really, to be honest."

"Bullshit," Will said, looking him over. "You need to eat, my friend. You look like a fuckin' coat hanger."

Hall forced a laugh, but it came out as more of a snort. "Thanks again."

Will went over to the kitchen area and mixed some things around in two frying pans. "So, nothing's changed since we spoke over the phone? Still want to cut wood for a month?"

"Yeah," Hall said. He put his hands in his pockets and watched Will cook. He felt out of place. He looked around for a liquor cabinet, but he knew he would not find one.

"Good," Will said. "The main attraction up here is the winter sports. Lots of cross-country skiing and snowmobiling, so the first couple months of snow is always the busiest. You any good with an axe?"

"I can swing one," Hall said.

"Well, you'll be swingin' like a pro by the end of tomorrow." Will laughed. "Just you wait. So, Wright says you were on the sauce pretty hard. Anything else?"

"Yeah, a couple other things."

"Like what?"

"Cocaine mostly."

"Ah, we're men of similar tastes, my friend." Will smiled, and when he smiled, his handlebar moustache widened around his mouth. "That was my mix. I was always old school. Always went with the bottle of Jack and a bag of fuckin' coke."

"Yeah," Hall said, forcing another laugh. "It's the cornerstone of a good Friday night."

"Friday night? It was the cornerstone of every fuckin' night for me. I loved it. I loved the ritual of it, you know? Opening the little bag, crushing it up with a credit card, chopping up some sexy lookin' lines, rolling up a bill, and chasing it back with Jack on the rocks. Then it's fucking game time." He talked loudly and excitedly, and his deep, good-natured voice filled the room with the warmth and the smell of the potatoes, onions, and ground beef he was frying.

"So, how long you got sober?" Will asked.

"Well, if I'm gonna be honest with you, less than an hour."

Will turned on him. "You didn't bring any of that fuckin' shit into my cabin, did you?" His brow was furrowed, and he was looking at Hall very seriously.

"No, it's all gone. Sorry, I've been on a pretty hard run."

Will's face softened, and he turned back to the stove. "It's all good, my friend. Just remember what I said over the phone. If you want to work for me, you work sober."

"Yeah, absolutely."

"I like your style though," Will said, "pushin' it right to the finish line. I would've done the same thing." He broke out laughing. "You're gonna have one hell of a day tomorrow, buddy. You sleep last night?"

"No."

"Well, get some food into you, and get some rack time. We start at six. Dinner's ready."

Will filled up two plates, and they went to the chairs in front of the fireplace and the TV and ate. They ate seriously, not talking much. Hall was not hungry at first, but once he started, he did not stop until his plate was empty. He felt full and satisfied and warm and did not feel so nervous anymore.

He went outside, smoked a cigarette, and brought his things into his room. When he came out, Will was washing the dishes. Hall offered to help, but Will refused.

"No, just rack the fuck out, man. You'll need it. Oh, and John," he took his hands out of the sink and turned to him, "if you hear me making any noises in my sleep, just don't worry about it, okay?"

"Noises? What do you mean?"

"You'll know what I mean if you hear them. Just don't worry about it, all right?"

"All right," Hall said.

"All right. Goodnight."

"'Night."

Hall had a few Seroquel Kitty had given him. He took them with water and went to bed. Sleep came to him much quicker than he thought it would, and when it did, he slept straight through the night.

Chapter 37

Hall woke up to a banging on his door at 0600. A few minutes later when he came out, Will was frying some of the previous night's dinner and had a pot of coffee on. Hall drank two large glasses of water before he poured himself a cup of coffee, as Will suggested. Hall started Will's truck for him, and after they had eaten, they drove to the yard, which was a clearing in a copse of trees near the entrance of the cabin community. The snow had been cleared with a shovel, and what was left had been compacted by foot. Several piles of logs were covered with tarps and had collected snow, except for one pile, where the logs were exposed, and around that pile the snow was covered with sawdust. A little way past the clearing was a small wooden shed with a large padlock on it.

Will unlocked the shed. Inside were various tools, pieces of equipment, and some gas cans. He handed Hall a gas can and a chainsaw. For himself he took two axes and two pieces of what looked like gear chain.

They went back to the pile of logs. Hall filed the chainsaw, put the chain bar forward, and primed it, but he forgot where to put the choke. He did not want Will to think he did not know, so he yanked on it in all the different positions until it started.

"Up to cold start," Will said.

"Yeah, it's coming back to me," Hall said. He put the chainsaw down on the ground to let it warm up.

Back at the pile, Will picked a log, and they climbed on top of the pile and kicked it off. They climbed down and pushed the log farther back. Will moved his end easily, with only his arms it seemed, while Hall had to dig his feet into the snow and push with everything. They repeated the process until four logs were evenly spaced at the bottom of the pile.

Will put on a pair of safety glasses, picked up the chainsaw, and cut the first log into ten pieces, starting on one end and moving his way down. When he got to the last piece, it was the same size as all the rest. He handed Hall the chainsaw and the safety glasses.

"Remember, let the chainsaw do the work."

Hall stood over the second log as Will had done, revved the chainsaw, and brought it down carefully into the log. When it bit the wood, he came forward and back and angled the blade down when it was farthest from him and up when he brought it in close. He could smell the exhaust and the freshly cut wood. When the first cut was done, he moved on to the second, already feeling the strain in his back. By the fourth cut, he was starting to sweat. He was sore when he got to the last cut, but it was a good soreness, and when he finished, his last piece was almost the same size as the others.

"Good work," Will said, "but this is the easy part."

Will cut the third log, and Hall cut the fourth. They took a break, drank some water, and Hall smoked a cigarette. When he finished, Will showed him how to sharpen an axe. Will picked the largest, best-cut piece for his chopping block, stacked it, assumed a stance, brought the axe up, and let it come down, splitting the piece roughly in half. He cut the smaller half in two and the larger half in three, picked up one of the pieces and gave it to Hall.

"That's the size you want."

The first piece Hall picked to cut had a large knot, and his first swing only dug a few inches into the wood before the axe head got stuck in the knot. He had to wrestle with it to get it out. He kept going, but the axe head kept getting stuck.

"Toss it," Will said. "That knot's too big."

Hall threw the log to the side and went on to the next piece. His first swing severed about a quarter of the log off, and he worked the rest of it down to the sizes Will had shown him. He cut three of the ten pieces of the first log in the time it took Will to cut seven.

Hall cut four, and Will cut six of the next log, and the same with the log after that. When they came to the last log, Will showed Hall how to cut kindling. He stacked the block, picked up one of the chains, wrapped it around the wood, and latched it onto itself. He swung into it, split the log, and it stayed in place on the block, wrapped in the chain. He brought his hand up closer to the axe head, and with small, concise swings he split the wood into thin pieces.

After the last log was cut in this way, they took a break, and then stacked the wood and tarped it. Will said it would stay there for a year, dry out over the summer, and be ready to burn the following winter. He drove his truck next to a pile of seasoned wood, which he or someone else had cut the year before, and they pulled the tarp off the pile and loaded it into the truck.

They drove to each of the cabins, which all had wood bins near the road, and filled them up, as needed. They did not bother talking while they unloaded the wood, but they split a conversation between the short times they were in the truck driving between cabins.

"So, you were on tour with Wright?"

"Yeah," Hall said. "We were in the same platoon. You were on one of his tours too, weren't you?"

"Yeah, I was. I was on your tour, too."

"You were? I don't recognize you from battalion."

"I had hair on my head back then. Did they try to send you to spin dry?"

"Yeah," Hall said, "my sergeant major was pushing it on me. In hindsight I should've done it, but I got sober for a bit when I got out of the army. Not too long though, obviously. Did they try and send you?"

"They did send me," Will said.

"How'd that go?"

"It was fuckin' bullshit."

"Why?"

"Because I went there to sort some shit out that they couldn't fuckin' handle. I went there to sort out my PTSD, to sort out the cause of my drinking and coke habit, and they wouldn't touch it. Wouldn't go fuckin' near it. We had these little groups where everyone was supposed to pour their guts out, you know? Talk about their feelings and shit, but they told me I couldn't talk about anything that happened overseas, because, get this, they were worried it might traumatize the other clients."

Will's voice was rising. Hall heard the rubber on the steering wheel twisting under his grip.

"Don't you think if it's so traumatizing that other people can't even hear about it without being fuckin' traumatized, then I should probably fuckin' talk to somebody about it? Stupid fucks."

Hall started laughing and Will caught it, and Hall was glad he did, because it was not a strong laugh.

"You think that's why you drank and did coke?" Will asked.

"That was probably part of it," Hall said.

"You don't think tour affected you?"

"Yeah, it affected me. You don't go to a place like Afghanistan and not come back affected by it. I've just never had any PST, I mean, PTSD symptoms. Drinking has always been trouble for me."

"Yeah, me, too," Will said. He laughed. "Always."

By the time they finished working for the day, Hall was sore all over and felt nauseous. He had a hot shower while Will cut up and fried five chuck steaks with potatoes and onions. Hall was hungry when he came out of the shower and smelled the meal cooking. After they had eaten, he felt much better. He cleaned everything up and packed what was left away in the fridge for the next day. He went outside and smoked a couple of cigarettes and talked to Kitty on the phone for a while. It was not a good conversation. She was either high or coming down, and she did not seem interested in talking about anything. She asked him only one question.

"Are you doing good up there?"

"Yeah, babe. I'm doing great. Soon I'll be back, and we'll be doing great together."

"Okay," she said.

After they had hung up, Hall went back inside.

"How's the girl?" Will asked.

"Not great."

"No? What's up? Did she use with you?"

"She uses, yeah. Not coke though."

"What then?"

"Heroin."

"Jesus."

"Yeah."

"Did you know she was doing it when you started seeing her?"

"I had no idea until I found her half-dead in our apartment."

"Shit."

"Yeah," Hall said. "You got a woman?"

"I've got an ex-wife," Will said, "and a little girl."

He walked to his bedroom and came back with a picture. He handed it to Hall. In the picture, Will was on a beach, wearing sunglasses, his head clean-shaven, and on his shoulders was a girl, maybe ten or eleven, laughing, and he was smiling. The little girl had one hand wrapped around his head and the other held high in the air.

"She's pretty. What's her name?"

"Allison."

"How old is she?"

"She was ten there. She's thirteen now."

"She's with her mom?"

Hall handed the picture back to him. Will held it in both hands and stared at it. "Yeah, she is."

"When's the last time you saw her?"

Will looked up at the ceiling. "Sixteen months and fourteen days. The ex-wife got a restraining order against me."

"For what?"

"I had a bit of a meltdown. You know."

"Sorry, man."

"Yeah, thanks," Will said.

That night Hall woke up sometime early in the morning and went to the bathroom and then the kitchen for a glass of water. He drank it in the kitchen and from there he heard Will whimpering in his sleep. Will had a deep, masculine voice, but the sounds he was making then were high and shrill. The sounds came and went, and Hall stood in the kitchen, listening. Then a moaning started, and then there was a vicious, terrified scream that tightened Hall's skin and raised the hair on his neck and arms, and then it was over.

Hall refilled his glass and went back to bed.

Chapter 38

By the end of the first week, Hall had gained ten pounds, and he was not as sore at the end of the work days.

Will was friends with many of the people who stayed in the cabins, and he had an arrangement with one of them where he gave them free firewood and they gave him the use of their snowmobiles. At the end of the first week, they finished work early and took the machines out into the woods and through the trails. They found a small lake and raced each other across the ice. Hall had never driven a snowmobile before, and it had been hard keeping up with Will through the trails, but on the lake, he was free to practice at his own speed. Will kept coming straight for him and then carving away, spraying him with snow. Hall got away from him for a while, on the other side of the lake.

With about a kilometer between them, Hall started driving toward Will. As he got closer, he saw Will was driving toward him as well. He pushed the machine as fast as it would go, and the acceleration made him nervous, but once he got up to speed, he felt better and saw that Will was going as fast as him, if not faster, and they were heading straight for each other. He knew what Will wanted to do. The engine screamed, the cold wind stinging his cheeks under his goggles, numbing the skin, his fingers hot on the heated handlebars. Will was close now, growing larger, and he saw that they would collide. He leaned hard to the right, and their engines screamed together, and then Will was past him, and Hall slowed down, his heart pounding, his whole body tense. He forced himself to relax. He took his helmet off, and steam came out of his jacket and off his face and hair. He was breathing heavily, and he felt very good.

Will came around, stopped next to him, and took off his helmet. He was laughing.

"That was fucking incredible!" Hall said. "Fuck, man, what a rush."

"Fuckin' eh, buddy. Better than blow. Better than the biggest fuckin' Hollywood. Feels good, huh?"

"Yeah," Hall said, "I feel great."

"Good," Will said. "You pick the trails this time. Don't worry about getting lost; just go. I'll get us back."

Later, back in the cabin, they ate dinner, real steak this time, with the usual potatoes and onions. Hall cleaned up after, and they watched *Full Metal Jacket*. They took turns quoting the lines, and at some point during the movie, they started trading war stories.

Will told him about his friend, Brett Phillips. They had met in a bar when Will had first come to battalion for work up training. Two girls were sitting at the bar, and Will had started chatting with the one on the right as Brett approached the one on the left. Will and Brett were with separate groups of friends, and they had never met before then. As military men sometimes did for amusement, Will made up a new profession for himself and told his girl he was a professional gardener. He and his girl had been laughing about it, because she did not believe him. The girls went to the restroom together, leaving Will and Brett alone at the bar, and they introduced themselves. Brett had been playing the same game, and he had told his girl that he was a bird photographer. They were both immediately suspicious of each other, but to keep the bit going, they introduced themselves as they had done to the girls, and while the girls were in the washroom, they made up various things about birds and gardening until the two women came back and sat between them. The following Monday, they ran into each other at the battalion lines, both in uniform, and immediately became friends. It was a popular story, and Hall had heard a version of it before, and he knew about Brett Phillips.

"It blew one of his arms and some of his guts on top of this fuckin' mud hut about twenty meters from the blast," Will said, "so I had to climb on top of it to pick up the pieces. There was an opening in the roof, and there was a family inside the mud hut, and this little girl just fuckin' stood there looking at me. She just kept watching me as I collected all the pieces of him. There was a guy at the side of the mud hut holding a garbage bag open for me, so I put all the pieces of Brett in a pile beside me, on the edge of the hut, and I sat down next to the pile of pieces, and I had to carefully toss each piece, one at a time, into the garbage bag. Then I climbed down with his arm in my hand, and fuckin' rigor mortis had set in, and it was all stiff in the wrist and elbow. I held onto the arm and walked it back to the CCV, and while I was walking, it started loosening up, and the joints started working again. I had always thought that rigor mortis was permanent, but apparently, it's not. It's only temporary. It has to do with some chemical change in the muscles, and it only lasts for about an hour or so."

The movie finished and they put another one on, *Black Hawk Down*.

"I've never seen this before," Hall said.

Will laughed.

"Did you ever hear that story about Wright?" Hall asked.

"Which one?"

"The one with the axe handle and the mud hut."

"I haven't heard that one," Will said. "Which tour?"

"His second tour."

"No, I don't think so. How's it go?"

"Well, they took fire from this mud hut, and one of his buddies in his section got killed. I don't know if you know him; it was a guy named Louis or something like that."

"Lenny," Will said. "Yeah I knew Lenny. I was there. Wright didn't tell you we were in the same section?"

"Oh," Hall said. "No, he didn't. He just told me you were on tour together. Okay, so you obviously know the story then."

"No, no," he said, "I want to hear whatever version this is. Go ahead, tell it."

"All right, well, it goes that a couple days later, his section commander, or I guess your section commander, gave the OC false grids for a patrol, and they went out and went back to that hut, and they found two fighting-age males there and, well, Wright beat them to death with an axe handle. Or nearly to death. I don't know. Am I close?"

"It was a crowbar, not an axe handle."

"A crowbar?"

"A crowbar. And I can't say for sure if he killed them because it all happened pretty fast. We put security around the mud hut, and I was watching arcs right outside the front door, and our section commander and Wright and one other guy went inside. I heard some yelling and some banging around, so I went in, and Wright had them on the ground on their faces and was searching them. The sergeant took me back outside so we could radio up to higher, and as he was giving me the message, we heard this bashing, these fuckin' wet-sounding thuds, and we both went back in, and Wright was beating one of them on the head with the crowbar, and the other one was already unconscious or dead. So we grabbed him and pulled him out and got the fuck out of there. That was kept under wraps for years. I'm surprised it ever got out."

"It was more of a myth than anything," Hall said. "I've never asked Wright about it myself."

"Are you surprised that it's true?"

"Not really, no."

"I didn't think so."

They went back to the movie.

Something made Will think of Allison, his daughter, and he talked about her for a while. His ex-wife had given birth to her after they had only been dating a year, and when Allison was four, she was the flower girl for their wedding. During the first dance, she had run out from the crowd and jumped between them, and Will had danced with his daughter standing on his shoes between him and her mother.

Chapter 39

Halfway into the second week, Kitty stopped answering her phone. Hall did not think anything of it the first day, but after she did not text or call him back the second day, he called the dealer.

"Sorry man," the dealer said, "I haven't heard from her. How long has it been?"

"Only two days."

"Maybe she's just strung out. You know what that's like."

"Yeah, maybe."

"Although . . . ."

"What? What is it?"

"I've been out of down for about a week now," the dealer said.

"You're out of heroin?"

"Yeah, my guy got pinched."

"What about Jason? Is he still selling it?"

"Yeah, he is."

"Fuck. Okay, John, can you . . . uh . . . Fuck, give me a second."

"I'll tell you what," the dealer said, "I got a few guys who owe me money who went straight to Jason after I went dry. One of them is his buddy and goes into his house and everything. I could see if he's seen her there."

"She won't be there."

"You want me to swing by your place?"

"Can you?"

"No problem, dude. I'll get right back to you."

"Thanks, man."

The dealer texted him two hours later and said she was not answering the buzzer.

The next day, Hall brought it up with Will. He explained everything—about Kitty and about Jason.

"Would he hurt her?" Will asked.

"I don't know," Hall said.

"Is this a pride thing?"

"No, it's more than that. That guy is fucking rotten."

"That's a tough situation," Will said. "I mean, it sounds like if she's there, she went there willingly."

"Because she's hooked on fucking heroin, man," Hall said.

"Listen," Will said, "I wouldn't like it if I were you either. But they didn't kidnap her. This is her shit, and I know it upsets you, but you need to worry about your own shit. Were you any good to her when you were drunk off your ass and fucked up on coke?"

Hall made no reply.

"Well, you've got a good, safe place here for another two weeks. You leave here with a month sober, and you'll have a good chance of staying that way. Then you can help your girlfriend, and help her properly."

The next day Hall continued calling her, but her phone was off. The dealer sent him a text that night saying she was at Jason's house. Hall went outside, called the dealer, pressed him for details, hung up, and went back inside the cabin.

"Sorry, man, but I have to go," he said to Will.

"She's there?"

"Yeah. She's half-dead on a mattress in one of his spare bedrooms." Hall was breathing heavily and looking around the cabin. He could pack and be on the road to Edmonton in twenty minutes.

"You're sure about this?"

"Yeah, I'm sure," Hall said, and he started toward his room.

"You want a hand?" Will asked.

"No, I'm good. I didn't pack much."

"Not with your luggage. I mean do you want a hand with getting your girlfriend back."

Hall stopped and turned to him. "Yeah?"

"Yeah," Will said. "We'll make it a hard knock, just like old times."

Chapter 40

Wright brought his SUV to a slow stop half a block from the house. Will was in the passenger's seat, and Hall was in the back. Wright shut off the vehicle, and they waited with the windows down, listening and watching the house. It was early in the morning, and the neighborhood was dark and quiet. There were no lights on in Jason's house, but they saw the flicker of a television through a bottom window.

"Give me a quick one," Will said.

Hall picked the bottle of whiskey off the floor and handed it to Will. Will took a drink and passed it to Wright, who did the same, and Wright passed it back to Hall. Hall took a drink.

"How thick is that door?"

"It's not thin."

"Is it wood?"

"Yeah."

"It'll break then."

"It'll be loud."

"We'll have to be quick. No fucking around."

They were all whispering.

"Give me another one," Will said. Hall passed him the bottle. Will took another drink and passed the bottle around again. "Let's kit up," Will said.

Wright had provided three unregistered pistols, balaclavas, flashlights, and gloves.

"What time is it?"

"0412."

"Give me one more," Will said.

Hall passed him the bottle. Will put his pistol in his lap, pulled his balaclava up, and took a drink. He offered the bottle to Wright, but Wright shook his head. Will took another one and handed the bottle back to Hall, who took two, as Will had done.

"What time is it now?"

"0413."

"A few more minutes."

"Let's do it now."

"Now?"

"Now is good."

"You ready?"

"I'm ready."

"You ready?"

"What's left in the bottle?"

"One or two more."

"Pass it here."

Hall passed the bottle to Will, who pulled his balaclava up again and took another drink. There was one small one left in the bottle, and Hall drank it and put the empty bottle back on the floor.

"Ready?"

"Good."

"Yeah, good."

"Let's go."

Wright turned the engine on and drove straight toward the house, driving over the lawn so that Will and Hall's side of the SUV stopped a meter from the front door. They exited the vehicle, leaving the doors open. Will and Hall waited for Wright to get around to them. Wright went straight for the door and tried the handle.

"Locked."

Wright stepped back. Will walked toward the door, and on his last step, brought his right knee up into his chest, leaned forward and kicked the door near the handle. The wood splintered around the lock. Will recovered and kicked it again, and the door burst open. As he recovered from the second kick, Wright took the door.

Hall followed Wright, and Will followed Hall. Wright walked fast, his pistol up. They turned their flashlights on. The hallway was empty. They came to the living room and found a man and a woman there—the woman on the couch, the man walking toward the stairs, but when he saw them, he stopped and stared at Wright. His face was bright in Wright's flashlight. The man was thin, and the woman was fat. They both looked strung out and frightened. Hall did not recognize either of them. Wright grabbed a fistful of the man's hair, dragged him to the couch, and threw him against the woman.

"Oh my god!" The woman started crying. "Oh my god, I can't be here, no, I can't be here, I have nothing to do with this."

"Shut the fuck up," Wright said, standing over them. Will and Hall branched off from Wright and checked the back hallway. It was empty.

"I can't be here," the woman said, "no, I can't be here, please, I have nothing to do with this." She stood up off the couch and tried to walk past Wright, keeping her face turned away from him, but Wright stepped in front of her and struck her in the face. She crumpled to the floor and started moaning.

The man started to get up, but Wright pointed his pistol at him. "I will fucking execute you." The man sat back down.

Wright grabbed the woman by the hair and dragged her back to the couch next to the man. He started hitting the man until they were both bent over, cowering under him with their arms wrapped protectively around their heads.

"She'll be upstairs," Hall said to Will.

"We'll clear the basement first," Will said. He opened the basement door, and Hall followed him down the stairs. The basement was filled with garbage, and there was a dirty mattress on the floor, but it was empty. They went back upstairs to the main floor.

Wright was still standing over the man and the woman. Hall approached the main set of stairs, which led up in a switchback.

Will started to climb them, but Hall said, "Let me go first."

Will stepped to the side without looking back and let Hall pass. Hall kept his pistol held high and climbed to the top of the stairs. When he reached the upper level, a hallway opened up with two doors on the left, which were closed, and a bathroom with the door open. Another door was on the right. It was also closed.

"Go right," Will whispered, and Hall did.

Will came in behind Hall and stepped to the side. The room was empty. A large mattress was on the floor with a few small pieces of furniture around it and dirty clothes and garbage everywhere. They checked the bathroom quickly, then went back into the hall and took the next door.

Will went in first. Hall came in behind him and stepped to the side. A mattress was on the floor, and on the mattress was the large man with the thick brow and the spotted face. He was naked and asleep. The nightstand beside the mattress was covered in used needles, pieces of cotton, spoons, little baggies, and a tin can with an indent in it and holes poked into it. Between him and the nightstand, only half on the mattress, was a girl, also naked and asleep. Her chest was flat, her skin was a dirty, blotchy white, and the insides of both arms were purple and cratered with track marks. She was young. She did not look anything like Will's daughter, but Hall knew it did not matter. He knew that for Will, she might as well have been.

Will did not speak. He quietly put his pistol and flashlight away, kneeled down, and picked up the girl, one arm under her knees, one around her shoulders. He turned to Hall with her in his arms. "Take her downstairs."

Hall put his pistol and flashlight away and took the girl from him. He barely felt the weight of her. He turned around and walked back out into the hallway and down the stairs, careful not to bump her against anything. She moaned a little when he got to the second set of stairs and brought her hand up to her face.

He put her on the couch and looked for a blanket but could not find one. He found a sweatshirt on the floor and used that instead, and then he heard Will begin upstairs. Wright looked at Hall, and Hall could tell that Wright was smiling beneath his balaclava.

Hall went back up the stairs. The door had swung closed again, so he could not see what was happening in the room. He could only hear the sounds. He stood still for a moment, listening.

When he opened the door, he saw that Will had dragged the man to the other end of the mattress so that his head was hanging off the end of it. The man's nose was crumpled up and pushed off to the side, and his jaw was loose and hung at a strange angle. Will hit him three more times while Hall was in the room. Will had Kevlar knuckles on his gloves. After the last strike, only skin kept the jaw bone attached to the skull. Little red bubbles grew and popped around the mutilated nose, and the man made a shallow sucking sound.

Will looked at Hall. He was breathing hard. Only his eyes showed through his balaclava, and they were wet. Will looked back at the man on the mattress. Hall touched Will on the shoulder, went back into the hallway, and faced the last door. Will came out and stacked up behind him. They had their pistols out again.

Hall opened the door, and there she was. The room was much cleaner than the others, with nothing on the floors except the mattress and a nightstand next to it. Needles and baggies and other things were on the nightstand, but they were organized and neat. Kitty was under a blanket. Hall pulled the blanket back from her, and she stirred. He pulled the balaclava off his head, leaned over her, and touched her on the cheek.

"Let's go," Will said.

Chapter 41

Hall picked Kitty up from the detox center on a Saturday. He asked her if she wanted something to eat, but she said she just wanted to go home. He helped her unpack, and they put a movie on and sat on the couch together. He had her close to him and had his arm around her. They watched the first half of the movie in silence.

She started crying, and he held her, not saying anything. She cried for a long time, and he kept holding her, holding her hand, holding her head, wrapping his arms around her back, holding all of her. After she was finished, neither of them spoke, and they watched the rest of the movie until she fell asleep on his chest, his arms still around her, and the movie went back to its menu. He stayed still and let her sleep. But he could not leave it alone.

"Kitty," he said. He said her name three more times before she woke up.

"Yes?"

"You have to tell me what happened."

She did not say anything, just stayed with her face pressed against his chest.

"Kitty, did anything happen? Did anything happen with Jason?"

She started crying again, and he knew. He stayed there and let her finish. He kept holding her.

"Kitty, I love you," he said when she was finished. "I love you so fucking much." He had more to say, but he did not say it. He could not get it out. Everything was suddenly blocked.

"Your heart is beating so fast," she said.

"I need to go out for a bit," he said.

She came away from him, and he stood up and collected his things. He went to the front door and put on his shoes and jacket.

"John, you abandoned me," she said.

He had the door open, but he closed it and walked back into the living room. She was crying again.

"You left me," she said.

He did not say anything.

"After you hit me, I didn't know if it would ever be the same with us. And I was alone, John. I was so alone."

He turned away from her and left.

He called the dealer, but he did not pick up. He texted him and called him again, but there was still no answer. He drove to a bar, ordered a double rye and ginger, and sat at a corner table. He drank quickly and went back to the bar for another.

He thought about Jason with her on that mattress in the upstairs bedroom. He thought of Jason tying off her arm, Kitty on her back, lying on the mattress, him sitting beside her, rubbing the inside of her arm, finding her veins, massaging them out of her arm. Melting it, mixing it, sucking it up through a small piece of cotton into the syringe, picking a vein, pressing into it, piercing it, the nozzle of the needle going red, pulling back, dark red shooting into golden brown, all of it being pressed, pressed into her, her eyes closing, her head falling back, his hands pulling it out, untying the elastic, leaning over her, his hand feeling that arm, his arm then, his hands touching her leg, coming up her leg, coming for her.

He called the dealer again, but there was still no answer. He went back up to the bar and ordered another double rye and ginger. He drank two more and drove back to the apartment. He hit the driver's window three times with his elbow, but the glass did not break, so he hit the center console with his right fist three times, and the radio screen broke, and some of the buttons came off.

In war, death is not a very important thing. When it happens, the importance falls on how to solve it—who takes what job, what to do with the body, and how equipment is to be redistributed. If you are affected by it, you are expected to solve any resulting issues that might jeopardize your effectiveness as a soldier or inform your chain of command so that they can do it for you. In war, death is a stoppage. But in the civilized world, nothing is more important than death. Wallpaper and carpets can scream of it for years.

Hall walked into the lobby. There was an open elevator, and he took it up and thought of the things he was going to say. It was bright in the elevator. There were lights on the walls and the ceiling, and where there were no lights, there were mirrors. The hallway was darker. Their apartment was at the end of the first hall, at the corner.

All the lights were off, and through the window, the sun was setting. The river and the buildings by the river were blue, and the last light of the sun was red. When he found her, he knew immediately.

Hall went into the bedroom, and she was on the bed. He touched her hand and wrapped his fingers around hers. When he grabbed them, they were stiff, and when he tried to lift her hand, the wrist and elbow did not bend, and her arm lifted with her hand and started to lift her torso. He let go of her hand. It was only temporary, Will had said. It was a chemical change in the muscles. It only lasted for about an hour. It was only temporary.

Chapter 42

Hall did not drink or use at first. Not because it was what she would have wanted but because he knew being high would make him think of her. But then, six days after the funeral, he went to the dealer's house. He bought some cocaine and oxycontin, and the dealer crushed it all up and put it in a bag for him. After he left, he picked up a mickey of rye. He drank it straight from the bottle.

He borrowed one of the unregistered pistols from Wright, and Wright wiped it down before he gave it to him.

He sat in his car in front of the house. All the blinds had been drawn, and where there were no blinds, blankets had been pinned over the windows. He kept looking at the blinds and the blankets. There were four windows in total: two upstairs, one large one downstairs, and one in the front door. He drank the rye and stuck a rolled-up bill into the bag and took whatever came up. He did this several times, and when he had taken the right amount, when he was in the right place, he got out of the car and walked to the front door.

The door was still broken and swung open easily. He held the pistol down but straight-armed. He walked down the hallway and brought the pistol up a bit and came into the living room. Courtney was sitting there by herself in the center of the U-shaped couch. She had a piece of tinfoil out and she was heating it with a Zippo lighter.

She breathed in sharply after she had inhaled the smoke and held it in. She was sitting straight-backed on the edge of the couch, and her chest was up and out from the breath. She stared at him.

Hall stared back at her. He let the pistol down slightly. He quickly checked the back hallway and looked up the stairs and then brought his attention back to Courtney. She let the breath go.

"Where's Jason?"

"I don't know."

Hall took a step toward her. "Courtney," he said, "tell me where he is."

Her purple hair was longer than he remembered it. It looked healthy and straight, and she had it tied up in a ponytail. "He left," she said. "I told him you'd come back here for him, so he left. I thought you would have brought your friends again."

Her cellphone was sitting on the couch beside her. He leaned over her and picked it up and checked for recent calls or messages, but there were none. He put the phone in his back left pocket. The mickey of rye was in the right. He checked upstairs, and the bedroom where they had found the large man and the girl had not changed. It was still filthy, and the bloodstain was still on the carpet and the mattress. The room he had found Kitty in was also the same, still clean and organized.

He checked every room, bathroom, closet, and hallway, and then he went downstairs into the basement. It was dark, and the air was stale. He stopped halfway down the stairs and let his eyes adjust. Someone had cleaned up or, rather, made a clearing amongst the garbage, and in the center of the clearing was a canvas, face down on the cement floor. Hall went down the rest of the way and kneeled over it. He picked it up by a corner and turned it over.

He stood up and stared down at it. Something hard formed in the back of his throat. He sat down on the stairs but stood up again, took the mickey of rye and the cellphone out of his back pockets and sat back down. He put the pistol, the mickey, and the phone down on the step he was sitting on, and took the bag of cocaine and oxycontin out of his jacket pocket. It was almost empty and he poured what was left onto the back of his hand and snorted it. His heart was pounding in his chest. He felt it with his hand. He picked the pistol up again and felt the grooves of the grip against the skin of his palm and the cold metal of the barrel against his index finger. He pressed the magazine release with his thumb and gripped the bottom of the magazine with his thumb and index finger of his left hand and slid it down slowly and back up again, listening to smooth metallic sound it made, finally slamming it back into place with his palm. He breathed in through his nose and out through his mouth.

He stood up and took his jacket off. He sat back down on the step. With his left hand, he felt his beating heart through his chest, pressing his fingers hard into his skin and muscle, moving them in a circle, searching for where the beat was strongest. He looked down and noted the spot. Holding the pistol in his right hand, he pressed it against his chest, testing the angle, but his wrist was bent too far and it seemed unstable. He changed his grip and held the pistol backwards in his left hand, supporting it with his right. The thumb of his right hand stretched back, reaching for the trigger. He took a slow breath in through his nose and held it. He released it through his mouth and took another. He squeezed his eyes shut, released the breath slowly and pressed the pad of his thumb against the trigger and something cried from behind him.

He opened his eyes and turned around. The small white cat was standing at the top of the stairs, looking down at him. It cried again and started coming down the stairs. It came down slowly, unsure of itself, using both front legs with each small jump, stopping at each step and crying before it continued. When it reached him it climbed into his lap. Hall put the pistol down and held the small cat and started crying. He hunched forward, holding the cat carefully with both hands, pressing his wet face against its fur, and he felt its ribs expand and contract with every tiny breath.

He stayed there for a long time with the cat, and when he finally went back upstairs Courtney had not moved from her place on the couch. He had put his jacket back on and he had the pistol in one hand and the cat in the other. He went to the far couch and sat down facing Courtney. He put the pistol down on the cushion beside him and took the mickey out of his pocket. He took a drink and watched her. She emptied a little bag onto a piece of tinfoil. She heated it up and sucked the smoke into herself and stared at him as she exhaled. She laid back on the couch. The cat started crying and squirming in Hall's grip. He put it down on the floor and it went away somewhere.

"Were you high when you and your friends came in here?" Courtney asked.

"No."

"But you're high now."

He did not say anything. He took another drink.

"And drunk," she said. "So, tell me, what did you use when you were with her? What was your couple's combination? And what I really want to know is, what were you on when you hit her? How far under the influence do you need to be to hurt someone you supposedly love?"

He still did not reply.

"I can't imagine how awful you feel for doing that," she said. "You're very rough, you know that, John? Or at least you try to be. Kitty should have been smarter, but I suppose I can see why she liked you. All girls have a soft spot for the troubled ones. For the lost causes. Unfortunately, not all of us are smart enough to ignore it."

His silence meant nothing to her. She opened up another little bag.

"But you did fight a war. That counts for something. Do you think having fought a war made it easier to find your girlfriend dead in your apartment? And so shortly after you struck her, too. Kitty had never been hit by a man before. Did you know that? Even Jason never hit her. But you did. And now she's dead. It must be so hard not to blame yourself. Am I right, darling?"

She took another hit and held the smoke in, stood up, and walked over to him. She looked at the pistol on the cushion beside him. She blew the smoke out the side of her mouth and looked back at him. His right hand held the mickey on his knee. She moved her hand toward the pistol. He watched it. She touched it, wrapped her fingers around it, and before she took it, she looked at him for a long time, but he did not do anything. She picked up the pistol.

She sat back down and brought the pistol into her lap. She turned it around in her hands. She held it still for a moment, staring at him, then stood up and went to the far end of the couch and put the pistol down on a side table. She came back over to him and held her hand out. "Come here, poor darling."

He looked up into her eyes, took her hand, and stood up. She unzipped his jacket and put her hands on his chest, slid them over him, under the jacket, slowly peeling it off. She put a hand on his cheek, and her hand was warm. She moved it down his face and onto his chest and onto his arm. She went up and down his arm with her hand and then down his stomach. She took hold of his shirt and brought it up, and he finished it for her and threw it onto the couch behind him.

She touched his naked chest and arms and pushed him down on the couch. He watched her walk across the room and pick up a small black purse. She came over to him and went down on her knees between his legs.

She took everything she needed out of the black purse and prepared it on the coffee table behind her. She wrapped the rubber strip around his arm and tied it off. She took his hand and pulled his arm toward her. She said to make a fist, and he did. She pierced his skin, the nozzle went red as she pulled back on the plunger, and his blood exploded in the chamber like a tiny red smoke grenade. She took the rubber strip off his arm, pushed the plunger down, and he felt it immediately. He leaned back and let his head rest on the couch.

Hall laughed. It seemed like the only thing to do. Courtney climbed onto his lap with her legs on either side of him, and he leaned forward and put his head against her breasts.

She ran her fingers through his hair, and whispered into his ear, "Baby...."

* * *

Lightning Source UK Ltd.
Milton Keynes UK
UKHW01f2142010818
326642UK00002B/178/P